Beebo Brinker

Beebo Brinker

by Ann Bannon

CLEIS
PRESS

Published in the United States by Cleis Press Inc.,
P.O. Box 14684, San Francisco, California 94114.
Printed in the United States.
Cover design: Scott Idleman
Text design: Karen Quigg
Cleis Press logo art: Juana Alicia
10 9 8 7 6 5 4 3 2 1

❧

"Looking back from the mid-80s to the distant 50s and 60s, let me share a thought with you. The books as they stand have 50s flaws. They are, in effect, the offspring of their special era, with its biases. But they speak truly of that time and place as I knew it. I would not write them today quite as I wrote them then. But I did write them then, of course. And if Beebo is really *there* for some of you—and Laura and Beth and the others—it's because I stayed close to what felt real and right." — ANN BANNON

Beebo Brinker

Jack Mann had seen enough in his life to swear off surprise forever. He had seen the ports of the Pacific from the deck of a Navy hospital ship during World War II. He had helped patch the endless cut and bloodied bodies, torn every which way, some irreparably. He had seen the sensuous Melanesian girls, the bronzed bare-chested surfers on Hawaiian beaches, the sly stinking misery of the caves of Iwo Jima.

A medical corpsman gets an eyeful—and a noseful—of human wretchedness during a war. When it was over, Jack left the service with a vow to lead a quiet uncomplicated life, and never to hurt anybody by so much as a pinprick. It shot the bottom out of his plans to enter medical school, but he let them go without undue regret. He'd be well along in his thirties by the time he finished, and it didn't seem worth it any more.

So he completed the course he started before the war: engineering. And after he got his degree he took a job in the New York office of a big Chicago construction firm as head of drafting.

During those war years, when Jack was holding heaving sailors over the head and labeling countless blood samples, he had fallen in love. It was a lousy affair, unhappy and violent. But peculiarly good now and then. Good enough to sell him on Love for a long time.

He organized his life around it. He earned his money to pamper whatever passion came his way. That was the only real value his bank account held for him; that, and helping stray people out of trouble, the way others help stray cats.

But by the time Jack reached his thirties, there had been too many who took advantage of his generosity to swindle him; his confidence to cuckold him; his affection to torment him. He turned cynic. There was hope in him still, but he buttoned it down under his skepticism.

He wanted to stabilize his life, settle down with one person and live out a long rewarding love. But Jack Mann could only love other men: boys, to be exact. Volatile, charming, will-o-the-wisp boys, who looked him up Friday, loved him Saturday, and left him Sunday. They couldn't even spell "stabilize."

His emotional differentness had given Jack a good eye for people, a knack for sizing them up fast. He usually knew what to expect from a boy after talking to him twenty or thirty minutes, and he had learned not to give in to the type who brought certain suffering—the type who couldn't spell.

But Jack had also learned that he couldn't live his life only for love. The less romantic he got about it, the clearer his view of life became. It didn't make him happy, this cynicism. But it protected him from too much hurt, and gave him a sort of sour wit and wisdom.

Jack Mann was thirty-three years old, short in height, tall in mentality. He was slight but tough: big-shouldered for his size and deep-chested. His far-sighted eyes watched the world through a pair of magnifying lenses, set in tortoise-shell frames.

They were seeing sharply these days, for Jack was between lovers: bored and restless, but also healthy, wealthy, and on the wagon. When the new love came along—and it would—he would stay up most nights, blow his bankroll, and hit the bottle. It was nuts, but it happened every time. It seemed to preserve his lost illusions for a while, till the new "love" vanished and joined the countless old ones in his memory.

Jack lived in Greenwich Village, near the bottom of Manhattan. It was filled with aspiring young artists. Filled, too, with ambitious businessmen with wives and families, who played hob with the local bohemia. A rash of raids was in progress on the homosexual bar hangouts at the moment, with cops rousting respectable beards-and-sandals off their favorite park benches; hustling old dykes, who were Village fixtures for eons, off the streets so they wouldn't offend the deodorized young middle-class wives.

Jack was pondering the problem one May evening as he came up the subway steps at 14th Street. At six o'clock the air was still violet-light. It was a good time for ambling through the winding streets he had come to know so well.

He tacked neatly in and out through the spring mixture of tourists and natives: young girls with new jobs and timid eyes; older girls with no jobs and knowing eyes; quiet sensitive boys having intimate beers together in small boites. Shops, clubs, shoebox theaters. It always delighted him to see them, people and buildings both, blooming with the weather.

Jack stopped to buy some knockwurst and sauerkraut in a German delicatessen, eating them at the counter with an ale.

When he left, feeling sage and prosperous, he saw a handsome girl passing the shop, carrying a wicker suitcase in one hand. Her strong face and bewildered eyes contradicted each other. Jack followed a few feet behind her, intrigued. He had done this many a time, sometimes meeting the appealing person behind the face, sometimes losing the face forever in the swirling crowds.

The girl he was tailing appeared to be in her late teens, big-tall, with dark curly hair and blue eyes: Irish coloring, but not an Irish face. She walked with long firm strides, yet clearly did not know where she was. In her pocket was a yellow *Guide to Greenwich Village* with creased pages. Twice she stopped to consult it, comparing what she read to the unfamiliar milieu surrounding her.

A sitting duck for fast operators, Jack thought. But something wary in the way she held herself and eyed the crowd told him she knew that much herself. She was trying to defend herself against them by suspecting every passerby of ulterior motives.

At the first street comer she nearly collided with a small crop-haired butch, who said, "Hi, friend," to her. The big girl stared for a moment, surprised and uncertain, afraid to answer. She moved on, crossing the street and detouring widely around a Beat with a fierce beard who sat guarding his gouaches, watching her pass with a curious who-are-you? look.

Jack was amused at the girl's odd air of authority, the set of her chin, the strong rhythm of her walking. And yet, despite her efforts to look self-assured, she was clearly no native New Yorker. Her face, when he glimpsed it, was a map of confusion.

Rather abruptly, as if suddenly tired, she stopped, and Jack waited discreetly behind her, leaning against a railing and lighting a cigarette, watching her with a casual air.

She searched with travel-grimy hands for a cigarette in her pocket, but found only tobacco crumbs. Wearily she let herself sag against a shop window, evidently convinced it was silly to keep marching in the same direction, just because she had started out in it. Better to rest, to think a minute. Her gaze fell on Jack, who was studying her with a little smile. She looked square at him, and then her eyes dropped. He sensed something of her reaction: he was a strange man; she was a girl, forlorn and alone in a city she didn't know. And probably too damn poor to squander money on cigarettes.

Jack strolled over to her, pulling a pack from his pocket and extending it with one cigarette bounced forward for her to take. She looked up, startled. She was four inches taller than Jack. There was a small pause and then she shook her head and looked away, afraid of him.

"You'd take it if I were somebody's grandmother," he kidded her. "Don't hold it against me that I'm a man."

She gave him a tentative smile.

"Come on, take it," he urged.

She accepted one cigarette, but still he held the pack toward her. "Take 'em all. I have plenty. You look like you could use these."

She obviously wanted to, but she said shyly in a round low voice, "Thanks, but I can't pay you."

Jack chuckled. "You're a nice girl from a nice family," he said. "Know how I know? Oh, it's not because you want to pay for the pack." She looked at him with guarded interest. "It's because you're afraid of me. No, it's true. That's the mark of a nice girl, sad to say. Men scare her. I can hear your mother telling you, 'Dear, never take presents from a strange man.' Right?"

She smiled at him. "Close enough," she said softly, and inhaled some smoke with a look of relief.

"Well, consider this a loan," he said, gesturing toward the cigarettes, and then he tucked them in her pocket next to the *Guide*. She jumped at the touch of his hand. He felt it but did not say anything. "You're pretty new, aren't you?" he said.

"I'm pretty used, if you want to know," she said ruefully.

Jack laughed. "How old? Seventeen?"

"Do I look *that* young?" she asked, dismayed. There was intelligence in her regular features, but a pleasant country innocence, too. And she was uncommonly handsome with her black wavy hair and restless blue eyes.

"Do you have a name?" he asked.

"Do you?" she countered, instantly defensive.

He held out his hand affably and said, "I'm Jack Mann. Does that make you feel any better?"

She took his hand, cautiously at first, then gave it a firm shake. "Should it?" she said.

"Only if you live down here," he answered. "Everybody knows I'm harmless."

She seemed reassured. "I'm going to live here. I'm looking for a place now." She paused as if embarrassed. "I do have a name: Beebo Brinker."

He blinked. "Beebo?" he said.

"It used to be Betty Jean. But I couldn't say it right when I was little."

They smoked a moment in silence and then Beebo said, "I guess I'd better get going. I have to spend the night somewhere." And she turned a sudden pink, realizing the inference Jack might draw from her remark. "Everybody" might know Jack down here, but Beebo wasn't everybody. For all she knew he was harmless as a shark. The mere fact that he had a name wasn't all *that* reassuring.

"Looks to me like you need some food first," he said lightly. "There's always a sack somewhere."

"I don't have much money."

"Better to spend it on food," he said. "Anyway, what the hell, I'll treat you. There's some good Wiener schnitzel about a block back." He tried to take her wicker case to carry it for her, but she pulled away, offended as if his offer were a comment on her ability to take care of herself.

Jack stopped and laughed a little. "Look, my little friend," he said kindly. "When I first hit New York I was as pea-green as you are. Somebody did this for me and let me save my few bucks for a room and job hunting. This is my way of paying him back. Ten years from now, you'll do the same thing for the next guy. Fair?"

It was hard for her to resist. She was almost shaky hungry; she was worn out; she was lost. And Jack looked as kind as he was. It was a part of his success in salvaging people: they liked his face. It was homely, but in the good-humored amiable way that made him seem like an old friend in a matter of minutes.

Finally Beebo smiled at him. "Fair," she said. "But I'll pay you back, Jack. I will."

They walked back to the German delicatessen, Beebo with a firm grip on her suitcase.

She finished her meal in ten minutes. Jack ordered another for her, over her protests, kidding her about her appetite.

"Jesus," he said. "When did you eat last?"

"Fort Worth."

"Indiana?" Jack stared.

"Yes. I ate three sandwiches in the rest room, on the train. That was yesterday." Beebo drained her milk glass and put it on the table. The pneumatic little blonde waitress brought the second plateful. Jack, watching Beebo, who was watching the waitress, saw her wide blue eyes glide up and down the plump pink-uniformed body with curious interest. Beebo pulled back, holding her breath as the waitress leaned over her to set a basket of bread on the table, and there was a look of fear on her face.

Jack thought to himself, she's afraid of her. Afraid of that bouncy little bitch. Afraid of...women?

When she had finished eating, Beebo glanced up at him. For all her physical sturdiness and arresting face, she was not a forward or a confident girl.

"You eat like a farm hand," he chuckled.

"I should. I was raised in farm country," she said, looking away from him. Her shyness beguiled him. "Thank you for the food."

"My pleasure." He observed her through a scrim of cigarette smoke. "If I weren't afraid of scaring hell out of you, I'd ask you over to my place for a drink," he said. She blanched. "I mean, a drink of milk," he said.

"I don't drink," she told him apologetically, as if teetotaling were something hick-town and unsophisticated.

"Not even milk?"

"Not with strange men."

"Am I really that strange?" he grinned, laughing at her again.

"Am I really that funny?" she demanded.

"No." He reached over the table top unexpectedly and pressed her hand. She tried to jerk it away but he held it tight, surprising her with his strength. "You're a lovely girl," he said. It wasn't suggestive or even romantic. He didn't mean it to be. "You're a sweet young kid and you're lost and tired and frightened. You need one thing right now, Beebo, and the rest will take care of itself."

"What's that?" She retrieved her hand and tucked it behind her.

"A friend."

She gazed at him, sizing him up, and then began to move from the booth.

"I'm no wolf," Jack said, sliding after her. "Can't you tell? I just like to help lost girls. I collect them." And when she turned back with a frown of disbelief, he shrugged. "Everybody's got to have a hobby."

He bought some Dutch beer and sausage, paid the cashier, and walked with Beebo out the front door. On the pavement she stopped, swinging her wicker case around in front of her like a piece of fragile armor. Jack saw the defensive glint in her eyes.

"Okay, little lost friend," he said. "You're under no obligation to me. If this bothers you, the hell with it. Find yourself a hotel room, a park bench. I don't care. Well...I care, but I don't want to scare you any more."

Beebo hesitated a moment, then held out her hand and shook his. "Thanks anyway, Jack. I'll find you some day and pay you back," she said. She looked as much afraid to leave him as to stay with him.

"So long, Beebo," he said, dropping her hand. She walked away from him backwards a few steps so she could keep an eye on him, turned around and then turned back.

Jack smiled at her. "I'm afraid I'm just about your safest bet," he said kindly. "If you knew how safe, you'd come along without a qualm."

And when he smiled she had to answer him. "All right," she said, still clutching her wicker bag in both hands. "But just so you'll know: my father taught me how to fight."

"Beebo, my dear," he said as they began to walk toward his apartment, "you could probably throw me twenty feet through the air if you had to, but you won't have to. I have no designs on you. Honest to God. I don't even have a bunch of etchings to show you in my pad. Nothing but good talk and cold beer. And a bed."

Beebo stopped in her tracks.

"Well, the bed is good and cold too," he said. "God, you're a scary one."

"Did you go home to bed with the first stranger you met in New York?" she demanded.

"Sure," he said. "Doesn't everybody?"

She laughed at last, a full country sound that must have carried across the hay fields, and followed him again. He walked, hands in pockets, letting her curb her long stride to keep from getting ahead of him. But when he tried to take her arm at a corner, she shied away, determined to rely only on herself.

Jack unlocked the door of his small apartment, holding it with his foot while Beebo went in. The corridor outside was littered with buckets, planks, and ladders. "They're redecorating the hall," he explained. "We like to put on a good front in this rattrap."

He headed for the kitchen with the bag of sausage and the beer, set them on the counter, and sprang himself a can of cold brew. "What do you want, Beebo? One of these?" He lifted the can. When she hesitated, he said, "You don't really want that milk, do you?"

"Have you got something—weak?"

"Well, I've got something colorful," he said. "I don't know how weak it is." He went down on his haunches in front of a small liquor chest and foraged in it for a minute. "Somebody gave me this stuff for Christmas and I've been trying to give it away ever since. Here we are."

He took out an ornate bottle, broke the seal and pulled the cork, and got down a liqueur glass. When he up-ended the bottle, a rich green liquid came out, moving at about the speed of cod-liver oil and looking like some dollar-an-ounce shampoo for Park Avenue lovelies. The pungent fumes of peppermint penetrated every crack in the wall.

"What is it?" Beebo said, intimidated by the looks of it.

"Peppermint schnapps," Jack said. "God. It's even worse than I thought. Want to chicken out?"

"I grew up in a town full of German farmers," she said. "I should take to schnapps like a kid to candy."

Jack handed over the glass. "Okay, it's your stomach. Just don't get tanked on the stuff."

"I just want a taste. You make me feel babyish about the milk."

He picked up his beer and the schnapps bottle, and she followed him into the living room. "You can drink all the milk you want, honey," he said, settling into a leather arm chair, "before the sun goes over the yardarm. After that, we switch to spirits."

He turned on a phonograph nearby and turned the sound low. Beebo sat down a few feet from him on the floor, pulling her skirt primly over her knees. She seemed awkward in it, like a girl reared in jeans or jodhpurs. Jack studied her while she took a sip of the schnapps, and returned her smile when she looked up at him. "Good," she said. "Like the sundaes we used to get after the Saturday afternoon movie."

She was a strangely winning girl. Despite her size, her pink cheeks and firm-muscled limbs, she seemed to need caring for. At one moment she seemed wise and sad beyond her years, like a girl who has been forced to grow up in a hothouse hurry. At the next, she was a picture of rural naïveté that moved Jack; made him like her and want to help her.

She wore a sporty jacket, the kind with a gold thread emblem on the breast pocket; a man's white shirt, open at the throat, tieless and gray with travel dust; a straight tan cotton skirt that hugged her small hips; white socks and tennis shoes. Her short hair had been combed without the manufactured curls and varnished waves that marked so many teenagers. It was neat, but the natural curl was slowly fighting free of the imposed order.

Her eyes were an off-blue, and that was where the sadness showed. They darted around the room, moving constantly, searching the shadows, trying to assure her, visually at least, that there was nothing to fear.

"What are you doing here in New York, Beebo?" Jack asked her.

She looked into her glass and emptied it before she answered him. "Looking for a job," she said. "Me and everybody else, I guess."

"What kind of job?"

"I don't know," she said softly. "Could I have a little more of that stuff?" He handed the bottle down to her. "It's not half as bad as it looks."

"Did you have a job back home?" he asked.

"No. I—I just finished high school."

"In the middle of May?" His brow puckered. "When I was in school they used to keep us there till June, at least."

"Well, I—you see—it's farm country," she stammered. "They let kids out early for spring planting."

"Jesus, honey, they gave that up in the last century."

"Not the little towns," she said, suddenly on guard.

Jack looked at his shoes, unwilling to distress her. "Your dad's a farmer, then?" he said.

"No, a vet." She was proud of it. "An animal doctor."

"Oh. What was he planting in the middle of May—chickens?"

Beebo clamped her jaws together. He could see the muscles knot under her skin. "If they let the farmer's kids out early, they have to let the vet's kids out, too," she said, trying to be calm. "Everyone at the same time."

"Okay, don't get mad," he said and offered her a cigarette. She took it after a pause that verged on a sulk, but insisted on lighting it for herself. It evidently bothered her to let him perform the small masculine courtesies for her, as if they were an encroachment on her independence.

"So what did they teach you in high school? Typing? Shorthand?" Jack said. "What can you *do?*"

Beebo blew smoke through her nose and finally gave him a woeful smile. "I can castrate a hog," she said. "I can deliver a calf. I can jump a horse and I can run like hell." She made a small sardonic laugh deep in her throat. "God knows they need me in New York City."

Jack patted her shoulder. "You'll go straight to the top, honey," he said. "But not here. Out west somewhere."

"It has to be here, even if I have to dig ditches," she said, and the wry amusement had left her. "I'm not going home."

"Where's home?"

"Wisconsin. A little farming town west of Milwaukee. Juniper Hill."

"Lots of cheese, beer, and German burghers?" he said.

"Lots of mean-minded puritans," she said bitterly. "Lots of hard hearts and empty heads. For me…lots of heartache and not much more."

"Why?" he said gently.

She looked away, pouring some more schnapps for herself. Jack was glad she had a small glass.

"Why did you ditch Juniper Hill, Beebo?" he persisted.

"I—just got into some trouble and ran away. Old story."

"And your parents disowned you?"

"No. I only have my father—my mother died years ago. My father wanted me to stay. But I'd had it."

Jack saw her chin tremble and he got up and brought her a box of tissues. "Hell, I'm sorry," he said. "I'm too nosy. I thought it might help to talk it out a little."

"It might," she conceded, "but not now." She sat rigidly, trying to check her emotion. Jack admired her dignity. After a moment she added, "My father—is a damn good man. He loves me and he tries to understand me. He's the only one who does."

"You mean the only one in Juniper Hill," Jack said. "I'm doing my damnedest to understand you too, Beebo."

She relented a little from her stiff reserve and said, "I don't know why you should, but—thanks."

"There must be other people in your life who tried to help, honey," he said. "Friends, sisters, brothers—"

"One brother," she said acidly. "Everything I ever did was inside-out, ass-backwards, and dead wrong as far as Jim was concerned. I humiliated him and he hated me for it. Oh, I was no dreamboat. I know that. I deserved a wallop now and then. But not when I was down."

"That's the way things go between brothers and sisters," Jack said. "They're supposed to fight."

"You don't understand the *reason.*"

"Explain it to me, then." Jack saw the tremor in her hand when she ditched her cigarette. He let her finish another glassful of schnapps, hoping it might relax her. Then he said, "Tell me the real reason why you left Juniper Hill."

She answered at last in a dull voice, as if it didn't matter any more who knew the truth. "I was kicked out of school."

Jack studied her, perplexed. He would have been gently amused if she hadn't seemed so stricken by it all. "Well, honey, it only happens to the best and the worst," he said. "The worst get canned for being too stupid and the best for being too smart. They damn near kicked me out once....I was one of the best." He grinned.

"Best, worst, or—or different," Beebo said. "I was different. I mean, I just didn't fit in. I wasn't like the rest. They didn't want me around. I guess they felt threatened, as if I were a nudist or a vegetarian, or something. People don't like you to be different. It scares them. They think maybe some of it will rub off on them, and they can't imagine anything worse."

"Than becoming a vegetarian?" he said and downed the rest of his beer to drown a chuckle. He set the glass on the floor by the leg of his chair. "Are you a vegetarian, Beebo?" She shook her head. "A nudist?"

"I'm just trying to make you understand," she said, almost pleading, and there was a real beacon of fear shining through her troubled eyes.

Jack reached out his hand and held it toward her until she gave him one of hers. "Are you afraid to tell me, Beebo?" he said. "Are you ashamed of something? Something you did? Something you *are?*"

She reclaimed her hand and pulled a piece of tissue from her bag, trying to keep her back straight, her head high. But she folded suddenly around a sob, bending over to hold herself, comfort herself. Jack took her shoulders in his firm hands and said, "Whatever it is, you'll lick it, honey. I'll help you if you'll let me. I'm an old hand at this sort of thing. I've been saving people from themselves for years. Sort of a sidewalk Dorothy Dix. I don't know why, exactly. It just makes me feel good. I like to see somebody I like, learn to like himself. You're a big, clean, healthy girl, Beebo. You're handsome as hell. You're bright and sensitive. I like you, and I'm pretty particular."

She murmured inarticulately into her hands, trying to thank him, but he shushed her.

"Why don't you like yourself?" he asked.

After a moment she stopped crying and wiped her face. She threw Jack a quick cautious look, wondering how much of her story she could risk with him. Perversely enough, his very kindness and patience scared her off. She was afraid that the truth would sicken him, alienate him from her. And at this forlorn low point in her life, she needed his friendship more than a bed or a cigarette or even food.

Jack caught something of the conflict going on within her. "Tell me what you can," he said.

"My dad is a veterinarian," she began in her low voice. "Everybody in Juniper Hill loved him. Till he started—drinking too much. But that wasn't for a long time. In the beginning we were all very happy. Even after my mother died, we got along. My brother Jim and I were friends back in grade school.

"Dad taught us about animals. There wasn't a job he couldn't trust me with when it came to caring for a sick animal. And the past few years when he's been—well, drunk so much of the time—I've done a lot of the surgery, too. I'm twice the vet my brother'll ever be. Jim never did like it much. He went along because he was ashamed of his squeamishness. But whenever things got bloody or tough, he ducked out.

"But I got along fine with Dad. The one thing I always wanted was to live a good life for his sake. Be a credit to him. Be something wonderful. Be—a doctor. He was so proud of that. He understood, he helped me all he could." She drained her glass again. "Some doctor I'll be now," she said. "A witch doctor, maybe." She filled the glass and Jack said anxiously, "Whoa, easy there. You're a milk drinker, remember?"

She ignored him. "At least I won't be around to see Dad's face when he realizes I'll never make it to medical school," Beebo said, the corners of her mouth turned down. "I hated to leave him, but I had to do it. It's one thing to stick it out in a place where they don't like you. It's another to let yourself be destroyed."

"So you think you've solved your problems by coming to the big city?" Jack asked her.

"Not all of them!" she retorted. "I'll have to get work, I'll have to find a place to live and all that. But I've solved the worst one, Jack."

"Maybe you brought some of them with you," he said. "You didn't run as far away from Juniper Hill as you think. People are still people, no matter what the town. And Beebo is still Beebo. Do you think New Yorkers are wiser and better than the people in Juniper Hill, honey? Hell, no. They're probably worse. The only difference is that here, you have a chance to be anonymous. Back home everybody knew who you were."

Beebo threw him a sudden smile. "I don't think there's a single Jack Mann in all of Juniper Hill," she said. "It was worth the trip to meet you."

"Well, I'd like to think I'm that fascinating," he said. "But you didn't come to New York City to find Jack Mann, after all. You came to find Beebo Brinker. Yourself. Or are you one of those rare lucky ones who knows all there is to know about themselves by the time they're seventeen?"

"Eighteen," she corrected. "No, I'm not one of the lucky ones. Just one of the rare ones." Inexplicably, it struck both of them funny and they laughed at each other. Beebo felt herself loose and pliable under the influence of the liqueur. It was exhilarating, a floating release that shrouded the pain and confusion of her flight from home and arrival in this cold new place. She was glad for Jack's company, for his warmth and humor. "You must be good for me," she told him. "Either you or the schnapps."

"You're going pretty heavy on that stuff, friend," he warned her, nodding at the glass. "There's more in it than peppermint, you know."

"But it tastes so good going down," she said, surprised to find herself still laughing.

"Well, it doesn't taste so good when it comes back up."

"I haven't had that much," she said and poured herself some more. Jack rolled his eyes to heaven and made her laugh again.

"You know I could take advantage of you in your condition," he said, thinking it might sober her up a little. But his fundamental compassion and intelligence had put her at ease, led her to trust him. She was actually enjoying herself a little now, trying to forget whatever it was that drove her into this new life, and Jack hadn't the heart to stir up her fears again. He wondered if she had left a scandal or a tragedy behind her in Juniper Hill.

"I was going to be a doctor once myself," he said.

She looked at him with a sort of cockeyed interest. "What happened?"

"Would have taken too long. I wanted to get that degree and get out. And I wanted love. But you can't make love to anybody after a long day over a hot cadaver. You're too pooped and the sight of human flesh gives you goose pimples instead of pleasant shivers. Besides, I spent four years in the Navy in the Second World War, and I'd had it with blood and suffering."

Beebo drank the schnapps in her glass. "That's as good a reason as any for quitting, I guess," she said.

"You could still finish up high school and go on to college," he said, trying not to sound pushy.

"No. I've lost it, Jack. That ambition, that will to do well. I left it behind when I left my father. I just don't give a double damn about medicine, for the first time in my life."

"Because a bunch of small-minded provincials asked you to leave their little high school? You make it sound like you were just squirming to be asked."

"You're saying I didn't have the guts to fight them," she said, speaking without resentment. "It isn't that, Jack. I did fight them, with all I've got. I'm tired of it, that's all. You can't fight everybody all the time and still have room in your life to study and think and learn."

"Was it that bad, Beebo?"

"*I* was that bad—to the people in Juniper Hill."

Jack shook his head in bewilderment and laughed a little. "You don't happen to carry the bubonic plague, do you?" he said.

She knew how curious she had made him about herself, and she hadn't the courage to expose the truth to him yet. So she merely said, "That's over now. My life is going to be different."

"Different, but not necessarily better," he said. "I wish to hell you'd come clean with me, honey. I can't help you this way. I don't know what you're running away from."

"I'm not running away from, I'm running *to*," she said. "To this city, this chance for a new start."

"And a new Beebo?" he asked. "Do you think being in a new place will make you better and braver somehow?"

"I'm not chicken, Jack," she said firmly. "I left for Dad's sake as much as my own."

"I didn't say you were, honey," he told her gently. "I don't think a chicken would have come so far to face so much all alone. I think you're a decent, intelligent girl. I think you're a good-looking girl, too, just for the record. That much is plain as the schnapps on your face."

Beebo frowned at him, self-conscious and surprised. "You're the first man who ever called me 'good-looking,'" she said. "No, the second. My father always thought..." Her voice went very soft. "You know, it kills me to go off and—and abandon him like this." She got up from the floor and walked a little unsteadily to the front window.

"Why don't you write to him?" Jack suggested. "If he was so good to you—if you were so close—he deserves to know where you are."

"That was the whole point of leaving," she said, shaking her head. "To keep it secret. To relieve him."

"Of what?"

"Of myself. I was a burden to him. He did too much for me. He tried to be father and mother both. He indulged me when he should have been stern. He never could bear to punish me."

She stood looking out his front window in silence, crying quietly. Her face was still, with the only movement the rhythmic swell and spill of tears from her eyes.

"My father," she said, "is no angel. Much as I love him, I know *that* much." Jack sensed a whole raft of sad secrets behind that brief phrase.

He stood up, crushed his cigarette, and looked at her for a moment. She stood with her legs apart and well-defined by her narrow cotton skirt. Her hair was tousled and damp with sweat, and there was a shine in her wet eyes reflected from the lamplight that intensified the blue. She had left her schnapps glass on the floor and her empty hands hung limp against her thighs. She lifted them now and then to brush away tears. Her head inclined slightly, like that of a youngster who has grown too tall too fast and doesn't want to tower over her classmates.

Her face, sensitive and striped with tears, was in many ways the face of a boy. Her stance was boyish and her low voice too was like a boy's, balanced on the brink of maturity. And there it would stay all her life, never to plumb the true depth of a man's.

She became aware of Jack's eyes on her and turned to pick up her glass, but bumped against a corner of a table and nearly fell. Jack reached her in two big steps and pulled her straight again while she put both hands to her temples. "I feel as if I'm dreaming," she murmured. "Am I?" She looked quizzically at him.

"You're not, but I am," he said, taking her elbow and steering her toward the bedroom. "I'm a dream walking. I'm dreaming and you're in my dream. When I wake up, you'll cease to exist."

"That would solve everything, wouldn't it?" she said, leaning on him more than she realized. She tried to stop him in the center of the room to get her liqueur, but he kept pushing till she gave up.

"Come on, let Uncle Jack bed you down," he said. He took one of her arms across his shoulder, the better to balance them both, pulled her into the bedroom, and unloaded her on his double bed. Beebo spread-eagled herself into all four corners with a sigh, and it wasn't till Jack had all her clothes off but the underwear that she came to and tried to protest. Jack removed her socks with a yank.

"Why, you lousy man," she said, staring at him. But when he smelled the socks, she laughed.

"God, what an exciting creature you are," he grimaced, surveying her muscular angles with all the ardor of an old hen.

"So I'm not your type," she said, getting to her feet. "I can still take off my own underwear." She tried it, lost her balance, and sat down summarily on the bed.

Jack tossed her a nightshirt from his dresser. It was scarlet and orange cotton flannel. "I like flashy sleepers," he explained.

She put it on while he washed in the bathroom. But when he returned he found her leaning on the dresser, dizzily close to losing the schnapps.

Jack guided her to the bathroom and got her to the washbowl before it came up.

"I had no idea there was so much in the bottle," Jack said when she had gotten the last of it out. At last she straightened up to look in the mirror. "By God, Beebo, you were the same color as the schnapps for a minute there."

He made her rinse her mouth and then dragged her back to bed, where he washed her unconscious face and hands. He sat and gazed at her before he turned out the light, speculating about her. Asleep, she looked younger, adolescent: still a child, with a child's

19

purity; soon an adult, with adult desires. Did she know already what those desires would be? And was that why she fled from Juniper Hill? The knowledge that her desires and her adult self would shock the town, shock her father, shock even herself?

Jack thought so. He thought she knew what it was that troubled her so deeply, even though she might not know the name for it. It wasn't just being "different" that she hated. It was the kind of differentness. Jack wanted to comfort her, to explain that she wasn't alone in the world, that other people were different in the same way she was. But he couldn't speak of it to her until she admitted it first to him.

He smoothed the hair off her forehead, admiring her features and her flawless skin without the least taint of physicality. He felt sorry for her, and scoffed at himself for wishing she were the boy she resembled at that moment. Then he lay down beside her and went to sleep.

Beebo slept for fourteen hours. She wakened with a glaring square of sunshine astride her face. When she rolled over to escape it, she felt a new sensation: the beginning beat of the long rhythm of a hangover—her first.

The thought of the peppermint schnapps nauseated her for a few moments. She looked around the room to forget it and clear her head, and found a note pinned to the pillow next to hers. It gave her a start to realize Jack had spent the night in bed with her. And then it made her laugh and the laugh sent aching echoes through her head.

The note said, "I'm at work. Home around 5:30. Plenty of feed in refrig. You don't want it but you NEED it. White pills in medicine chest for head. Take two and LIVE. You're a devil in bed. Jack."

She smiled, and lifted herself with gingerly care from the bed. It was two-thirty in the afternoon.

When Jack came home with a brown bag full of groceries, she was smoking quietly and reading the paper in his kitchen.

"How are you?" he said, smiling.

"Fine."

"I don't believe it."

"Well, I'm clean, and you can believe *that.* I took a bath."

"On you it looks good," he said, putting food away.

Beebo shook her head a little. "I was just thinking...you're about the only friend I have, Jack. I've been kicking myself all day for not thanking you. I mean, you listened to me for hours. You've been damn nice about my problems."

"That's my style," he said, but he was flattered. "Besides, us frustrated doctors have to stick together. It's nice to come home to a welcoming committee that thinks I'm the greatest guy in the world."

"You must have a lot of friends down here," she said, curious about him. Beebo had done all the talking since they met. But who was Jack Mann, the guy who did all the listening? Just a good-hearted young man in a strange town who gave her a drink and a bed, and was about to give her some dinner.

"Oh, plenty of friends," he said, lighting the oven.

"You made me feel safe and—and *human* last night, Jack. If that doesn't sound too silly."

"Did you think you weren't?" He put the ready-cooked food in the stove to warm.

"I'm grateful. I wanted you to know."

"Marry me and prove it," he said.

She looked at him with her mouth open, astonished. "You're kidding!" she said.

"Nope. I always wanted a dozen kids."

Beebo began to laugh. "I'd make a lousy mother, I'm afraid," she said.

"You'd make a dandy mother, honey. Nice girls always like kids."

"Is that why you want to get married? Just to have kids?"

"When I was in the Navy, I was always the sucker who put on the whiskers and passed out the popsicles on Christmas Day in the Islands. Hot? Mamma mia! I nearly passed out myself. Melted almost as fast as the goo I was giving away. But I loved those kids."

"Then why aren't you married? Why don't you have some kids of your own?" she prodded. It seemed peculiar to her that so affable a man, especially one who liked children, should be single.

"Beebo, my ravishing love, why don't *you* get married and have some kids?" he countered, disconcerting her.

"A woman has to do the having," she said. "All a man has to do is get her pregnant."

"All," Jack repeated, rolling his eyes.

"Besides, I don't want to get married," she added, her eyes veiled and troubled.

"Hell, everybody gets married," Jack said, watching her closely. Maybe she would open up a bit now and talk about what really mattered.

"Everybody but *you,*" she said.

He hunched his shoulders and grinned. "Touché," he said. Then he opened the oven door to squint at the bubbling ravioli, and drew it out with a potholder, spooning it onto their plates.

They sat down at the table and Jack told her, "This is the greatest Italian food you'll ever eat. Pasquini on Thompson Street makes it up." He glanced up and found Beebo studying him. "What's the matter? Don't like pasta?"

"Jack, have you ever been in love?" she said.

Jack smiled and swallowed a forkful of food before he answered. She was asking him, as circuitously as possible, to tell her about life. She didn't want him to guess it, but that was what she wanted.

"I fall in love twice a year," he said. "Once in the fall and once in the spring. In the fall the kids come back to school, a few blocks from here. There are plenty of newcomers waiting to be loved the wrong way in September. They call me Wrong Way Mann." He glanced up at her, but instead of taking the hint, she was puzzled by it.

"I didn't know there was a wrong way," she said earnestly.

"In love, as in everything else," he said. "I just—well. Let's say I have a talent for goofing things up." He wondered if he ought to be frank with her about himself. It might relieve her, might make it possible for her to talk about herself then. But, looking at her face again, he decided against it. The whole subject scared her still. She wanted to learn and yet she feared that what she learned might be ugly, or more frightening than her ignorance.

He would have to go slowly with her, teach her gently what she was, and teach her not to hate the word for it: Lesbian. Such a soft word, mellifluous on the tongue; such a stab in the heart to someone very young, unsure, and afraid.

"And in the spring?" she was asking. "You fall in love then, too?"

"That's just the weather, I guess. I fall in love with everybody in the spring. The butcher, the baker, the candlestickmaker." He smiled at her face. She was amused and startled by the male catalog, and afraid to let her amusement show. Jack took her off the hook. "Good, hm?" He nodded at the food.

Beebo took a bite without answering. "What's it like to live down here? I mean—" She cleared her throat. "In the Village?"

"Just one mad passionate fling after another," he said. "Try the cheese." He passed it to her.

"With the butcher and the baker?" she said humorously and made him laugh.

At last he said, "Well, honey, it's like everyplace else. You eat three squares a day, you sleep eight hours a night, you work and earn money and obey the laws...well, *most* of the laws. The only difference between here and Juniper Hill is, we stay open all night."

She laughed. And suddenly she said, "You know, this *is* good," and began to eat with an appetite.

"So's the salad." He pushed the bowl toward her. "Now you tell me something, Little Girl Lost," he said. "Were *you* ever in love?"

She looked down at her plate, uncomfortably self-conscious.

"Oh, come on," he teased. "I'm not going to blackmail you."

"Not real love," she said. "Puppy love, I guess."

"That kind can hurt as much as the other," Jack said, and Beebo was grateful for his perception. "But it ought to be fun now and then, too."

"Maybe it ought to be, but it never was," she said. "I guess I'm like you, Jack. I goof everything up."

He pointed his fork at her plate. "You've stopped eating again," he said. "I want you to taste your future employer's cooking."

"My what?" she exclaimed.

"Pasquini needs a delivery boy. Can you drive?"

"I can drive, but can I be a boy?" she said with such a rueful face that he laughed aloud.

"You can wear slacks," he said. "That's the best I could do. The rest is up to you."

His laughter embarrassed her, as if perhaps she had gone too far with her remark, and she said as seriously as possible, "I learned to drive on a truck with six forward gears."

"This is a panel truck."

"Duck soup. God, I hope he'll take me, Jack. I have exactly ten bucks between me and the poorhouse. I didn't know what I was going to do with myself."

"Well, you haven't got the job yet, honey. But I told Pasquini you had lots of experience and you'd do him the favor of dropping by in the morning."

"Some favor!" she grinned. "Me, who couldn't find Times Square if my life depended on it, making deliveries in this tangled-up part of town."

"You'll catch on."

"What are the Pasquinis like?" she said.

"You'll like Marie. She's Pete's wife. Does all the cooking. It's her business, really. It was just a spaghetti joint when Pete's dad ran it. After he died Pete took over and damn near went bankrupt. Then he married Marie. She cooks *and* keeps the books—like nobody can. She used to be a pretty girl, too, till she had too many kids and too much pizza."

"What about Pete?"

"I don't know what to tell you about that guy. I've known him slightly for the past ten years, but no one knows him very well. As far as Marie's concerned, he's her number one delivery boy. As a husband and a father, he's her idea of a bust."

"You mean he cheats?"

"He's out every night of the week with weird girls on his arm. As if he were proud of it. He picks out the oddballs—you know, the ones who haven't cut their hair since they were four years old, and wear dead-white make-up and cotton lisle stockings."

"Lousy taste," Beebo said, but when Jack smiled she looked away. She wasn't going to give him the chance to ask what her own taste might be.

Jack paused, sensing her reticence, and then he went on, "Pete used to run a gang when he was in his teens. He was our local color."

"You mean he's a juvenile delinquent?" Beebo asked naively. "Are you sending me to work for a crook?"

"He's an *ex*-j.d.," Jack chuckled. "He went on to better things the day they broke his zip gun."

"My God! Is he a criminal, Jack?"

"No, honey, don't panic. He's just a kook. He's more of a loner now. It comes naturally to him to skulk around. But as far as I can tell, he only skulks after dark. And after Beat broads. He hasn't been arrested since he was nineteen, and that's been ten years."

"He sounds like the ideal employer," Beebo cracked.

"You could do worse; you with ten bucks in your pocket," Jack reminded her. "Besides, he's lived here all his life. He may be odd but you get used to him."

"Just how 'odd' is he?"

"Honey, you've *got* to be a little odd down here, or you lose your membership card," he said. "Besides, I'm not asking you to cut your veins and mingle blood with him. Just pass out the pizzas and take his money once a week."

Beebo shook her head and laughed. "Well, if you say so," she said. "I guess I'm safe as long as I don't wear cotton lisle stockings."

She got the job. Pete Pasquini had more deliveries than he could handle alone. Marie's sauces, salads, preserves, and pastas were making a name and making a pile. The orders were going up so fast that it would take a second driver to deliver them all.

Beebo, dressed in a clean white shirt, sweater, and tan slacks, faced Pete at eight in the morning. She was somewhat intimidated by the looks of him and by Jack's thumb sketch of the night before. He was a dour-faced young Italian-American with blue jowls and a down-turned mouth. If he ever smiled—Beebo doubted it—he would have been almost handsome, for his teeth were straight and white, and he had a peculiarly sensual mouth beneath his plum-dark eyes. He looked mean and sexy—a combination that instantly threw Beebo high on her guard.

"You're Beebo?" he said, looking up at her with an order pad and pencil poised in his hands.

"Yes," she said. "Jack Mann sent me. I—he—said you needed a driver."

He smirked a little. Probably his smile for the day, she thought. "You're as tall as I am," he observed, as if pleased about it; pleased at least to make her self-conscious about it.

"Would you like to see me drive? I'm a good driver," she said resentfully.

"How come you're so tall, Beebo? Girls ain't supposed to be so tall." He put the paper and pencil down and turned to look her over, leaning jauntily on a linoleum-covered counter as he did so.

Beebo folded her arms over her chest in a gesture that told him to slow down, back off; a very unfeminine gesture that ordinarily offended a man's ideals. "I can drive. You want a driver," she said curtly. "Let's talk business." She had learned long ago to stand her ground when someone taunted her. Otherwise the taunting grew intolerable.

To her amazement, she made Pete Pasquini laugh. It was not a reassuring sound. "You're a feisty one, ain't you?" he grinned. "You—are—a—*feisty*—one." He separated each word with slow relish, enjoying her discomfiture. For though she stood tall and bold in front of him, her hot face betrayed her embarrassment. She gave him a withering look and then turned and strode toward the door till she heard his voice behind her, accompanied by his footsteps.

"No offense, Beebo," he said, "I'm gonna be your boss. I wanta be your friend, too. I don't want people workin' for me don't like me. Shake hands?"

She turned around slowly, unconvinced. Maybe he really thought he was ingratiating himself with her. But she didn't like his method much. It was the thought of her nearly empty wallet that finally prompted her to offer him her hand. He took it with a rather light loose grasp, surprising Beebo, who was used to the hearty grip of the farmers in her home county. But when he lifted her hand up and said, "Hey, that's big, too!" she snatched it away as if he had burned her.

"Okay, okay, all you got to do is drive, you don't have to shake hands with me all day," he said, amused by her reaction. "I can see it ain't your favorite game."

It seemed peculiar enough to Beebo that they shake hands at all. They were not officially employer and employee yet, and even if they were, they were still man and girl. It made her feel creepy. She assumed that Pete had to get his wife's approval before he could hire her. Marie was supposed to run the business.

"Well, come on, I'll show you where things is," Pete said.

"You mean it's settled?" She hesitated. "I'm hired?"

"Why not?" He turned back to look at her.

"Well, I thought your wife? I mean—?" She stopped, not wishing to anger him. His face had turned very dark.

"My wife *what?*" he said. "You never mind my wife. If I say you're hired, you're hired. I don't want no back talk about the wife. You dig?"

She nodded, startled by the force of his spite. She made a mental note not to press that sore spot again. He apparently needed and wanted the money Marie's succulent concoctions brought in, but he hated surrendering control of the shop to her. Yet it was the price of their success. She knew what she was doing, in the kitchen and in the accounts, and he was afraid to interfere.

Beebo stood frowning at the sawdust floor.

"What's the matter, kid? Something bugging you?" Pete asked.

She glanced up at him. It was strange that he should hire her on the spot without the slightest idea if she could drive worth a damn. "Do you want me to start deliveries this morning?" she said.

"I'll take you around, show you the route," he said. "First we got to make up the orders."

He walked toward the back of the store with Beebo behind him. "Mr. Pasquini, there's just one thing," she said.

"It's Pete. Yeah, what thing?" He handed her a large cardboard carton to pack a grocery order in.

"How much will it pay?" Beebo asked, standing there with the box, unwilling to start working till she knew what she was worth.

"Fifty a week to start," he said, without looking up. He lifted some bottled olive oil down from a nearby shelf. "Things work out good, I'll raise you. You want it, don't you?" He looked at her then.

There was a barely noticeable pause before she answered, "I want it." But she spoke with a sliver of misgiving stuck in the back of her mind.

Pete accompanied her on the delivery route that morning and again in the afternoon, watching her handle the truck, showing her where the customers lived. She had spent the night before with Jack studying a map of New York City and Greenwich Village, but what had seemed fairly logical on paper bogged down in colorful confusion when she took to the streets.

Pete swung an arm up on the seat behind her, his knees jutting toward her legs, and now and then when she missed a direction he would grab the wheel and start the turn for her. She disliked his closeness extremely, and throughout the day she was aware of his eyes on her face and body. It almost made her feel as if she had a figure, for the first time in her life, and the idea shocked her.

Beebo had broad shoulders and hardly a hint of a bosom. No man had ever looked at her appreciatively before, not even Jack Mann, who obviously liked her and enjoyed her company. She was not sure whether Pete admired her or was merely interested because she was so different from other girls.

He can't possibly like me, she thought. Not the way men like women. The notion was so preposterous that it made her smile and reassured her. Till Pete noticed the smile and said, "What's so funny, kid?" He looked too eager to know and she brushed it off. He let it go, but watched her more attentively, making her squirm a little.

It was a relief to climb down from the truck that afternoon—and a blow to feel the heavy clap of a masculine hand on her shoulder. "You did real good, Beebo," Pete said, and the hand lay there until she spun away from him and walked inside to meet his wife.

Marie Pasquini was twenty-six, the overweight and over-worked mother of five little Pasquinis. She did most of the cooking while Pete's mother tended her kids, and the two women fell into several pan-rattling arguments per day. Beebo could hear the soprano squeals of young children upstairs in the apartment above the store, and a periodic disciplinary squawk from Grandma Pasquini.

Marie greeted Beebo with a big smile, revealing the shadow of the pretty face concealed beneath the fat.

"Your accent is French, isn't it?" Beebo said.

"You got it," Marie beamed. "Smart girl." She moved about the kitchen while they got acquainted, eating, working, and talking incessantly. Pete slouched against the kitchen door chewing a wooden matchstick and watching Beebo.

Marie worked hard and she ate hard and she was going all to hips. But she was friendly and cheerful, and Beebo liked her.

"That's a good boy, that Jack," Marie said. "He comes in here two, three times a week, buys my food. Tells his friends, 'Eat Pasquini's stuff,' and by God, they eat."

"He gave me some last night," Beebo said. "It's good."

"You bet." Marie stirred her sauce and glanced at Beebo. "You live with him now?"

"Well—temporarily," Beebo said, taken aback both by the question and by Pete's silent laughter.

"About time he got a girl," Marie said briskly. "Even one in pants." And she glanced humorously at Beebo's tan chinos.

Beebo colored up. "Well, it's not quite like that," she protested.

"Oh, don't tell me," Marie said, holding up two spattered hands. "A boy and a girl...well...!" and she gave a Gallic chuckle.

"What you want to do, embarrass the kid?" Pete demanded suddenly with mock anger. "She don't sleep with no lousy fag."

"Shut that big mouth, Pete," Marie said sharply, without bothering to look at him. "She don't want to hear dirty talk, neither."

Beebo was burning to ask what a fag was, but she didn't dare. She could hear in her imagination the cackling it would provoke from Pete.

Marie stirred in silence for a moment. "I never saw a boy put up with so much," she said finally. "He got people in and out, in and out, every damn day, eating him out of house and home." Beebo squirmed guiltily. "His only trouble, he got too big a heart. Don't never take advantage of him like the others, Beebo."

"What others?"

"You don't know?" Marie looked at her, puzzled.

"Well, I've only known Jack a little while. I mean—"

"Oh." Marie nodded sagely. "Well, he got too many fair-weather friends. Know they can have whatever he got they want. So they take. And he lets them. Can't stand to see people go without. He's a good boy. Too good."

"He ain't all *that* good, Marie," Pete drawled, grinning at Beebo. "You just like him because he comes in here and gives you that swishy talk about what a good-looking dame you are. All that proves is, he got bad eyes. Now, Beebo here might have trouble with him, you never know. If I was her, I wouldn't climb in his bed."

"Pete, you got a mind even dirtier than your mouth," Marie said. "Get out of my kitchen, I don't want the food dirtied up too. Out, *salaud!*"

Beebo was amused by her accent, comically mismated with the ungrammatical English she had learned from Pete.

Marie threw a potlid at her husband. "See?" Pete shrugged at Beebo, catching the lid. "I try to say a few words and what do I get? Pots and pans. And she wonders why I go out at night."

"Out!" Marie stamped her foot and he left them, disappearing bizarrely like a wraith into the gloom of the darkened store. After nearly a full minute had elapsed Beebo became aware with a silent start that the fingers of his left hand were curled around the door frame: five orphaned earthworms searching for the dirt.

Beebo stared at them with something very near loathing. She wondered if she was supposed to see them, and if he thought they would please her for some obscure reason. Or was he hiding, thinking the fingers out of sight? No, he knew damn well she could see them, and would. They were his gesture of invitation, unheard and unseen by his wife.

Beebo began to sweat with alarm and revulsion. She chatted determinedly with Marie for almost fifteen minutes before those five pale fingers retreated from their post. Maybe it was supposed to be a gag, Beebo told herself. She didn't want to mention it to

Marie. It would make her look a fool, perhaps even hysterical, if the whole thing was only a joke.

That's what it is, Beebo told herself firmly. That's what it has to be. She stood up and thanked Marie, accepting a bag of hot fresh-cooked chicken to take home for dinner, and walked through the front of the shop. She held herself together tightly, and if she had seen the least movement, heard the least whisper, she would have lashed out in abrupt terror. She had the uncanny feeling that Pete was somewhere waiting with those loathsome hands. But she couldn't see him, she didn't hear him, and she reached the door and the outside with a gasp of relief.

The relief was so deep that it turned into a laugh, soothing her and making her a little ashamed of herself. Away from Pete she could scold herself for her aversion to him. Maybe it wasn't fair. He was just a guy, not a ghost, not a snake. He was spooky, but Marie seemed as healthy and normal as her good foods.

Beebo was disturbed by the strangeness of Pete's manner, but she could never believe that any man would truly desire her, no matter how creepy he was. Not even a nut like Pete Pasquini. For his own reasons he was making a study of her, but beyond that he would never go. She began to feel safe and comfortable again as she rounded the corner to Jack's street. She felt unassailable in the fortress of her flat-chested, muscular young body. It was not the stuff that male dreams are made of.

As Jack explained to her later, it was himself and others like him who had talked the Pasquinis' shop into a financial success. Rather abruptly, Pete and Marie found themselves making money, and Pete, after an adolescence full of alley wars and hock-shop heists, found himself taking a belated interest in the dough: not the flour kind, the folding kind.

He had married Marie overseas when he was in the service

and brought her back to his inheritance: the foundering grocery shop his father had left him. Undismayed, Marie set out to bear his kids and learn his mother's recipes. By a combination of luck, sense, and skill, Marie pulled them out of the dumps.

It was still nominally Pete's business, yet he did little more than run his wife's errands and pocket all the money Marie would let him have. He always demanded more, but he respected her French thrift. The money she refused to give him went back into the business and made it possible for him to insist on more gradually as time went on.

This arrangement galled Pete, but he preferred it to poverty. Still, he had to get even with her. So he did it by openly sniffing up skirts around Greenwich Village. He would even flaunt a girl at Marie now and then and she, stung, would call him half a man, who played with other girls because he didn't have what it took to keep one good woman satisfied. Or else she ignored him entirely, which enraged him.

It was not a quiet cozy family. Pete did not know or like his children very well. He got on famously with his mother, but his mother and his wife were lifelong enemies. Beebo began to learn about them as she worked near them in the shop.

Pete watched Beebo move around during the first week, making her feel clumsy as a young colt; getting in her way deliberately (she was sure) to make her dodge around him; turning up in out-of-the-way corners where she didn't expect to see him. Her antipathy to him was lively, but fortunately she didn't see much of him. Filling orders took less time than delivering them and she was out of the shop most of the day. In the truck she was disposed to be pleased with her job. She liked to drive. She liked to talk to people, and the customers were friendly. She even liked the chore of carrying the heavy cartons up and down all day. It pleased her to feel strong, equal to the task.

A week ago all her hopes had been crashing around her. She had retreated in disgrace from a cruel predicament. Then she found Jack Mann, a friend; a job; and some self-respect, one right after the other. She was grateful, full of the resilient optimism of youth.

Without any specific words on the subject, Beebo and Jack came to an understanding that she would live with him for a while, till she could afford a place for herself. "You'll be better off with a roommate," Jack advised her casually. "I'll have to introduce you to some of my upper-class female friends."

"Sure," she grinned. "'Pamela, this is my lower-class female friend, Beebo Brinker.' And she'll say, 'Dahling, you're absolutely crashing, but I can't possibly share my apartment with those pants.'" She made Jack laugh at her. "Besides, Jackson," Beebo added rather shyly, "I've already got a roommate. He only has one fault—he won't let me pay my half of the rent."

"I like to pay bills," Jack said. "Gives me a sense of power."

"Marie says you've got too big a heart," Beebo told him. "And she's right."

"Marie's a good girl," he said. "How are you getting along with Peter the Wolf?"

"Fine, as long as he's out of my sight."

Jack grinned. "You can handle him, honey. Just keep a can of corn beef in your pocket. If he tries to lift your wallet, clobber him."

"It's not my wallet I'm worried about," she said. "There's nothing in it, anyway. It's just that he's always under my feet when he should be on the other side of the store."

"I suspect it's for Marie's benefit," Jack said. "Every female who comes into the store gets the once-over from Pete—provided Marie is looking. And most of the time, she is. She likes to keep score, I guess."

"There was a girl today," Beebo said. "She came in the shop about noon, when Marie was fixing lunch. I waited on her." Her face became intent as she summoned the girl's image in her mind's eye.

"What about her?" Jack said curiously.

But Beebo, coming to herself at the sound of his voice, said, "Oh, nothing. But she was more Pete's type...*any* man's type."

"What was she like?"

"She had long black hair," Beebo said, as if it were very special. "People don't let their hair grow like that any more. It was lovely. She let it hang free down her back. And her face..." She was gone again, seeing it in her imagination.

"She must have been a looker," Jack said, frustrated by the reticence between himself and Beebo. He knew what hundreds of questions she needed to ask, what a wealth of help she would be wanting soon. But she didn't dare start asking and because she didn't, Jack dared not force the answers on her yet.

"She was absolutely gorgeous," Beebo said with a certain wonderment and innocence that touched him. "I never saw such a girl in my life before." There was a small silence. Beebo's words hung in the air like a neon sign and reduced her abruptly to confusion. To cover up, she said, "She wasn't a very nice girl, though. Not by your standards."

"My standards?"

"She's not afraid of boys," Beebo grinned. "At least, she wasn't afraid of Pete. But I think they knew each other from somewhere. He called her...Mona." She spoke the name self-consciously. "It sounds old-fashioned, doesn't it?"

"I wonder if it's Mona Petry," Jack said. "She has black hair, but I didn't think it was that long. Still, I haven't seen her for a while."

"Who's Mona Petry?" Beebo asked, her eyes intent on Jack.

"Old flame of Pete's," Jack said. "She used to come into the store a lot three or four years ago. She and Pete got quite a charge out of putting poor Marie on. Mona isn't the charitable type. She likes to land a man who belongs to some other woman—more to spite the other woman than because she wants the man. As soon as she won Pete, she dumped him like a sack of meal. For some reason, Pete never fought back. Makes me think she really meant something to him. God knows, none of the other broads do."

"Is she one of those man-hungry girls that can't get enough?" Beebo said. "I forget what they're called, but there's a name for it."

"The name is nymphomaniac," Jack said. "But Mona doesn't love men. She just plays around with them. They're good ego builders." He lighted a cigarette, seeing, without seeming to, the concentration on Beebo's face. The question was there on her tongue, in her mind, but she couldn't get it out. *If Mona doesn't love men,* she was thinking...*then who?*

"There's another word for Mona," Jack said. Beebo tensed up. "Bitch." He threw her a grin and made her laugh with nervous relief. "Actually, Mona loves girls," Jack went on, speaking in a smooth casual flow, a conversational tone that bespoke no shock, no disapproval, nothing but ordinary interest. He deliberately looked at the front page of the evening paper as he spoke.

Beebo answered huskily, "What do you mean? What girls?"

"Lesbians," he said. "Want to freshen this up for me, pal?" He handed her his highball glass. She took it with astonishment still plain on her face. When she returned from the kitchen with the new drink, she asked him, "Aren't they sort of—*immoral?* I heard the word once before. I thought you weren't supposed to say it."

At that, Jack looked up. "Lesbian? You mean you thought it was a dirty word?" he exclaimed, and laughed in spite of himself. Beebo was momentarily offended until he cleared his throat and said, "Forgive me, honey, but that's the bloodiest nonsense I've heard in a long time. Whoever in the hell told you it was dirty?"

"Doesn't it mean loose women?" Beebo asked.

He shook his head. "It means *gay* women," he said. "It means homosexual women. It means women, Beebo, who love other women. The way heterosexual women love men."

His words put a focus on Beebo's fascination. She stared at him from the sofa with her lips parted and her eyes fixed steadily on his. "You said Mona was a bitch," she said finally, softly. "And then you said she was a Lesbian. Doesn't that make her cheap? Q.E.D.?"

"Some of the staunchest Puritan ladies I know are double-dyed bitches," Jack said briskly. "And just because Mona is a bad apple doesn't mean all the gay girls in the world are full of worms. Mona would be bitchy anyway, gay *or* straight."

"What's 'straight'?"

"Heterosexual," Jack said.

"Where did you learn all those words?" Beebo said, bewildered.

"I'm a native. I speak the lingo," he said, but instead of catching his implication, she thought he meant only that he had lived in Greenwich Village so long he had picked it up, like everyone else.

"Does it ever happen that a nice girl is a Lesbian?" she asked him shyly.

"All the time," he said, opening up the paper and gazing through the ball scores.

"Did you ever meet any?"

"I've met most of them," he chuckled. "They're just as friendly and pleasant as other girls. Why not?"

"But can't you tell by looking at them that they're—" She rubbed a hand over her mouth as if to warn herself not to speak the word, and then said it anyway: "—Lesbian?"

"You mean, do they all wear army boots and Levis?" Jack said with a smile. "Does Mona Petry look like a buck private?"

Beebo shook her head. "That's why it's so hard to believe she's what you say she is."

"Gay? Why hell, she's slept with more girls than she has men. And let me tell you, that's damn near enough girls to elect a lady president."

Beebo laughed with him, and yet she felt a strange obsession with the whole idea. She half resented Jack's merriment on the subject, although she was relieved that he displayed no contempt for Lesbians as a group. Only for Mona Petry. She was surprised to find herself wanting to defend Mona, whom she knew so little. And yet she trusted Jack's judgment. Still, what a pity to think a girl that pretty was that hard.

Jack sipped his drink and picked up his cigarette, still with his eyes on the paper. "There are some nice little gay bars around the neighborhood," he said. "We'll have to take some of them in. Maybe this weekend, hm?" He didn't look at her. His cigarette waggled between his lips as he talked.

"Is it all right to go there?" Beebo asked. "Don't the police make raids on those places?"

"Now and then!" he conceded. "Of course, if you'd rather not..."

"Oh, I'd like to go," she said, so quickly that he smiled into the newsprint. "But aren't they just for men—the gay bars?"

"Men, girls, and everything in between," he assured her.

"Do you ever go there, Jack?"

Again he was tempted to be honest with her, and still again he restrained himself. "I go when the mood is on me," he said. Beebo became silent at once, as if she suspected she was trying to learn too much too fast. But she spent the remaining weekdays waiting impatiently for a tour of the bars with Jack.

Jack took her to three or four of his favorite places, and to one strictly Lesbian bar where they admitted only the faces they recognized, through a window in the door. Beebo followed him around quietly, watching, listening, almost breathing in the atmosphere. She said little, and most of what she did say was interrogatory.

Jack answered her calmly while he sipped one beer after another. He would order one for her and let her work at it, but he usually ended up finishing it himself. In every bar he was kept busy greeting people, trading jokes, laughing. Beebo trailed along in his wake, smiling and shaking hands with the strangers who were Jack's friends, and promptly forgetting their names.

But not their faces. Toward the end of the evening she began to feel that she had seen more faces in one night than she had seen in a lifetime in Juniper Hill. And these faces seemed different to her: rare and beautiful, sharers of a special knowledge. They had bright eyes and young smiles, no matter how old they were.

"They make a big thing of keeping young down here," Jack told her. "The men are worse than the girls. Nobody loves an old queen."

It was almost one in the morning when they left the last co-ed bar and Jack asked if she was game for one more. "This one is just for Lesbians," he said.

She nodded, and a few minutes later they were being admitted to a basement bar saturated with pink light, paneled with mirrors, and filled with girls. More girls, more sizes, types, and ages, than Beebo had ever seen collected together in one place. The place was called the Colophon and it was decorated with the emblems of various famous publishing houses.

Jack fought his way through the crush at the bar, absorbing a lot of pointed merriment directed at his masculinity.

"Sour grapes," he cried good-naturedly and inspired a chorus of laughter and catcalls. Beebo, pushing in behind him, became aware suddenly that she was the object of mass curiosity. She could look over the heads of most of the girls and her height made her visible from all directions.

Abashed, she closed in on Jack, who was hollering an order to the bartender. "Maybe we ought to go. I—I mean—" She didn't know how to explain herself to him. He was looking at her with a startled frown. "They don't seem to like having a man in here," she said lamely.

Jack began to laugh. "You want me to go, honey? Okay. Just give me two bits to see a movie."

She gasped. "That's not what I meant!" she objected. "I don't want to be in here alone!"

"Why not?" He reached between two girls at the bar to grab his beer. "You'll make out. I might cramp your style."

"Jack, damn it, if you go, *I* go."

"Okay, pal, I won't ditch you," he said, glimpsing her anxious face. "Relax. We'll have one more and then cut out."

She had had quite a bit of beer already, even with Jack finishing them for her. But she couldn't stand there with all those eyes on her and do nothing. Better to drink a beer than gape back at the gapers. She poured some into her glass and drank it. And then drained the glass and poured some more.

Jack took her elbow. "I see some friends over there," he said, guiding her toward a table near the back. There were introductions all around, but to Beebo, things seemed different. The other bars had been all male or mixed. In this one, Jack Mann and the two bartenders, and a small scattering of "Johns," were the only men in a big room solidly packed with women. It excited Beebo intensely—all that femininity. She was silent, studying the girls at the table while Jack talked with them. When she shook hands with them, a new feeling gripped her. For the first time in her life she was proud of her size, proud of her strength, even proud of her oddly boyish face. She could see interest, even admiration on the faces of many of the girls. She was not used to that kind of reaction in people, and it exhilarated her. But she didn't talk much, only answering direct questions when she had to; smiling at them when they smiled at her; looking away in confusion when one or another tried to stare her down.

They had been there half an hour when somebody came over from another table and asked her to dance. Beebo turned around, her stomach in a knot. "Are they dancing?" she asked.

"Sure," said the girl. "By the jukebox."

Beebo had heard music without looking to see where it came from. She got up from the table and went to the back room, realizing as she stood up how much beer she had drunk. At the back of the crowd surrounding the dance floor, there was room to stand and watch.

The music was rhythmic and popular. The floor was jammed

with a mass of couples...a mass of girls, dancing, arms locked around each other, bodies pressed close and warm. Their cheeks were touching. Quick light kisses were exchanged. And they were all girls, every one of them: young and lovely and infatuated with each other. They touched one another with gentle caresses, they kissed, they smiled and laughed and whispered while they turned and moved together.

There was no shame, no shock, no self-consciousness about it at all. They were enjoying themselves. They were having fun in the most natural way imaginable. They were all in love, or so it seemed. They were—what did Jack call it?—gay.

Beebo watched them for less than a minute, all told; but a minute that was transfixed like a living picture in her mind for the rest of her life. She was startled by it, afraid of it. And yet so passionately moved that she caught her breath and held it till her heart began to pound in protest. Her fists closed hard with the nails biting into her palms and she was obsessed momentarily by the desire to grab the girl nearest her and kiss her.

At that point she murmured, "Oh, God!" and turned to flee. She felt the way she had in childhood dreams when she was being chased by some vague terrible menace, and she had to move slowly and tortuously, with great effort, as through a wall of water, while the monster gained on her from behind.

She caught Jack's shoulders in her big hands and squeezed them hard. "Let's go, let's go," she said urgently.

He looked at her as if she had lost her senses. "I just ordered another round," he said.

"Jack, please!" She pulled him to his feet.

"Jesus, can't you wait a little while, honey?" he said, and triggered an outburst of merriment at the table. But she meant it, and he was not too high to see her panic. He picked his jacket off the back of his chair, apologizing to his friends. "When she wants it, she wants it now," he grinned, shrugging.

"Who are you kidding?" they laughed.

Beebo was already pushing her way to the exit and Jack had a battle to catch her. He found her waiting for him outside by the door.

"Hey," he said, and put a friendly hand on her shoulder as they started to walk toward his apartment. "What happened?"

"I don't want to go back there, Jack," she blurted.

"What's the matter with it? Too much fun?"

"It was awful," she said, not even knowing why she said it.

"You liked the other places."

She wouldn't answer, only striding along so fast in her haste to leave the Colophon behind that Jack had to run to keep up.

"Was it the dancing?" he said.

She whirled to answer him, her face flushed with emotion. "I suppose you've seen it so many times you think nothing of it," she cried. "Well, it's—it's *wrong!*"

"Who the hell do you think you are to call it wrong?" Jack demanded. "Those are damn nice girls. If they want to dance with each other, let them dance. You don't have to watch."

Beebo listened, her anger fading, to be replaced by a fearful desire.

"Did it make you feel...that way, Beebo?" he said gently.

"It made me feel..." She turned away, unable to face him. "Funny inside. As if it was wrong. Or too right. I don't know."

"It's not wrong, pal," he said, speaking to her back. "You've been brought up to think so. Most of us have. But who are they hurting? Nobody. They're just making each other happy. And you want their heads to roll because it makes you feel funny."

She covered her face with her hands and rubbed her eyes roughly. Through her fingers she said, "I don't want to hurt them. I just don't want to stand there and watch them."

"Well, why didn't you dance?" he said. "Hell, I don't like being a wallflower, either."

"Jack, I can't dance like that," she said in a hushed voice.

"Why can't you?" She refused to answer, so he answered for her. "You can. You just won't. But you know something, my little friend? One of these days, you will."

"You're no prophet, Jack. Don't predict *my* future." She started walking again.

He followed her, throwing up his hands. "Okay, okay. It shook you. But not because it was vulgar and indecent. Because it was beautiful and exciting. Besides, you envied those kids on the dance floor. Didn't you?"

Her confession never came. They walked in silence the rest of the way to Jack's apartment. He closed and locked the front door and turned on the living room light, tossing his jacket into a chair.

"Beebo," he said, lighting a cigarette. "You've been living with me almost a month now—"

"If you want me to move, I'll move." She was surly and defensive.

"I want you to stay. When you move, it'll be because you want to," he said. "Besides, that's not what I want to talk about. In the past month, you have never once told me the most important thing about yourself, Beebo."

She felt a flash of fear, piercing as sudden light in darkness. "I don't know what you mean," she said.

Jack gave her the freshly lighted cigarette and she hid gratefully behind a smoke screen. "You know," he said. "But I'm not going to insist on it. I think you want to talk to me, but you're afraid. I'm trying every way I know to show you that it won't offend me, Beebo. You think about that. You think about the people who are my friends—people I enjoy and respect—and then you ask yourself what you have to fear."

There was a long pause. At last she said, "It isn't that easy, Jack. I should know what I am. But I don't know myself at all. Especially here in this new place. Back in Juniper Hill, I could only see what other people saw, and I was afraid and ashamed. But here, I look all different. I even feel different." She looked at her hands. "Don't push me, Jackson." And she rushed past him suddenly, to cry in the privacy of the bathroom; to wonder why the girls she had seen that night had moved her so dramatically.

She did not fall asleep until very late. And when she did, she dreamed of sweet, supple, smiling-faced girls, dancing sensuously in each other's arms; glancing at her with wide curious eyes; beckoning to her. She saw herself glide slowly, almost reluctantly, over the floor with a girl whose long black hair hung halfway down her back; a girl with an old-fashioned name: Mona. Beebo touched the hair, the long dipping curve of the back till her hands rested on Mona's hips.

The next thing she knew, Jack was shaking her awake. "Wake up! Jesus!" he said, grinning at her in the early light. "You're beating hell out of the mattress."

Her eyes flew wide open and she stared at him, stuttering.

"Funny thing about dreams," he said softly. "They let you be yourself in the dark. When you can be yourself in the morning, too, you'll be cured."

"Cured of what?" she said in a disgruntled whisper.

Jack chuckled. "Dreams," he said. "You won't need 'em."

Beebo was relieved when he went back to sleep. There was no escaping now what she was. The dancing lovers in the Colophon had impressed it indelibly on her. And yet Jack wanted her to confirm it in so many words, and the idea terrified her. It would be like accepting a label for the rest of her life—a label she didn't even understand yet.

And there was no one to tell her that the time would come when the label wouldn't frighten her; when she would be happy simply to be what she was.

They went a while longer without discussing it. Jack was on the verge of confronting Beebo a dozen times with his own homosexuality. But she would catch the look in his eye and warn him with tacit signs to keep still. He began to wonder if she understood about him at all. He had tried to make it obvious the night they went barhopping. He wanted to say to her, "Okay, I'm gay. But that doesn't make me less human, less moral, less *normal* than other men. You've got the same bug, Beebo; only with you, it's girls. Look at me: I'm proof you can live with it. You don't need to hate yourself or the people you're attracted to."

But if she saw it she kept it to herself. *She's too wrapped up in discovering herself to discover me too,* he thought. He tried to kid her. "You think it's all right for the other girls but not for Beebo," he said, but she wouldn't give him a smile. He felt stumped in front of her stubborn silence; aching to help her, afraid of scaring her into an emotional crack-up.

She was very tense. And then one evening, about a week after her night out with Jack, over dinner she said, "Mona was in the shop again. I talked to her."

Jack looked up in surprise. "What about?"

"I asked if she was Mona Petry. She is." She seemed afraid to elaborate.

"Is that all?" he smiled.

"You were right about her—she's gay." She looked up to catch the smile.

"Did she say so?" he asked.

"No, Pete said so after she left. He said he used to date her but he dropped her when he found out."

"Well, he's got it backwards, but never mind. The point is, Mona's a slippery little bitch. She's good to look at but she isn't any fun. She's out to screw the whole damn world. If I were you—"

"Jackson, I don't give a damn what you think of Mona Petry," Beebo said.

"Then why bring her up?"

She colored, and put down a few more bites of the dinner they were eating. Finally, slowly, with her face still pink, she said, "Do you think it would be all right if I went out tonight? I mean—alone?"

"If you eat all your spinach."

"I am asking you," she said hotly, "because I value your judgment. Not because I'm an addlepated child."

"All right," he said, smiling into his napkin. "Where do you want to go?"

She looked at her plate. "The Colophon," she said, making him strain to hear it.

"Why? Want to drop a bomb on the dance floor?"

She sighed. "Pete says Mona hangs out there."

"In that case, I don't think it's safe," he said flatly. "But it should be educational."

She said, "Jack, I'm scared. I don't think I've ever been so scared of anything in my life."

"It's no disgrace to be scared, Beebo. Only to act like it."

"I feel as if that damn silly bar—the people in it—are a sort of challenge," she said, fumbling to express it justly. "As if I have to go back or I'll never know…" She shook her head with a self-conscious smile. "That's a hell of a place to go looking for yourself."

"Hell of a place to go looking for Mona," he said. "I don't know though, pal. It has to come sooner or later. It's time you learned a thing or two. You're naïve, but you're no fool. Go on—but go slow."

Mona was not at the Colophon that night, or for many nights afterward. In a way, Beebo was relieved. She wanted to meet her, but she wanted time to meet other people too, to see other places, and cruise around the Village without any pressure on her to prove things to herself. Or to a worldly girl like Mona Petry. Beebo was still a stranger in a strange town, unsure, and grateful for a chance to learn unobserved.

She would sit and gaze for hours at the girls in the bars or passing in the streets. She wanted to talk to them, see what they were like. She was often drawn to one enough to daydream about her, but she never mentioned it to Jack. Still, she was eagerly curious about the Lesbian mores and social codes. The gay girls seemed so smooth and easy with each other, talking about shared experiences in a special slang, like members of an exclusive sorority.

Beebo, watching them as the days and weeks passed, became slowly aware how much she envied them. She wanted to join the in-group. And she would watch them longingly and wonder if their talk was ever about her. It was.

A few of Jack's friends, who had met her in his company, would come up and talk with her, and knowing for certain that they were Lesbians gave Beebo a vibrant pleasure, whether or not the girls themselves were exciting. Looking at one she would think, *She knows how it feels to want what I want. I could make her happy. I know it.* Even the word "Lesbian," which had offended her before, began to sound wonderful in her ears.

She shocked herself with such candid thoughts, but that was only at first. Little by little, it began to seem beautiful to her that two women could come together with passion and intelligence and make a life with and for each other; make a marriage. She dreamed of lovely, sophisticated women at her feet, aware even as she dreamed that she hadn't yet the *savoir faire* to win such a woman. But she was afire with ambition to acquire it.

She would walk into a bar, order a beer, and sit alone and silent through an evening. In her solitude, she seemed mysterious to the laughing chattering people around her. They began to point her out when she came in.

At first, ignorance and inexperience kept Beebo aloof. But she quickly understood that her refusal to be sociable made her the target of a lot of smiling speculation. When she got over being afraid of the situation, it amused her. The fact that she attracted girls, even ones she knew she would never pursue, was almost supernaturally strange and exciting to her. She submitted to their teasing questions with an enigmatic smile until she realized that one or two had worked themselves up to infatuation pitch over her.

There followed a period of elation when she walked into Julian's or the Cellar and saw the eyes she knew had waited all night to look into hers turn and flash in her direction. She always passed them by and went to a seat at the bar. But each time she came closer to stopping and answering a smile or asking someone to join her in a beer. And still, she couldn't find Mona.

The only wrong note in the tune was a boy, slight and fine-featured, who watched her and seemed to have persuaded himself that he loved her. He fell for her with an awkward crush that embarrassed them both. Often, at the end of an evening when he was pretty high, he would approach her and timidly offer to buy her a drink.

Beebo kept turning him down, kindly but firmly. He always flinched when she said no, and she pitied him. He had a gentle appealing face, fair in the way of extreme youth. She guessed he must be a couple of years younger than she, and wondered how he could buy drinks in a bar.

"I'm sorry, I'm just leaving," she would tell him.

And he would watch her go, wistfully. He looked tired and malnourished, and she wondered once if it would offend him to be offered a free sandwich. She never quite got up the nerve to find out.

At home, Jack did not press her. But her silence regarding her activities at night worried him and put a strain between them. She knew that Jack was waiting for her to talk about it, and she wanted to be honest with him more than ever. He had been patient, humorously tolerant with her. And she knew that he was a man of the world. He had made it clear that he enjoyed the friendship of many delightful gay women, that he approved of them, and that he thought she might enjoy their company.

But he had not said, "Oh, come on, Beebo. You're gay. Admit it. We both know it." He had, however, come closer than she knew to saying it. And it was hard for Jack himself to realize that his hints and jokes were couched in a language still foreign to her in many ways. Often they went over her head or were taken at face value; saved and worried over, but never fathomed.

So she found herself hung up on a dilemma: she was sure of his friendship as long as she was an observer of the gay scene, not a sister-in-the-bonds. But what would he say if she told him she had a desperate crush on Mona Petry with the long black hair? Or that she got dizzy with the joy of being in a crowd of gay girls; near enough to touch, to overhear, to look and look and look until they whirled through her dreams at night?

Would he say, *You can play with the matches but don't get burned?* Would he pity her? Turn on his wit? Would he—could he— take it with the easy calm he showed in other circumstances?

She thought he could. She felt closer to him now that she had spent nearly two months under his roof. She knew his heart was big, and she had seen him in a Lesbian bar talking with his friends there. He was not being condescending. He valued them.

Perhaps more than anything, she was persuaded by the need to talk it out; the need for help and comfort. And that was Jack's forte.

Beebo and Jack were watching a TV show one evening when he asked her, during the commercial, why she wasn't going out that night. "Don't tell me you gave up on Mona," he teased.

Instead of answering, she told him about the boy who was in love with her. "His name is Pat," she said. "The bartender told me. He looks hungry, as if he needs to be cared for." She laughed. "I was never much for maternal instincts—but he seems to bring them out."

"I'd like to meet him. He might bring mine out, too," Jack said.

"Why don't you come with me Friday? He's always at Julian's."

Jack looked away. "I've been trying to give you a free rein," he said. "You don't want me along. I'll find him myself."

"I do want you along," she said. "I like your company."

"More than the girls'?" he grinned.

She felt herself tense all over. There had been so many chances lately to talk to him, and she had run away from them all. Now, she felt a surge of defiance, a will to have it out. He had a right to know at least as much about her as she knew about herself. He had earned it through his generosity and affection.

"I read a book once," she said clumsily. "Under my covers at night—when I was fifteen. It was about two girls who loved each other. One of them committed suicide. It hit me so hard I wanted to die, too. That's about as close as I've come to reality in my life, Jack. Until now."

He leaned over and switched off the television. The room was so quiet they could hear themselves breathing.

"I was kicked out of school," she went on hesitantly, "because I looked so much like a boy, they thought I must be acting like one. Chasing girls. Molesting them. Everything I ever did to a girl, or wanted to do or dreamed of doing, happened in my imagination. The trouble was, everybody else in Juniper Hill had an imagination, too. And they had me doing all these things for real." She shut her eyes and tried to force her heart to slow down, just by thinking about it.

"And you never did?" he said. "You never tried? There must have been girls, Beebo—"

"There were, but all I had to do was talk to one and her name was mud. I wouldn't do that to anybody I cared for."

Jack stared at her, wondering what geyser of emotion must be waiting to erupt from someone so intense, so yearning, and so rigidly denied all her life.

"My father tried to teach me not to hate myself because I looked like hell in gingham frills," she said. "But when you see people turn away and laugh behind their hands... It makes you wonder what you really are." She looked at him anxiously, and then she said it. "I've never touched a girl I liked. Never made a pass or spoken a word of love to a single living girl. Does that make me normal, Jack?...And yet I know I could, and I think now I will, and God knows I want to desperately. Does that make me gay?" She spoke rapidly, stopping abruptly as if her voice had gone dead in her throat at the word "gay."

"Well, first," he said kindly, "you're Beebo Brinker, human being. If you *are* gay, that's second. Some girls like you are gay, some aren't. Your body is boyish, but there's nothing *wrong* with it." His voice was reassuring.

"Nothing, except there's a boy inside it," she said. "And he has to live without all the masculine trimmings other boys take for granted. Jack, long before I knew anything about sex, I knew I wanted to be tall and strong and wear pants and ride horses and have a career...and never marry a man or learn to cook or raise babies. Never."

"That's still no proof you're gay," he said, going slowly, letting her convince herself.

"I'm not even built like a girl. Girls are knock-elbowed and big-hipped. They can't throw or run or—look at my arm, Jack. I was the best pitcher on the team whenever they let me play." She rolled her sleeve back and showed him a well-muscled arm, browned and veined and straight as a boy's.

"I see," he murmured.

"It was the parents who gave me the worst of it," she said. "The kids weren't too bad till I got to high school. But you know what happens then. You get hairy and you get pimples and you have to start using a deodorant."

Jack laughed silently behind his cigarette.

"And the boys get big and hot and anxious, like a stallion servicing a mare."

Jack swallowed, feeling himself move. "And the girls?"

"The girls," she sighed, "get round and soft and snippy."

"And instead of round and soft, you got hot and anxious?"

"All of a sudden, I was Poison Ivy Brinker," she confirmed. "Nobody wanted whatever it was I had. My brother Jim said I wasn't a boy and I wasn't a girl, and I had damn well better be one or the other or he'd hound me out of school himself."

"What did you do?"

"I tried to be like the rest. But not to please *that* horse's ass." Her farmer's profanity tickled him. "I did it for Dad. He thought I was adjusting pretty well, and that was his consolation. I never told him how bad it was."

"So now you want to find Mona Petry," Jack said, after a small pause, "and ask her if you're gay."

"Not *ask* her. Just get to know her and see if it could happen. She makes me wonder so.... Jack, what makes a feminine girl like that gay? Why does she love other girls, when she's just as womanly and perfumed as the girl who goes for men? I used to think that all homosexual girls were three-quarters boy." She hung her head. "Like me, I guess. And that they were all doomed to love feminine girls who could never love them back. It seems like a miracle that a girl like Mona could love a—" she stopped, embarrassed.

"Could love a girl like you," he finished for her. "Take it on faith, honey. She doesn't have to look like a Ram tackle to know that her happiness lies with other women. The girls you see around town aren't all boyish, are they?"

"They're not all gay, either."

He ground out his cigarette. "Tell me why they ran you out of Juniper Hill. The whole story. Was it really just a nasty rumor about you and the Jones girl?"

Beebo lay down, stretched out on the sofa, and answered without looking at him. "They'd been hoping for an excuse for years," she said. "It was in April, last spring. I went to the livestock exhibition in Chicago with Dad and Jim. I was in the stalls with them most of the time, handling some of the steers from our county. Sweaty and gritty, and not thinking about much but the job. And then one night—I'll never know why—I took it into my head to wear Jim's good clothes.

"I knew it was dangerous, but suddenly it was also irresistible. Maybe I just wanted to get away with it. Maybe it was the feel of a man's clothes on my back, or a simple case of jealousy. Anyway, I played sick at dinnertime, and stayed in the hotel till they left.

"Jack, it was as though I had a fever. The minute I was alone I put Jim's things on. I slung Dad's German camera over my shoulder and took his *Farm Journal* press pass. On the way over, I stopped for a real man's haircut. The barber never said a word. Just took my money and stared.

"I looked older than Jim. I felt wonderful." She stopped, her chin trembling. "A blonde usher showed me to the press section. She was small and pretty and she asked me if I was from the 'working press.' I said yes because it sounded important. She gave me a seat in the front row with a typewriter. It was screwed down to a stand. God, imagine!" She almost laughed.

"I really blitzed them," she said, remembering the good part with a throb of regret. "Everybody else was writing on their machines to beat hell, but I didn't even put a piece of paper in mine. After a while I took out the camera and made some pictures. The girl came back and said I could work in the arena if I wanted to, and I did. It was hotter than Hades but I wouldn't have taken that tweed jacket off for a fortune.

"I guess I took pictures for almost three hours...just wandered around, kidding the girls on horseback and keeping clear of the Wisconsin people." She hesitated and Jack said, "What happened then?"

"I got sick," she whispered. "My stomach. I thought it was bad food. Or that damn heat. Awful stomach cramps. In half an hour I was so miserable I could hardly stand up and I was scared to death I might faint. If I'd had any sense I'd have gone back to my seat and rested. But not Beebo. I didn't want to waste my moment of glory. It would go away—it *had* to.

"Well, I was right about one thing—I fainted, right there in the arena. The next I knew, I was strangling on smelling salts and trying to sit up on a cot in the Red Cross station. The doctor asked how I felt and I said it was indigestion. He wanted to have a look.

"I was terrified. I tried to laugh it off. I said I was tired, I said it was the heat, I said it was something I ate. But that bastard had to look. He thought it might be appendicitis. There was nothing I could do but cover my face and curse, and cry," she said harshly. Jack handed her a newly lighted cigarette, and she took it, still talking.

"The doctor saw the tears, and that was the tip-off. He opened my shirt so fast the buttons flew. And when he saw my chest, he opened the pants without a word. Just big bug-eyes." She gave Jack a look of sad disgust. "I had the curse," she muttered. "First time."

After a moment she went on, "I never meant to hurt anybody or cause a scene. But I hurt my father too much. He suffered over it. I had to wait till my hair grew out before I could go back to school, but I could have saved myself the bother. They let me know as soon as I got back I wasn't wanted. Before Chicago, they thought I was just a queer kid. But afterwards, I was really queer. There's a big difference."

Jack listened, bound to her by the story with an empathy born of his own emotional aberration.

"The principal of the high school said he hoped he could count on me to understand his position. *His* position. I wanted to ask him if he understood *mine*." There was hopeless bitterness in her voice.

"They never do," Jack said quietly. "Still, that's not the only high school in the world. You could finish up somewhere else and go on to pre-med, Beebo."

"You didn't," she reminded him. "You got fed up and quit. But me—I've been expelled. I'm not wanted anywhere."

"Do you think a job as a truck driver is worth sacking a medical career for?"

"What did you sack yours for?" He was making her defensive.

"My story's all over," he said. "But there's still time for you. Beebo, do you know what you're trying to do? Get even with the world. You're so mad at it and everybody in it for the bum deal you got, you're going to deny it a good doctor some day."

"I'd be a rotten doctor, Jack. I'd be scared. I'd be running and hiding every day of my life."

"Hell, plenty of doctors are gay. They manage." He was surprised at the importance it was assuming in his own mind. He really cared about it. It depressed him to think of what she might be and what she was in a fair way now of becoming. "You're thinking that if people are going to reject you, by God you're going to reject them first. If they make it hard for you to be a doctor, you'll make damn sure they never *get* that doctor. You've been keeping score and now you're avenging yourself on the world because most of the people in it are straight. You keep it up and you'll turn into a joyless old dyke without a shred of love in her heart for anyone."

Beebo sat up and frowned at him, surprised but not riled. "Are you telling me to go to hell because I—I think I'm gay?" she asked.

"I'm telling you to go to college," he said seriously.

"Jack, you goofed your chance for an M.D. for reasons a lot flimsier than mine. What are you trying to do? Push me into school so you can make peace with your conscience? You're the one who wants to give that good doctor to humanity. If it can't be yourself, better it should be Beebo than nobody. And Jack Mann will have made a gift to his fellow men. Jack, the Great Humanitarian. And you won't even have to crack a book." She spoke wryly, but without rancor.

Jack was stunned into silence by her flash of insight.

"I hit it, didn't I?" she said. "Jack, you don't know what you're asking me to do: wear a skirt for the rest of my life. Forget about love till my heart dries up. Go back and face the father I destroyed and the brother who hates me...well, I can't. I'm no martyr. I'm not brave enough to try to be a doctor now, just because you tried and failed. And feel bad about it."

He took her hands and rubbed them. "You hit it dead on, little pal, but only part of it," he said. "Sure, I'd like to see you with a medical degree and know I'd had something to do with it. But forget me. Be selfish about it. A degree would protect you, not expose you to more trouble. Knowledge, success, the respect of other doctors—that would be your defense against the world."

"There's no protection against myself. My feelings. I didn't tell you about the girls back home, Jack, walking down country lanes after school with their arms around the boys, kissing and laughing. The girls I couldn't touch or talk to or even smile at. The girls I'd grown up with, suddenly filling out their sweaters and their nylons, smooth and sweet with scented hair and pink mouths. I didn't tell you how I ached for them."

He got up and crossed the room, looking out his front windows. "I don't want you to end up an old bull dyke in faded denims, letting some blowsy little fem take care of you," he said acidly. "You're not a bum."

"I don't want that, either. But Jack, I can't spend the rest of my life wondering!" She went to his side, speaking urgently, wanting him to root for her, not against her. "They call this life gay," she said softly, following his gaze out the windows. "I need a little gaiety."

"They call it gay out of a perverted sense of humor," he said.

Across the street two young women were walking slowly in the mild evening air, arms around each other's waists. "There," Beebo said, nodding at them. "That's what I want. I've wanted it ever since I knew girls did such things."

"You mean Mona?" he said.

Beebo shoved her hands into her pockets, self-conscious as always when that name came up. "You have to start somewhere," she said.

"You have quite a thing about her, don't you?" he said.

Beebo's cheeks flushed and she looked at the floor. "I never dared to admit that I wanted a girl before, Jack. Maybe I picked the wrong time. Or the wrong audience."

"Pal, you just picked the wrong girl."

"I don't want you to pity me. That's why I held out so long. I need you, Jack. You're the first friend—the first brother—I ever had."

Jack was touched and embarrassed. "I feel no pity for you, Beebo," he said. "You don't need pity. I feel friendship and...anxiety. If you've made up your mind to stay here, I'll do anything to help you, teach you, take you around. But, honey—not Mona. She doesn't believe in anything but kicks. She'll charm the pants off you and then leave you standing naked in front of your enemies."

"Are you trying to say you disapprove of Mona, but not of the fact that I'm—I *must* be—gay?" she said.

"Why would I disapprove of that?" he said and then he laughed. "I swear to God, Beebo, you can be thicker than bean soup. I've done everything but sing it for you in C sharp."

"I know you've tried to be tolerant and all, introducing me to your friends. I thought it was because you suspected about me and you wanted to be a good sport."

"I'm trying to explain about *me,* not you," he said, throwing out his hands and still chuckling.

Beebo smiled back, mystified. "Let me in on the joke, will you?"

"The joke's on me this time," he said.

She studied him a moment, her smile yielding to perplexity. And then she said, "Oh!" suddenly and lifted a hand to her face. She went back to the sofa and sat down with her head in her hands.

"Well, you don't need to feel badly about it, pal," he said, joining her. "I don't. There are even days when I feel sorry for the straight people."

"Jesus, I should have seen it," she murmured.

"No, you shouldn't. I'm a genius at hiding it."

"Jack, I'm sure a fool. I've been up to my eyes in my own troubles."

He shook his head. "I couldn't believe you wouldn't figure it out. It's hard to realize the kind of life you've been leading up to now. How little you've been allowed to see or understand."

She looked up at him. "Thanks for being patient," she said. "I mean it. Jack, how long have you been gay? How did you find out about yourself?"

"I didn't. I was told. In the Navy, by a hairy little gob who kept climbing into my bunk at night and telling me fairy stories. When he got a rise out of me, he made the diagnosis. I told him to go to hell, but the next night, I was climbing into *his* bunk."

It made her smile. "Can you forgive me?" she said.

"Nothing to forgive. And I'll let you back into my good graces on one condition. Do you think your friend Pat will be in bloom tonight?"

"Probably," she said, seeing him through her new understanding as through a rainbow curtain. He was a new shape, a new color, a new man. She was vastly relieved, and just a little awed. And ashamed of her bean-soup intuition.

"Let's go look at him," Jack said.

The night was hot and damp, with a low black sky that had looked menacing in the daylight, but was soft and close as dark came down, floating over the neon merriment below.

Beebo was quiet as they walked, preoccupied with a new attitude toward Jack and an almost unbearable sense of anticipation. Pat was usually at Julian's. When they arrived, the bar was crowded but there was standing room at one end. They squeezed in and ordered drinks, and Beebo began to pick out the faces that searched for her.

"Is he here?" Jack asked, glancing around.

She discovered him right away. "Over there in the blue shirt," she said, nodding.

"They all have blue shirts," Jack said, squinting through the smoke.

"The blond one."

There was a pause and Jack's face puckered thoughtfully. "He looks pretty young," he said in a bemused voice.

"You mean, you like his face?" Beebo smiled at him.

"It's a face," he said noncommittally, and when she laughed he shrugged and added, "Okay. A nice face. Beebo, I think you're playing cupid."

"I wouldn't know how," she said. "Besides, you told me you only fell in love in the fall or the spring. This is midsummer." But she wondered suddenly what would happen if he broke his rule. It made her heart drop. Jack's apartment was small, with just one bed. Even if he didn't ask her to leave, how welcome would she be if he invited a third party to share it with them? She'd have to bow out, out of simple consideration. But where could she go? She had avoided making any friends, and the Pasquinis with their five kids were out of the question. She would have preferred a park bench anyway to a room with Pete Pasquini in it.

Beebo and Jack were both caught unaware by the sudden quiet interruption. There he was, Beebo's boy, standing behind and between them. He had come over in the moment it took them to discuss him and now they looked at him in surprise.

He paled a little and started to back away, but Jack put a hand on his shoulder. "Don't panic. We're harmless when we're drinking," he said. "What's your name?"

"Pat Kynaston," said the boy, staring into his beer. He supposed Beebo had Jack with her this time to show him she was taken, and he was crushed.

"Pat? That's a girl's name," Beebo kidded.

Pat swallowed some beer and moved the sawdust under his shoes.

"Have a drink, honey," Jack said, and Beebo felt a stir of strange interest in the endearment. And yet Pat seemed more like a child than a man, and it was easy to call him fond names. In spite of his light beard he had a child's face, full of a child's hardy trust. He smiled at Jack, reassured.

"He looks as green as you did last May," Jack told Beebo. "How long have you been here, Pat?"

"Oh, since seven-thirty, I guess."

"No, I mean in New York?" Jack grinned.

"Oh. January." Pat's eyes remained on Beebo while he answered Jack. But when she returned the look, he glanced down to her belt. "I left school then," he said.

"Sounds like the story of my life," said Beebo. "How old are you?"

"Twenty-seven."

Jack cleared his throat and Beebo's mouth dropped open. "With that face?" Jack protested. "You mean your *father* is twenty-seven."

Pat laughed a little and shook his head.

"Besides, what is a twenty-seven-year-old child doing in school? You should be through."

"I was working on a doctorate in entomology."

"Bugs? You don't look like a bug collector," Jack said with a grimace, and they laughed while the drinks came up. Jack pulled Pat between himself and Beebo and teased him for a while, making him blush and answer questions. But when it came out that Pat was working as a garbage-collector for the New York City Department of Sanitation, Jack stopped laughing.

"God! A frail kid like you? You shouldn't do work like that," he declared.

"It was all I could get. Nobody wants an entomologist *manqué,*" Pat said. "I guess that's why I'm skinny. I look at those rotting scraps all day and when I get home the stuff in my icebox looks just as bad."

Jack tapped Beebo on the shoulder. "Do we have any of Marie's chicken tetrazini in the refrigerator?"

"Plenty."

"Let's go." Jack threw a couple of bills on the counter and took Pat by the elbow. Beebo took the other and they walked him out of Julian's and down the street.

Beebo had been elated to learn that Jack, too, was gay. But now she felt the first twinge of misgiving. Jack was the older brother she never really had; one she could learn from, look up to, even love. It was a valuable feeling, new to her. For as fiercely as she resented Jim, she had always harbored a secret regret that they could not have been friends.

They walked toward Jack's place with Pat clinging in bewildered pleasure to Beebo, the object of what had seemed so long a futile attraction. But Beebo was lost in herself, wondering if she could make it yet in the city on her own. She was strong and handsome, and she walked, gestured, even swore with a boyish gusto that made her seem more experienced than she was. But she was still untutored in the ways of metropolitan gay life and that fact undermined her self-confidence.

They put Pat, who was high enough to be sleepy, on Jack's sofa and looked at him. He dozed a little, his fair face averted, and the two roommates were struck with the beauty of his features. Beebo was unnerved to find herself suddenly wanting a girl with blast-furnace intensity.

"I'll heat the bird," she offered to Jack, "if you'll mind the patient."

"You're on," he said.

But she was sorry to have to leave them alone together. Jack was entirely too taken with the boy. Beebo moved pensively around the kitchen, preparing the food with unaccustomed hands.

Jack brought Pat to the table when she called them. Pat looked so slender and peaked that she felt a good doctor's desire to stuff him full of nourishment.

He leaned against the door frame, gazing at Beebo. "Who are you, anyway?" he asked, drunk enough to be brave.

"Sit down, Hungry," Beebo said, smiling at him.

Abashed, but unappeased, he obeyed.

"You know what's wrong with you, Pat? Malnutrition," she said. "If you had any food under your belt, you wouldn't give two bits for me." He turned a baffled face to her. "Why hell, the damn bugs eat better than you do," she told him. "They get all the garbage that ruins your appetite."

She tried to feed him but he turned away. "I can't," he said. The excitement of coming home with this girl he had admired so fervently for a couple of months was too much; that, and all the beer he had drunk...and a new gentle feeling stirring in him for Jack Mann.

"Sure you can," Beebo said, and began to feed him as if he were a sick lamb, while Jack cut the chicken bits for her. When Pat tried to protest she popped a mess of spicy meat between his teeth and shushed him, wishing all the while that she were ministering to a lovely girl instead of a lost boy.

Beebo stole a look at Jack, afraid of what she might see. But he was regarding Pat with compassion, the same he had shown to her when he found her...and just a trace of desire, tightly controlled. Jack had kindly instincts. It was one of the things Beebo admired most in him. He took care of people because it made him happy. No one was to blame if, when the person was a beautiful young boy, it made him very happy indeed.

Beebo got the chicken down Pat and made him drink his milk, which he did out of pure infatuation for her. And then Jack filled the silence with one word: "Bedtime."

But Pat seemed to be in a sort of trance, brought on by fatigue, fascination, and a full stomach. "Are you conscious?" Jack asked him with a smile.

"I was just thinking," Pat murmured, blinking at Beebo. "Maybe I'm straight."

They laughed at him, till he got indignant and tried to explain that even Beebo's marginal femininity didn't discourage him.

"You need some sleep, buddy," Jack told him, and took him off to the sofa. "And no damn trash cans for you in the morning."

"What if I lose my job?" Pat said.

"That would be the best thing that could happen to you."

"I'll starve," Pat whispered.

"Not while I'm around," Jack said. Pat smiled at him sleepily, and then shut his eyes and turned on his side.

Beebo climbed into Jack's bed feeling like an impostor. But she was embarrassed to make an issue of it; more than that, afraid. If she offered to take the sofa herself, Jack might grab the chance to have Pat beside him all night.

Beebo felt no physical attraction to Pat; only sympathetic interest. But his puppy love had scorched her a little; just enough to keep her moving and twisting on the warm sheets for an hour, obsessed with the growing need for a girl. A girl to curl in her lap and kiss her and talk away her fears.

Pat's loneliness shocked her. She saw herself mirrored in his predicament. Who was more alone than a lost and defenseless soul, hungry for something it couldn't find? Couldn't even define? It was enough to warp the heart, deform the soul.

It was enough to get her out of bed at midnight that night, make her dress in silence and leave the apartment, undetected by Jack or Pat.

She was almost as surprised to find herself on the street as Jack would have been to see her there. And yet the cool night air washed gratefully over her face and cleared her thoughts. She wandered aimlessly a while, as if trying to ignore the one place she wanted to visit: the Colophon.

But her feet took her there anyway, and she found herself ringing the bell. The owner opened the peek-through in the door and nodded to her. She felt a momentary country-girl shame at being recognized in such a place. But she was glad enough to gain entrance. The glow inside was the color of fluorescent Merthiolate. It seemed almost antiseptic to Beebo, who had painted the undersides of countless cows and sows with disinfectants the same shade prior to a delivery.

She took a seat at the bar. "Scotch and water," she said.

While the barman got it, she gazed idly into the mirror behind him, picking out the interesting girls surrounding her. She felt uncomfortable here in the pants she usually wore to work; in her hair that had just been cut and was too short again.

Do they think I'm funny? she wondered. *Or—exciting?* She drank in silence, and ordered another, thinking that the solitude and uncertainty she felt now were worse than those she felt with Jack. For a minute, almost anything seemed better than having to leave Jack, with only fifty bucks a week to spend, no friends, and no place to live.

The bartender brought her another drink while she searched for the last cigarette in her pack. It was empty. The girl sitting next to her immediately offered her one, but Beebo declined. It was partly her shyness, partly the knowledge that it was better to be hard-to-get in the Colophon.

"Do you have cigarettes?" she asked the bartender.

"Machine by the wall," he said.

She got up and sauntered over, ignoring the outrage on the face of the girl at the bar. The machine swallowed her coins and spit out a pack of filter-tips. Beebo noticed the jukebox, looked at her change, and fed it a quarter, good for three dances. She liked to watch the girls move around the floor together, now that the initial revolt had worn off.

But when she regained her seat, she found most of the patrons paying attention to her, not the tunes. She looked back at them, surprised and wary. The cigarettes in her hand were an excuse to look away for a minute and she did, lighting one while the general conversation died away like a weak breeze. She lowered her match slowly and glanced up again, her skin prickling. What in hell were they trying to do? Scare her out? Show her they didn't like her? Had she been too aloof with them, too remote and hard to know?

She had started the music, and it was an invitation to dance. They were waiting for her to show them. It wasn't hostility she saw on their faces so much as, "Show us, if you're so damn big and smart. We've been waiting for a chance to trap you. This is it."

She had to do something to humanize herself. There was an air of self-confidence and sensual promise about Beebo that she couldn't help. And when she felt neither confident nor sensual, she looked all the more as if she did: tall and strong and coolly sure of herself. She had turned the drawback of being young and ignorant into a deliberate defense.

It didn't matter to the sophisticated girls judging her now that she was a country girl fresh from the hayfields of Wisconsin, or that she had never made love to a woman before in her life. They didn't know that and wouldn't have believed it anyway.

Beebo recognized quickly that she had to start acting the way she looked. She had established a mood of expectation about herself, and now it was time to come across. The music played on. It was Beebo's turn.

The match she held was burning near her finger, and because she had to do something about *it* and all the eyes on her, she turned to the girl beside her and held out the match.

"Blow," she said simply, and the girl, with a smile, blew.

Beebo returned the smile. "Well," she said in her low voice, which somehow carried even into the back room and the dance floor, "I'm damned if I'm going to waste a good quarter." She got up and walked across the room toward the prettiest girl she could see, sitting at a table with her lover and two other couples. It was exactly the way she would have reacted to student-baiting at

Juniper Hill High. The worse it got, the taller she walked. Her heart was beating so hard she wanted to squeeze it still. But she knew no one could hear it through her chest.

She stopped in front of the pretty girl and looked at her for a second in incredulous silence. Then she said quietly, "Will you dance with me, Mona?"

Mona Petry smiled at her. Nobody else in Greenwich Village would have flouted the social code that way: walked between two lovers and taken one away for a dance. Mona took a leisurely drag on her cigarette, letting her pleasure show in a faint smile. Then she stood up and said, "Yes. I will, Beebo." Her lover threw Beebo a keen, hard look and then relapsed into a sullen stare.

Beebo and Mona walked to the floor single file, and Mona turned when she got clear of the tables, lifting her arms to be held. The movement was so easy and natural that it excited Beebo and made her bold—she who knew nothing about dancing. But she was not lacking in grace or rhythm. She took Mona in a rather prim embrace at first, and began to move her over the floor as the music directed.

Mona disturbed her by putting her head back and smiling up at her. At last she said, "How did you know my name?"

"Pete Pasquini told me," Beebo said. "How did you know mine?"

"Same answer," Mona laughed. "He gets around, doesn't he?"

"So they say," Beebo said.

"You mean you don't know from personal experience?"

"Me?" Beebo stared at her. "Should I?"

Mona chuckled. "No, you shouldn't," she said.

"Did I—take you away from something over there?" Beebo said.

"From some*body*," Mona corrected her. "But it's all right. She's deadly dull. I've been waiting for you to come over."

Beebo felt her face get warm. "I didn't even see you until I stood up," she said.

"I saw you," Mona murmured. They danced a moment more, and Beebo pulled her closer, wondering if Mona could feel her heart, now bongoing under her ribs, or guess at the racing triumph in her veins.

"Did you ask Pete about me?" Mona prodded.

"A little," Beebo admitted. And was surprised to find that the admission felt good. "Yes," she whispered.

"What did he say?"

"He said you were a wonderful girl."

"Did you believe him?"

Beebo hesitated and finally said, huskily, "Yes."

"You're a good dancer, Beebo," Mona said, knowing, like an expert, just how far to go before she switched gears.

"I dance like a donkey," Beebo grinned, strong enough in her victory to laugh at herself.

"No, you're a natural," Mona insisted. "A natural dancer, I mean."

"I don't care what you mean, just keep dancing," Beebo said.

Mona put her head down against Beebo's shoulder and laughed, and Beebo felt the same elation as a man when he has impressed a desirable girl and she lets him know it with her flattery. Mona—so elusive, so pretty, so dominant in Beebo's dreams lately. Beebo was holding her tighter than she meant to, but when she tried to loosen her embrace, Mona put both arms about her neck and pulled her back again.

For the first time, Beebo had the nerve to look straight at her. It was a long hungry look that took in everything: the long dark square-cut hair and bangs; the big hazel eyes; the fine figure, slim and exaggeratedly tall in high heels. But it was still necessary for her to look up at Beebo.

"It's nice you're so tall," Mona told her.

"Who's the girl you're with?" Beebo said. "I think she wants to drown me."

"No doubt. Her name's Todd."

"Is she a friend?"

"She was, till you asked for this dance," Mona smiled.

Beebo didn't want to make trouble. "I'm sorry," she said.

"Are you?" Mona was forward as only a world-weary girl with nothing to learn—or lose—could be. And yet she seemed too young for such ennui—still in her twenties. "Are you sorry about Todd?" she pressed Beebo.

"I'm not sorry I'm dancing with you, if that's what you mean," Beebo said.

"That's what I mean," Mona smiled. "Would you like to dance without an audience, Beebo?"

Beebo frowned at her. "You mean ditch your friends?"

Mona could see that Beebo was offended by such a suggestion of two-timing; and Mona was interested enough in this big, beautiful, strange girl not to want her offended. "They aren't true friends," Mona said plaintively, "that you can count on, anyway. It's all over between Todd and me, too. We just came here to bury the corpse tonight. This is where we met five months ago."

"Five months? That's not very long to be in love with somebody," Beebo said.

"I wasn't," Mona said.

"Was she?" It seemed indescribably sad to Beebo that one partner be in love and the other feel nothing. She wanted everyone to be happy on this night full of sequin-lights and clouds of music: even Todd.

"I never meant much to Todd," Mona said. "Talk about ditching, Beebo. I'm the one who's getting ditched."

"You?" Beebo held her tightly, glad for the excuse. "How could anyone ever do that to you?"

Mona swayed against her, smiling with her eyes shut, and Beebo was too immersed in her to notice the look on Todd's face.

"She likes to torment her lovers," Mona whispered. "She uses them, as if they were things. When she gets tired of them, she puts them in a drawer and pulls them out to show off, like trophies. That's all she does—collect broken hearts."

"She sounds like a female dog," Beebo commented. And yet the little speech recalled disturbingly some of Jack's remarks about Mona; as if Mona were amusing herself by describing her own faults to Beebo and pretending they were Todd's.

The music ended and they stood on the floor a moment, arms still clasped about each other. "Wait at the bar," Mona whispered into Beebo's ear. "I'll get my coat." Beebo glanced doubtfully at the table, but Mona said, "It'll be better if I tell her alone. Go on."

Beebo released her reluctantly, went to her seat, and sipped at her drink till Mona came up. She let Mona lead the way, feeling a sudden wild exhilaration as she followed, lighting a cigarette, holding the door for Mona, taking the street side when they reached the sidewalk.

"Was Todd angry?" she asked.

"No one wants to look the fool," Mona said lightly, with a smile.

"I'm sorry. I wouldn't like to get you up the creek, Mona," Beebo said. "I didn't want trouble."

"I make my own trouble, Beebo. I thrive on it. The way I see it—" she paused to give Beebo her arm, and Beebo took it smoothly, with a sense of power and burgeoning desire, "—life is flat and dreary without trouble." Mona dodged a puddle, then continued. "Good trouble. Exciting trouble. You can't just walk across the Flats forever, doing what's expected of you. Excitement. That's everything to me." Mona stopped in her tracks to look at Beebo with bright sly eyes. "Being good isn't exciting. Right?"

"I'm no philosopher," Beebo said.

"I'll prove it to you. You're a good person, aren't you? You felt bad about Todd. You've been good all your life. But are you happy?"

"I am right now. Are you telling me to be bad?" Beebo said, laughing.

"Would making love to me be bad?" Mona asked her, so directly that Beebo wondered if she were being made fun of. There was no respect in Mona for the innate privacy and mystery of every human soul. She saw them all as part of the Flats—unless they could make beautiful trouble with her. Then, she was interested. Then, she saw an individual.

"Making love to you," Beebo said slowly, "would have to be good."

"I'll make it better than good." Mona reached up for Beebo's shoulders, pulling her back into the dusk of a doorway. They stood there a moment, Beebo in a fever of need and fear, till Mona's hand slid up behind her head, cupped it downward, and brought their lips together.

Beebo came to life with a swift jerking movement. Mona's kiss had been light and brief, until Beebo caught her again in a violent embrace and imprisoned her mouth. She forgot everything for a few minutes, holding Mona there in her arms and kissing her lips, pressing her back against the doorway and feeling the whole length of her body against Beebo's own.

It wasn't till she became aware that Mona was protesting that she let her go. She stood in front of Mona, still trembling and weak-kneed, her breath coming fast and her head spinning, and she felt oddly apologetic. Mona had started it, but Beebo had carried it too far. "I'm sorry," she panted.

"Stop saying you're sorry all the time," Mona told her in a sulky voice. And, with a briskness that all but shattered the mood, she turned and started walking off, her heels snapping against the asphalt. Beebo stared after her, shocked. Was this the end of it?

But Mona turned back after a quarter of a block and called her. "You aren't going to spend the night there, are you?" she said crisply.

Beebo hurried after her, and they walked for two more blocks without exchanging a word. Beebo could only suppose she had done something wrong. Yet she didn't know what, or how to make amends.

Mona stopped at a brownstone house with six front steps. "I live here," she said.

Beebo glanced up at it. "Shall I leave?" she said.

"Do you want to?"

"Don't answer my questions with more questions!" Beebo said, a tide of anger releasing her tongue. "Damn it, Mona, I don't like evasions."

"All right. Don't go," Mona said, and smiled at the outburst. She went up the steps with Beebo coming uneasily behind her, opened the door, and went to the first-floor apartment in the back. At her door she pulled out her key and waited. Beebo was looking around at the hall, old and modest, but cleanly kept. The apartments in a place like this could be astonishingly chic. She had seen some belonging to Jack's friends.

Mona let her take it in till Beebo became aware of the silence and turned to her quizzically.

"Approve?" Mona said.

Beebo nodded, and Mona, as if that were the signal, turned the key in the lock. She walked over the threshold, switched on a light, and abruptly backed out again, preventing Beebo from entering.

"What's wrong?" Beebo said, surprised.

"There's someone in there," Mona said.

Without thinking, Beebo made a lunge for the door. She had thrown prowlers out of her father's house before. A situation like this scared her far less than being in that room alone with Mona—much as she wanted it.

But Mona caught her arm. "It's a friend of mine!" she hissed. "Beebo, please!" Beebo stopped, irritated, waiting for an explanation. "It's a girl. I told her Todd and I were breaking up," Mona shrugged. "I guess she came over to cheer me up. We've been friends a long time. Oh, it's nothing romantic, Beebo."

"Well, send her home," Beebo said. It was one thing to be afraid of Mona, but another entirely to forfeit the whole night in honor of a hen party.

"I can't." Mona looked up at her in pretty distress. "She's my one real friend and I owe her a lot. She's had some bad times in her own life lately. Beebo, look—here's my phone number. Call me in an hour. Maybe we can still make it." She took a scratch pad from her purse and scribbled on it.

Beebo took it, feeling rebuffed and insulted. But Mona stood on tiptoes and kissed her lips again. And when Beebo refused to embrace her, Mona took her wrists and pulled them around her and gave Beebo a luxurious kiss. "Forgive me," she said. "It would be tough if she knew I'd brought someone home—it really would." She slipped out of Beebo's arms and put a hand on the doorknob. "Be sure to call me," she said. And then she disappeared inside her apartment.

Beebo stood in the hall a while, leaning on the dingy plaster and trying to make sense out of Mona. There was no sound from the apartment. Perhaps Mona and the girl had gone into a bedroom to talk. The idea made Beebo angry and jealous. She went slowly down the front hall. There was a pay phone by the entrance. Beebo went outside and sat on the front stoop for about forty-five minutes, and then went in to call.

She had lifted the telephone receiver and was about to drop in a dime, when she heard a bang from the end of the hall, as if someone had dropped something heavy. It seemed to come from Mona's door, and Beebo rushed toward it. But at the threshold, she froze.

Mona's voice, muffled as if through the walls of several rooms, but discernible, penetrated the wood. "And you! You sneak in here like a rat with the plague! God damn, how many times do I have to say it? *Call* first. Are you deaf or just stupid?"

Beebo's mouth opened as she strained to hear the answer. It came after a slight pause: "Rats don't scare you, doll. You already got the plague."

Beebo whirled away from the door as if she had been burned, and stood with her knuckles pressed angrily against her temples.

The voice belonged to a man.

It was several days before anything happened. Beebo went back to work as usual. There were no calls, no notes, no effort on Mona's part to get in touch with her and explain. Or apologize.

Beebo worked dully, but gratefully. Keeping busy was a balm to her nerves. She took pleasure in driving, taking corners faster and making deliveries in better time as she learned the routes. During the morning she took out groceries. In the afternoon, it was fresh-cooked, hot Italian food in insulated cartons.

Mona and her male visitor were on Beebo's mind so constantly that she didn't even take time to worry about Jack, or the possibility that he might fall in love with Pat. She saw them every evening, but said little and saw less.

She was full of a boiling bad temper: half-persuaded to go out on the town with as many girls as she could find, sure that Mona would hear about it; and half-toying with the idea of dating a man out of sheer spite. It would be nice irony—almost worth the embarrassment and social discomfort.

She was mad enough at Mona, in fact, to be nice to Pete. After all, Mona had stood him up too, long ago. He was still under her feet, and although he had never made any indecent proposals, he managed to always look as if he were just about to. Beebo was comforted to see that he gave the same look, and likely the same impression, to every woman in range of his sight, except his wife.

One day at noon, she went deliberately to the table in the kitchen where he was eating and pulled up a chair, while Marie served them. Pete looked at her with his somber eyes and stopped munching for a minute. She ordinarily managed her schedule so she could eat before or after he did. Marie noticed the change, as she noticed everything, but whatever she thought, she kept her own counsel.

"How is it with Jack and Pat?" Marie said conversationally.

Beebo straightened around. "How did you know about that?" she said, surprised.

"They was in earlier. Pat says he knows about bugs. Maybe he can stomp out my roaches.... He is a nice boy? I never did trust blonds."

Beebo felt threatened, as if Marie had just announced the end of Beebo's life with Jack. "Sure. Very nice," she said, and swallowed her stew. She was conscious of Pete's piercing gaze on her face.

"So?" Marie said, nodding. "He got a friendly style."

Beebo recounted mentally her evenings in the past week. Since Jack and Pat had met they had been together every night. Pat was in the apartment all day—no matter what hour Beebo dropped in during her deliveries. What about his job? And Jack? Jack Mann was a charming and persuasive man, and the fact that his face was plain did not alter the fact that his strong body was clean and pleasing, nor that his wits were quick and could make you learn and laugh.

"What's the matter, Beebo? You don't like rabbit?"

She started at Pete's voice and pulled away. His face was too close. But she was glad for the diversion. He aimed a big spoon at her stew. "Maybe you like a cheese sandwich?"

"No, this is fine," she said, forcing a social smile...and then wishing it were possible to retract it. Pete was examining her curiously.

She ate with concentration for several moments, still seeing Pat and Jack in her mind's eye. Pat liked Jack already. He was afraid of the city, and he abominated his job. If he didn't get back to it fast, he wouldn't have it any more, and she knew he didn't give a damn—as long as somebody fed and loved him. He was like a pet: a big lovable goddamn poodle. She knew his liking for Jack would grow to fondness, if not love. She could see it coming, especially at night when Jack let him talk his heart out. Nobody listened or comforted more intelligently than Jack.

And when they fall in love—then where do I go? Shack up with Mona and her stable of strange men? she wondered. Jack's remarks about Mona's past were haunting her days and ruining her nights.

"Beebo," said a quiet male voice into her ear. "You want the afternoon off?"

It was an indecent proposal, all right. His voice made it one.

"No thanks," she said frostily.

"You look bad."

"I'm all right," she snapped.

"You could've fooled me," he said. And when she didn't answer, he went on, unwilling to let the conversation die, "The way you was acting, I thought you was sick."

"Maybe I am," she said sardonically. "I've got the plague."

"The plague?" He stopped eating, his teeth poised around a bite, and grinned. "Plague, like the rats bring?"

"Yeah." Beebo frowned at him.

"I got a friend with an obsession about rats," he said. "You seen her in here once or twice. Mona. You know?" Beebo nodded, her eyes fixed on him. It was the longest she had looked at him squarely. "She tells every man she knows—and that's plenty—he's a rat. I asked her why once. Want to know what she said?" He paused, building suspense, while Beebo held her breath. "She says they're all hairy...filthy...and stupid. And they'll sleep with anything ain't already dead. You agree?" He grinned at her.

Beebo turned away. "I don't know any *men*," she said pointedly.

Pete threw his hands out. "Is that nice to say?" he demanded. "Jack, I can understand. All he got of man is his name. Your father, who knows? Another fag." Beebo got halfway out of her seat, but he protested elaborately at once. When she simmered down, he added confidentially, "But *me*...even Marie will admit that much, when she's feeling honest."

"Marie's in a position to have an opinion," Beebo said acidly. "But I don't think that's *it.*"

Pete folded his arms on the table and leaned on them, unoffended. "You want to be in that position too, Beebo?"

"Not for a million bucks," she said, and drank down her milk in a gesture of scorn.

"I know a lot of good positions," he said cozily, laughing at her.

Beebo had enough sense not to get visibly angry; not to make a scene. It wasn't worth it and it would only tickle Pete. If it did no more than embarrass the two women, he would be satisfied.

She put her glass down. "What do you do with all your women, Pete?" she asked him, making no effort to keep her voice from Marie. "Line them up in half-hour shifts? It beats me how one mighty male can keep so many women happy."

She picked up her plate and took it to the sink.

Marie tossed her a grin. "You tell him, Beebo," she said. "To hear him talk, he's sold out till next March."

"I'm selling nothing, bitch," Pete told her sharply. "What I got, I give away."

"Listen to Robin Hood," Beebo cracked, and walked out of the kitchen toward the truck with a load of Marie's packaged foods. Pete followed her. Marie turned and took a step toward them, thought better of it, and returned to brood over the stove. Beebo could handle him. She didn't need any help.

In the parking area, Pete took some of the load from Beebo and helped her put it in the truck. "You think I brag a lot, Beebo?" he said.

"I think you're a creep," she said.

He waited a moment, chagrined but not about to show it. "That mean you don't like me?" he said finally.

"Let's drop it, Pete."

"You *do* like me?" he pestered her.

"What do you want, a friendship ring?" she demanded.

Pete shrugged, staring at the low clouds, taking out a toothpick to spear the food specks stuck in his white teeth. "Just an opinion," he said.

"I told you. That's Marie's department. Now, if you'll get out of my way, I have some deliveries to make."

He turned to her. "Everybody got an opinion, Beebo. You worked for me over two months now. So say it. Say the truth."

Beebo swallowed her aggravation. This was a game of wits, and the first man to blow off, lost. She put on the same casual cloak Pete was wearing. "You're my boss. You keep clear of me, I keep clear of you, and we get along."

"You make a big thing of keeping clear," he said. "I smell bad, or something?"

"I wouldn't know. I never get that close," Beebo said.

Something in his eyes made her swing up into the driver's seat with unusual speed. She started the motor, but he came around the truck and pulled her door open.

"You want to know where Mona hangs out?" he said.

Beebo set her jaw. "Not from you," she said tautly.

Pete grinned. "Why not? My information is as good as the next guy's."

It made Beebo wildly impatient. She gripped the steering wheel in hard hands. "You through now, Pete?" she said, gunning the motor.

But he stood there, angled into the truck doorway so that she couldn't move without bending some of his bones the wrong way.

"It's okay, Beebo, don't get sore," he said, and put a hand on her knee. She picked it up and dropped it like a knot of worms, and he laughed. "You know why I do that?" he asked. "'Cause you put on such a good show. It really bugs you, don't it? When I touch you."

"You get the hell out of my truck or I'll roll you flat!"

He chuckled again. "Okay," he said. "I just got one piece of news for you, butch. Listen: 121 McDonald Street—Paula Ash. Tonight. For those as wants to locate Mona." He pulled away from the truck, and Beebo backed out in a rumble of dust and gravel.

It was nearly midnight before Beebo could bring herself to the McDonald Street address. She had debated it tempestuously throughout the evening, but without confiding in Jack. She could have gone to Mona's apartment instead, or called her and demanded an explanation. But something told her Pete Pasquini had an interesting motive for sending her here. She might get hurt; but she might also learn the truth, whatever that was, about Mona. So she took the chance.

She was in a don't-give-a-damn mood, expecting to find Mona with a man in the apartment, rented under an assumed name; or Mona making love to Paula Ash, whoever the hell she was; or even—best joke of all—Mona waiting for her alone, while Pete peeked through the keyhole.

She stood at 121 McDonald Street in a light drizzle, partially sheltered by an inset doorway, her hands shoved into the sleeves of her windbreaker, and tried to make up her mind to call the jest.

At last the chill drove her into the foyer to look at mailboxes. There was a Paula Ash, all right. Apartment 103. Beebo took a deep breath and pushed the buzzer.

The answer came after so long a wait that Beebo was just leaving in disgust, and had to turn back quickly to open the inner door. She had scarcely entered the hall when a door opened ahead and a girl looked out.

"Yes?" she said. She appeared very sleepy, as if she had been in bed for many hours already, even though it was not quite midnight.

"May I come in?" Beebo said. She walked down the hall looking Miss Ash over candidly. If Mona were going to stand her up, and Pete play jokes on her, the least she could do was fall into the pit with as much bravado as possible—and perhaps a pretty girl in her arms.

"I don't know," the girl said doubtfully, opening her eyes very wide as if the stretch would keep the lids up a few minutes more. "Who are you?"

"I'm Beebo." Beebo looked at her, standing about three feet away in the door, wondering if her name would register. The living room behind Paula looked inviting after the gray rain outside.

"Beebo Who?" The girl was beginning to wake up, staring at her visitor.

Beebo smiled. "Didn't Mona tell you?"

The girl gasped and rubbed her eyes open earnestly. "Mona!" she said, her voice husky. "Did Mona send you here?"

"Not exactly," Beebo said. "But I was made to think I'd find her here." The girl was so distressed that Beebo began to think Paula was the victim of whatever joke was afoot, and not herself. She was moved to apologize. "I'm sorry, Miss Ash," she said. "There must have been a mistake. I came expecting some sort of practical joke. I guess nobody let either one of us in on it."

"Will you come in, please," Paula Ash said unexpectedly. She was shy and looked at Beebo's shoulder when she spoke.

"Thank you," Beebo said, walking past her into the living room. "It's pretty cold outside." She took off her jacket and handed it to Paula, who hung it in her front closet.

"Will you have coffee?" Paula said.

"Thanks, that sounds good." Beebo watched her curiously while the girl busied herself in a small doorless kitchen. She had a delicately pretty face, different from Mona's slick good looks and more appealing to Beebo.

Paula ran an uneasy hand through her hair and bit her underlip as she stood by her stove, waiting for the water to boil. "Would you tell me," she asked timidly, "just what Mona told you?"

"I haven't seen Mona for a week," Beebo said. "A mutual acquaintance told me she'd be here tonight."

"Well, your mutual acquaintance has a queer sense of humor," Paula said. "Mona and I were never good friends. And lately we've been pretty good enemies."

"So that was it," Beebo said. "That's a hell of a note. I'm sorry, Miss Ash, I—"

"Paula, please. Oh, it wasn't your fault," Paula said. "Mona has done crazier things than meeting her new lovers in my living room. I've known her almost five years." She came back with two cups of hot coffee. She still seemed half-conscious, and when she stumbled a bit, Beebo got up and rescued the coffee.

Paula made a hissing sound of pain, pulling air between her teeth and looking at her left thumb.

"Did you scald it? Here. Under the cold water, quick." Beebo left the steaming cups on an end table and took Paula by the arm to the sink. She turned on the tap full force and held Paula's burn under the healing stream. Paula tried to pull away after a few seconds but Beebo held her securely. "Give it a good minute," she said.

And as they stood there, Beebo studied Paula at close range. She was a lovely-looking girl, even though she seemed *non compos* at the moment. "Are you sick, Paula?" Beebo asked kindly.

"No, no. Really. I'm just terribly tired. And then I took some sleeping pills. Probably too many. I haven't been sleeping well."

"If you're so tired, why do you take sleeping pills?" Beebo asked.

Paula's dainty face contracted around a private pain. "The doctor gave them to me. It's harder to sleep when you're too tired than when you're just tired." She weaved a little, and Beebo put an arm around her.

"Are you supposed to take so many they send you into a coma?"

"No. But one pill doesn't work. Three or four don't work any more. I just keep swallowing them till I drop off."

"That's dangerous," Beebo said. "One of these days you'll drop too damn far." She turned the water off and reached for a paper towel, blotting the injured hand gently. Suddenly, to her dismay, Paula pulled her hands away and hid her face in them to cry. Beebo watched, frustrated with the wish to touch and comfort her.

Paula's sobs were short and hard, and she pulled herself together with a stout effort of will. All Beebo could see for a moment was the top of her head, covered with marvelous rich red hair. And, when she looked up, a trail of pale freckles across her cheeks and nose. Beebo handed her a tissue from her shirt pocket, and Paula blew her nose and wiped her eyes.

She was a fragile, very feminine and small girl, wearing a pair of outsized, plaid-print men's pajamas.

Beebo took a bit of sleeve between her fingers with a smile. "You always wear these?" she asked.

"Only lately. They aren't mine. A former roommate left them behind when she moved."

"Oh," Beebo said. "I didn't think they were your type."

"They're not. They're hers. And she's gone, and this is all I have left of her." Paula shook out her smoldering curls and cleared her throat. "I'm better now. Shall we have the coffee?" she said. It was obvious that she had humiliated herself with the unplanned personal admissions, and Beebo did her the courtesy of dropping the subject and joining her in the living room.

They drank the coffee in preoccupied silence a while. Beebo lighted a cigarette and offered it to Paula, who refused. Finally she said lightly, hoping to cheer Paula up, "Seems to me those pajamas are the answer to your insomnia."

"What? How?" Paula looked at her as if suddenly remembering her presence in a room where Paula had thought herself alone with a ghost.

"Switch to nighties—your own—and get some rest," Beebo said. "If I had to wear a plaid like that, I'd have nightmares all night."

Paula smiled wanly. "I know," she said. "They're silly. I just needed somebody else to say it, I guess. It's hard to break away from a person you've been close to. You hang on to the stupidest things."

"Well, her old sleep gear won't bring her any closer," Beebo said. She pulled a sleeve out full length. "Did she play basketball?" Beebo said, and they both laughed.

"She wasn't a shorty," Paula admitted. Her laughter made her wonderfully pretty. She stopped it suddenly to say, "That's the first time I've laughed in a month." She gazed at Beebo with grateful astonishment.

"Looks like I got here just in time," Beebo said, not realizing till after she spoke what a hoary come-on that was. Paula's pink blush clarified things for her.

"I suppose you want to be getting home," Paula said shyly, rising from her chair. She was struck for the first time with Beebo's size. Stretched across the sofa, with her long legs thrusting out from under the cocktail table, Beebo looked too big for a nine-by-twelve living room.

To her surprise, Beebo found she didn't want to be getting home at all; not even to run interference between Jack and Pat. And thinking of Pat brought a flash of recognition to her mind. "You remind me of a friend," she told Paula, sitting up to scrutinize her. "A boy named Pat. A lovable thing. Shy and just a little childish. In the nice way, I mean."

"I remind you of a *boy?*" Paula stared.

"More of a child than a boy."

Paula didn't know quite how to take it. "In the nice way?"

"Yes. Trusting, affectionate. Still curious about people and life. It's a very—endearing quality."

"And you think *I'm* like that?" Paula asked.

"You obviously don't," Beebo chuckled.

"I've been told I'm nasty and spoiled and selfish...childish in the bad way."

"Who told you that? Your friend with the plaid pajamas?"

"Yes."

"If you were that way with her, she must have done something to deserve it. You look like a natural-born angel to me," Beebo said, surprising them both with her frankness.

"That's a very nice thing for a stranger to say," Paula said. "Thank you."

"My pleasure," Beebo said, blanketing her sudden confusion with an offhand nod.

There was a pensive pause while Beebo tried to remember the books she had read about Lesbian love. It wasn't always a question of sweeping girls off their feet and carrying them away to bed, as Mona had made it seem at first. How did you approach a sensitive, well-bred girl like this one? Mow her down with kisses? Certainly not.

Beebo began to wonder how to make herself welcome for the night. It seemed far better than going back to Jack's and stewing again until dawn about her future. She would be leaving Jack and Pat alone together all night for the first time, and yet it seemed less painful now than it had before. It would suffice Beebo if she and Paula did nothing but sit and talk all night.

"I suppose somebody's waiting for you?" Paula said.

"Nobody."

Paula frowned at her. "Your roommate?" she asked.

"My roommate is having an affair with a man," Beebo said and shocked Paula, until Beebo smiled at her and made her think she was kidding.

"Well...Mona?" she asked.

"Mona could be on the moon for all I know. I thought I'd find her here."

"And now you're disappointed," Paula said diffidently.

"Not at all. I'm relieved."

Paula drained her coffee cup and put it down with a nervous clink. "It must be—awkward—if your roommate is really in love with somebody else," she said, in a voice so soft it was its own apology for speaking.

"It is," Beebo said. "I hate to go home. I'm too long to sleep on the damn sofa."

"I'm afraid you're too long for mine, too," Paula said. There was a pause. "But I could sleep on it and you could take my bed, if you will."

It was such a completely disarming—almost quaint—invitation that Beebo smiled at her, prickling with temptation. Paula's bashfulness was enough to make Beebo self-assured.

"At least you're not too long for the pajamas," Paula said.

"I can't put you out like that," Beebo said.

Paula was flustered. She looked at her hands. "I don't mind," she said. "It's long and I'm short. We're used to each other."

"You and the sofa?" Beebo said, and stood up. She went to the closet and found her jacket. You can't take somebody's bed away just because you told a lie about sleeping on your own sofa. She pulled the jacket on and zipped it.

"You're a sweet girl, Paula," she said, not looking at her. "Miss Plaid Pajamas must be nuts. Find somebody who deserves you, and she'll never make you sleep alone on the sofa."

She started for the door but Paula, recovering suddenly, jumped up and put a restraining hand on her arm. Beebo turned around, a shiver of sharp excitement radiating through her. She was not—she was *never*—as sure of herself as she seemed.

"Beebo," Paula said, whispering so that Beebo had to bend her head to hear her. "I'd like you to stay. Make yourself welcome. Please."

Beebo was afraid to believe her ears. It had seemed almost easy, in retrospect, to storm the Colophon. She was not unaware that Mona was something of a catch, and when she went over the events of that night, she was satisfied at the way she had acted. Nobody, not Mona herself, knew how inexperienced and uncertain Beebo was, and nothing she had done gave her away. Unless it was her exuberance when Mona kissed her.

But now it seemed incredible that this exquisite stranger should reach out for her from the middle of nowhere. "Paula," she said, "I think we're both just lonely. I think it would be best if I go. You don't want to wake up tomorrow and hate yourself." She was still hedging about the ultimate test with a girl.

"I *was* lonely. I will be again if you go."

"Maybe you'd be better off lonely than sorry."

"Beebo, do I have to beg you?" Paula pleaded, her voice coming up stronger with her emotion.

Beebo reached for her in one instinctive motion, suddenly very warm inside her jacket. "No, Paula, you don't have to beg me to do anything. Just ask me."

"I did. And you didn't want to stay."

"I didn't want to scare you. I didn't understand."

"I thought it was Mona. She can make herself so—so tempting."

"I can't even remember what she looks like."

"Aren't you in love with her?"

Beebo's hands, with a will of their own, closed around Paula's warm slim arms. "I met her last week for the first time. You can't be in love with someone you just met."

"You can't?" Paula demurred cautiously, looking down at her big pajamas.

"I never was," Beebo said, feeling sweat break out on her forehead. She pulled gently on Paula and was almost dismayed when Paula moved docilely toward her. Beebo became feverishly aware that the plaid pajamas did not conceal all of Paula Ash. The sweeping curve of her breasts held the cotton top out far enough to brush Beebo's chest with a feather touch. Beebo felt it through the layers of her clothes with a tremor so hard and real it tumbled eighteen years of daydreams out of her head.

She held Paula at arm's length a moment, looking at this lovely little redheaded princess with a mixture of misgivings and want too powerful to pretend away. Paula took her hands and held them with quivering strength, returning Beebo's gaze. Beebo saw her own doubts reflected in Paula's eyes. But she saw desire there, too; desire so big that it had to be brave: it hadn't any place to hide.

Paula kissed Beebo's hands with a quick press of her mouth that electrified Beebo. She stood there while Paula kissed them over and over again and a passionate frenzy mounted in them both. Paula's lips, at first so chaste, almost reverent, warmed against Beebo's palms…and then her kitten-tongue slipped between Beebo's fingers and over the backs of her broad hands until those hands trembled perceptibly and Paula stopped, clutching them to her face.

Beebo reclaimed them, but only to caress Paula's face, bringing it close to her and seeing it with amazement.

"I never guessed I'd feel love for the first time through my hands," she murmured. "Paula, Paula, I would have done this all wrong if you hadn't had the guts to start it for me. I would have manhandled you, I—"

Paula stilled her with a finger over Beebo's mouth. "Don't talk now," she said.

And Beebo, who had never done more than dream before, slipped her arms around Paula and pulled her tight. It was a marvel the way their bodies fitted together; the way Paula's head tipped back naturally at so beckoning an angle, and rested on Beebo's arm; the way her eyes closed and her lips parted and her hair scattered like garnet petals around her flower-face.

Beebo kissed her mouth and kissed her mouth again, holding her against the wall with the pressure of her body. Paula submitted with a sort of wistful abandonment. Everywhere Beebo touched this sweet girl, she found thrilling surprises. And Paula, coming to life beneath Beebo's searching hands, found them with her.

It was no news to Beebo that she was tall and strong and male-inclined. But her voluptuous reaction to Paula shocked her speechless. Paula began to undress her and Beebo felt herself half-fainting backwards on the sofa into a whirlpool of sensual delight. The merest touch, the merest flutter of a finger, and Beebo went under, hearing her own moans like the whistle of a distant wind. Paula had only to undo a belt buckle or pull off a shoe, and Beebo responded with a beautiful helpless fury of desire.

It was no longer a question of proceeding with caution, of "learning how." The whole night passed like an ecstatic dream, punctuated with a few dead-asleep time-outs, when they were both too exhausted to move, even to make themselves comfortable.

Beebo had only a vague idea of what she was doing, beyond the overwhelming fact that she was making ardent love to Paula. She seemed to have no mind at all, or need of one. She was aware only that Paula was beautiful, she was gay, she was warmly loving, and she was there in Beebo's arms: fragrant and soft and auburn-topped as a bouquet of tiger lilies.

Beebo couldn't let her go. And when fatigue forced her to stop she would pull Paula close and stroke her, her heavy breath stirring Paula's glowing hair, and think about all the girls she had wanted and been denied. She was making up, this night, for every last one of them.

Paula whispered, "Do you still believe you can't love someone you just met?"

"I don't know what I believe any more."

And Paula said, "I love you, Beebo. Do you believe that?"

Beebo lifted Paula's fine face and covered it with kisses while Paula kept repeating, "I love you, I love you," until the words—the unadorned words—brought Beebo crashing to a climax, rolling over on Paula, embracing her with those long strong legs.

She felt Paula sobbing in the early dawn and raised up on an elbow to look at her. "Darling, did I hurt you?" she asked anxiously, not stopping to think that she had never called a girl "darling" before, either.

"No," Paula said. "It's just—I've been so unhappy, so confused. I thought the world had ended a month ago, and tonight it's just beginning. It's brand new. I'm so happy it scares me."

Beebo held her tenderly and brushed the tears off her cheeks. Paula put her head in the crook of Beebo's arm and gazed at her. "You must have been born making love, Beebo."

"How do you know?" Beebo had no intention of setting the record straight just then.

"I don't, really. It's just that I never reacted to anybody the way I have to you. I never did this with anybody before."

"Never made love?" Beebo said, surprised almost into laughter. *The blind leading the blind,* she thought.

"No, I've made love before," Paula said thoughtfully. "With men, too. It's just that I never.... You'll think I'm making this up, but it's the truth. I never—oh, God help me, I'm frigid. I mean, I was, till tonight."

Beebo lay there in the dark, holding her, torn between the wish to accept it and the suspicion that she was fibbing.

"You don't believe me," Paula said resignedly. "I shouldn't

have told you. It's enough that it happened."

Beebo petted her, smoothing her hair and letting her hands glide over Paula's silky body. "Okay, you never came before," she said. "Now I'll tell you a fish story. I never made love before."

Paula laughed good-naturedly. "All right, we're even," she said. "That's a real whopper. Mine was the truth."

Beebo laughed with her, and it didn't matter any more whether she had been lied to or not. It was the truth in spirit, and only Paula knew if it was the truth in fact. Her attraction to Beebo was so real that it took shape in the night, surrounding her like the aura of her perfume. Beebo kissed her while she was still laughing. "You have such a mouth, Paula. Such a mouth…"

"Does it please you?"

"You please me. All of you," Beebo said, and she meant it. Paula was wholly feminine, soft and submissive. She was finely constructed, looking somehow as breakable, as valuable—and as durable—as Limoges china. Beebo wanted to protect her, accomplish things for her.

She kept touching her admiringly. "You're so tiny," she said. "I'm going to feed you lasagna and put some meat on your bones."

"Will you buy me a new wardrobe when I get too fat for my old one?"

"I'll buy you anything. Mink coats. Meals at the Ritz. New York City," Beebo said.

"All of it?"

"Just the good parts."

Paula clutched at her suddenly, first laughing, then trembling. "Beebo, don't leave me," she said. "I do love you." She seemed dumbfounded. "It frightens me, it makes me believe all over again in my childhood dreams. Did you ever feel like that?"

"Only on the bad days. My childhood wasn't that pretty," Beebo said.

"When are the bad days?"

"Never any more. Not with Paula around."

They got up at noon the next day, and it was some time before Beebo could think rationally about her job. She should call Marie, she should call Jack and tell him where she was. But it was impossible to get out of the bed while Paula was in it. And every time Paula sat up, Beebo pulled her down.

"Let me make breakfast," Paula smiled, and after wrestling a moment, pulled free and scampered halfway across the bedroom, pulling a sheet after her. She stood with her dazzling naked back, delicately sugared with freckles, to Beebo, who admired it in infatuated silence.

Paula ruffled through her closet looking for a negligee until Beebo said, "Paula, are you in love with me or that sheet?"

"I don't want you to see me," Paula confessed. "You said I was too thin."

"I said 'tiny.' And beautiful. Honey, I felt you all over; I know you with my hands. Would it be so awful if I know you with my eyes, too?" When Paula hesitated, Beebo threw the covers off and stood by the bed.

Paula studied her in silence. "You're wonderful," she breathed at last.

"I'm homely," Beebo answered. "But I'm not ashamed of it."

"You are many things, Beebo, but homely isn't one of them," Paula declared. She faced Beebo sheet-first, like a highborn Roman girl in her wedding chiton. "How many girls have admired you like this?"

"Never a one," Beebo said. She crossed the room toward Paula and saw her flinch. "Are you afraid of me?" she said, surprised.

"A little."

"No, Paula." Beebo reached her, touching her with gentle hands. "I'd never hurt you. Don't you know that?"

"Not with your hands, maybe," Paula said, bending her graceful neck to kiss one. "But I'm so in love...it would take so little. And

89

scores of other girls must want you, Beebo. It would hurt me awfully if you ever wanted *them*."

"What girls?" Beebo scoffed.

"Well, for a starter—Mona."

"Paula, I kissed Mona twice. She stood me up twice. That's the end of that," Beebo said flatly. Abruptly, she pulled Paula's sheet off and gazed delightedly on the fresh fair curves beneath. And before Paula had time to blush, Beebo picked her up, grateful at last for the uncomely strength in her arms, and placed her on the bed.

"Beebo," Paula whispered, her arms locked tightly around Beebo's neck. "How old are you?"

Beebo couldn't blurt idiotically, "Eighteen." Instead she asked, "How old do I look?"

"Like a college kid," Paula sighed. "Which makes me older than you. I'm twenty-five, Beebo."

"An ancient ruin." Beebo kissed her nonchalantly, but she was secretly surprised. Nonetheless it pleased her to have won an older girl.

They made love again, lazily now. There was no wild rush, no fear on Beebo's part that it would hurt and disillusion her. They rolled in caresses like millionaires in blue chips...ran their fingers over each other, and kissed and tickled and laughed and blew in each other's ears.

And all the while Paula kept repeating, with the transparent affection that is the crown of femininity, "I love you, Beebo. I love you so much."

Beebo couldn't answer. She couldn't have been happier, or hotter, or more rapturously charmed with the girl. She could hardly believe she had found one so lovely, so generous, so responsive, so single.

But there was a lot of roaming restless curiosity in Beebo, and while she was willing and eager to make love to and romanticize Paula, she was not willing to fall in love with her.

It wasn't Paula's fault, though Paula, with a woman's quick awareness of emotions, sensed the situation. It was just that Beebo wasn't ready for it. Paula had come too early in Beebo's life. And that fact alone made Paula realize how young Beebo must be. Beebo had caught Paula in a vulnerable state, on the rebound from an unhappy love affair with the girl in the plaid pajamas. But it was the culmination of a lot of bad affairs with both sexes that had left Paula drained and skeptical; hopeless about her future and unable to cope with her present. She had nearly taken the whole bottle of sleeping pills the night before, instead of the four that knocked her out.

Beebo was too good to be true, too young to know herself, too masculine to be faithful. But how strong she was, how sensual and sure; in some ways, wise beyond her years with that hard-won maturity Jack had perceived months before.

Paula tried to tell herself, as she lay in Beebo's embrace, that she had nothing more than a hot crush that would end as suddenly as it began, and make her laugh to think she had called it love. She wanted very much to believe it, because it would have spared her the pain of losing Beebo Brinker to another girl—a pain she was in no condition to take safely then.

They ate together in Paula's kitchen, and Paula obligingly sat on Beebo's lap and let Beebo feed her. They were enchanted with each other. It was the kind of day everybody ought to have once in a while; if you knew it was coming, you could bear the boredom and solitude in the interim.

Paula told Beebo about her young years in Washington, D.C., and the shock that accompanied her suspicions that she was a Lesbian. Because it was Paula speaking, and because Beebo had never talked heart-to-heart with another Lesbian, the story seemed remarkable. She held Paula on her knees, answering with sympathy and affection, troubled and touched by it...and stirred by the warmth of Paula's close, firm bottom.

They were startled when the phone cut in on them late in the afternoon.

Paula answered it over Beebo's protests. "Hello?" she said, and as she listened her eyes went to Beebo in surprise. Finally she held out the receiver. "It's for you," she said. "Jack Mann."

Beebo stood up, concerned. "How did he know I was here?"

"You're his roommate, he says. Roommates ought to keep track of each other," Paula said, teasing but with just a trace of chill in her voice. "Why didn't you tell me you were straight, Beebo?"

Beebo took the phone with a comical grimace. "You would have guessed, anyway," she said. "Hey—do you know Jack?"

"Everybody knows Jack," said Paula.

Into the receiver Beebo said, "Jackson?"

"I hear you've been out stupefying the female population of Greenwich Village," Jack said. "You must have something. Paula's usually a deep freeze."

"How did you know I was here?" Beebo said.

"My spies are everywhere. And a damn good thing, too. I would have given you up for dead. Listen, pal, I just got an S.O.S. from Marie. There's a very large customer on Park Avenue who wants a very large pizza right now. Marie is whipping it up and Beebo will whip it over to said customer."

"Park Avenue is Pete's territory," Beebo said. "He won't like it."

"He's out somewhere, as usual. Marie can't find him and besides, she's afraid to look."

"You want me to leave now?" Disappointment growled in her voice.

"I know Paula, honey; she's a good girl. If she likes you enough to sleep with you, she likes you enough to wait for you."

"You mean you knew this beautiful girl all along and didn't tell me about her?" Beebo said, grinning at Paula.

"Well, hell, you waited two months to tell me you *wanted* one. Come on, Marie's in a hurry. Show her what you're made of."

"I'm made of sugar and spice, like the rest of the girls," Beebo said sourly. "It doesn't mix with cheese and anchovies."

"Get your ass over there, Beebo," Jack said. "This order goes to Venus Bogardus."

The name rang in Beebo's head. "The actress?" she said, frowning. "She's not one of our customers."

"She is now."

"But Jack, my God. Venus Bogardus!"

"The original. The girl with the bosom that just won't stop. Can you take it?"

"It's worth it just for a look," Beebo grinned. "Okay, call Marie and tell her I'm coming. And Jack—I know I should have called you. I'm sorry."

Beebo hung up and walked to Paula, expecting to embrace her and explain. But Paula was quite pale. "What's all this about Pete and Marie? Do you mean the Pasquinis?"

"Yes. I work for them. Marie wants me to deliver a pizza to—"

"—to Venus Bogardus. I heard. Beebo, why didn't you tell me about Pete?"

"There's nothing to tell," Beebo said, mystified. "Honey, are you mad at me? Why?"

"Pete and Mona are thick as thieves. What Mona does, Pete does; what Mona thinks, Pete thinks—unless they're quarreling. If they don't like you, they'd as soon exterminate you. They wouldn't cut you down if you were hanging."

Beebo laughed a little at this explosion. "I know you don't like Mona, honey. But Pete's just a twerp. He's the one who sent me over here last night. I'll admit it wasn't exactly ethical."

"Then Mona knows you're here. How charming," Paula said sourly.

"So what's Mona, the Wicked Witch?" Paula scowled and Beebo said, "Okay, Pete's a slob; and my opinion of Mona is slipping fast. But I can't be mad at anybody who sent me to you, Paula, no matter what their motives were."

"Now they'll do everything to take you away from me," Paula said, looking fearfully at Beebo.

"There's no way they could do that, sweetheart," Beebo said, pulling Paula down beside her on the bed. "Paula, I'll be back in an hour. I won't do anything but deliver the pizza."

Paula clung to her. "Promise," she said. "And if Milady Bogardus walks into the room, you have to shut your eyes and run."

"At the same time?"

"Yes."

"You want me to break my neck?" Beebo laughed.

"Better your neck than my heart," Paula whispered.

At the door Beebo took Paula's hands and kissed them the way Paula had first kissed hers. "I never liked Venus Bogardus," she said. "I read somewhere that her curves are built into her clothes. She's about as sexy as a hatrack under the finery—and a cool forty-eight years old."

"Come back," Paula said seriously. "That's all I ask."

They parted and Beebo left the building with a soaring pride and satisfaction that seemed to lift her clear of the pavement.

Marie Pasquini was waiting in the shop when Beebo arrived. She had just argued with her mother-in-law and it made her visage long and dark.

"Thank God, a happy face," she said when she saw Beebo.

"Maybe we ought to find Pete, Marie," Beebo said. "He considers Park his street."

"*His* street!" Marie spat. "It's too good for him. An alley full of donkey-do is too good for him."

"Too bad for you there ain't no such alleys handy," said Pete's voice from the front of the shop, approaching the kitchen. "You'd be right at home in one. Like the one where I found you in Bordeaux." He appeared in the kitchen doorway, making Beebo wonder how long he had been lurking there. Unaccountably, he gave her a case of gooseflesh.

"Here he comes," said Marie to Beebo. "Captain Marvel. Okay, Captain, here's an order. You want to deliver?"

"That depends on Beebo," Pete said, meandering unsteadily toward her. "Where were you today, butch? I had to make all the deliveries myself." His grin made her want to hit him.

"I was indisposed," she said.

"Indisposed," he mimicked in a fussy voice. "Well, ain't that a shame. I understand Paula Ash was indisposed today, too." His breath smelled of zinfandel.

Beebo stared at him with cold-eyed loathing and then stalked toward the back door.

"Wait a minute!" Pete called.

"Not for you," Beebo said.

"Beebo!" It was Marie's voice this time. "He's full of dry red. He can't drive. Please, I don't want to lose Venus Bogardus. Nor the truck, neither," she added, with a significant glance at Pete.

At the sound of that famous name, Pete burst into winy laughter. "Go on, Beebo, go on. Maybe she'll fall for you, too," he said. "How you gonna keep two of 'em happy at the same time? You want a few lessons?"

Beebo took the wrapped pizza from Marie and stormed out of the kitchen. She could hear the opening blast of a real wingding behind her.

Beebo drove through a light rain that was quickly slicking down the city streets. It was Midwestern weather. Her father's face crossed her mind, obscuring some of her revulsion against Pete. *I wonder where Dad thinks I am now?* she mused despondently.

She punished herself by picturing her father: a tan solid man, with the lines of worry and weather on his face, delivering a foal to its snorting, laboring mother; stooping with the burdens of alcohol and anxiety over his strange young daughter.

Beebo felt a surge of guilty love for him as she neared the address Marie had given her. She almost drove past. It was a big chilly building that looked loftily down on the summer sprinkle.

Beebo went up on the service elevator, her head full of whirling images: Paula, of the glorious red hair and sweet mouth. The big kindly father whose love had made her strong and himself weak. The people who had lately come to matter in her life in the city.

She knocked on the back door, becoming aware as she did so of strident voices within: a woman's, bright and soprano with anger; a boy's breaking with resentment; another woman, refereeing timidly for the first two.

"All right, all right, answer the goddamn door!" cried the soprano.

"Mother, do you have to swear like a whore?" the boy cried. "In front of delivery boys?"

"What do you care what I do with delivery boys, darling?"

Beebo recognized the celebrated voice, just as the door opened. "Are you the pizza?" asked a gray dumpling of a woman.

"No, but I have one with me," Beebo grinned. Her voice stilled the argument momentarily. "Five bucks," Beebo told the Dumpling, who wore a white uniform like a nurse, or nanny. Beebo waited for the money, suddenly full of springy laughter that might go off any second like a string of firecrackers.

"Five bucks?" said Venus Bogardus. "I haven't got a damn dime."

With a thrill of recognition, Beebo suddenly saw her. She was wearing a scarlet, silk-jersey dress. When she moved, she proved there was nothing beneath it. The hatrack story lay down and died. But Beebo was still so full of Paula that the sight of Venus Bogardus was little more than an entertainment.

Toby, the boy, turned his pockets inside out. "I gave you all my money yesterday," he said, glum and embarrassed. To Beebo he said, "I'm sorry," with the pathetic air of a child who is struggling to assume the responsibilities of dissipated parents. He was a good-looking boy; in his early teens, Beebo guessed, and finding life with a movie-star mother a stormy combination of high excitement and humiliation. He was not the type to take it lightly.

"Toby, don't you have something in your piggy bank, dear?" Venus persisted, aware of Beebo now.

"You threw my piggy bank down the incinerator shaft," he mumbled.

"I did?" She blinked at him with incredible blue eyes, encircled by long black lashes.

"A year ago," Toby said wearily.

"God, that was careless. Was there anything in it?" Venus said.

"Two-fifty in pennies. I was saving up for a catcher's mitt."

"Well, that wouldn't be enough anyway. For the pizza, I mean."

"Excuse me—why don't you charge it?" Beebo said. She was somewhat abashed to have walked in on a Love Queen in the midst of a common little argument.

"Do you think they'd let me?" Venus said, turning to Beebo at last, her voice melting off her tongue like buckwheat honey. Toby slammed out of the kitchen in utter disgust.

"I think so," Beebo said, smiling.

Venus came to take the pizza from her, opening the container for a taste. "Somebody said it was 'peerless pasta.' Is it *that* bad?"

"It's good."

Venus put it on the breakfast table and tore off a bite. "You're right," she said. "Want some?"

"No thanks," Beebo said, staring at her. Perhaps now was the time to back out and run, as Paula suggested.

"Don't be shy," Venus said. "Toby, come back and eat, dear," she called through the kitchen door. "We have a guest." Toby shuffled in while Venus explained to Beebo, still hesitating at the back door, "No cook tonight. She just quit for the hundredth time. Bring some plates, Mrs. Sack. I'll get the milk for these growing children."

"Miss Bogardus, I can't possibly stay; I—" Beebo said, but Venus interrupted her, as if she hadn't heard her, with a stream of cordial inanities.

Toby's face colored. "Mother, will you listen?" he said in an angry hiss. "She doesn't *want* to stay."

"I know, darling. Now shut up and sit down, all of you."

They did. It seemed to be the thing to do. But Beebo had a tingling feeling that the whole building would fold under her as soon as she touched down on the seat.

Venus opened the refrigerator and a loud smell came out. "God, look at the mess!" she cried. "I'll bet that bitch hasn't cleaned it for weeks."

"If you'd come home long enough to look at it once in a while, she would have," Toby said.

"Darling, I look at it every day, when I put the champagne in to cool."

She joined them, passing the milk around, and badgered Beebo to eat more than Beebo wanted. Toby couldn't stand it.

"Leave her alone, Mother!" he said, rising from his seat.

"Don't behave like a nervous girl, Toby," Venus reproved him breezily.

"I'm not a girl," he said in real anguish.

"Of course not, dear. Boys wear pants and girls wear skirts. That's how I've always known you were a boy."

Beebo became abruptly conscious of her chino slacks and found it hard to keep eating naturally.

"I'm sorry," Toby said again to Beebo. "My mother's a little cracked. It comes from getting her own way all the time."

"God, how dreadful to be fourteen," Venus said, gazing at her son pityingly. "I don't know how I lived through it myself." She ate for a minute quietly while Beebo plotted an escape. "I'll have to tell Leo about this; it's really marvelous," Venus said, cutting another bite.

"Leo's her husband," Toby said, making a face.

"You'd think they loathed each other," Venus said, glancing at Beebo. "Actually, Toby gets along better with Leo than with any of the others."

"It's a good thing *I* get along with him, because *you* sure don't," Toby flared, to the accompaniment of horrified shushings from Mrs. Sack.

"One more crack like that and you can leave the table," Venus said sharply. "God! What do you do with children that age?"

"I don't know. What do they do with you?" Beebo said.

Toby turned to her with an amazed grin.

"And how old are *you,* darling?" Venus asked Beebo, her eyes shining through their black fringe like hard chips of sapphire.

"Fourteen," Beebo said, and evoked a chuckle of relief from Toby. Beebo smiled at him, and suddenly they were in league; two friendly conspirators subverting Venus's authority.

"I'd have said twelve, to judge from your table manners," Venus cooed.

And unruffled, she continued eating, giving Beebo a chance to study her surreptitiously. Her face had been called the most perfect in the world when she was a starlet twenty years before. And still she was very lovely, even without make-up on her face. The lines about her eyes and mouth were faint and fine. You had to look for them, and somehow they made her beauty the more poignant, emphasizing as they did the perishability of human loveliness. She was probably in her late thirties, Beebo guessed.

"Tell me, darling," Venus said unexpectedly, startling Beebo. "Do you live in town somewhere with your mommy and daddy? I mean, surely a fourteen-year-old child isn't out delivering pizzas for a living."

"I live in town," Beebo said. "My father lives back in Wisconsin."

"How primitive," Venus said, with a smile that told Beebo she was aware of her own oversophisticated nonsense. She made it rather charming. "Just one father?" she said. "Toby has six."

"That must be a record," Beebo said quietly, trying to focus on her food.

"It's Mother's record, not mine," Toby said. "As far as I'm concerned, you can throw all six in the East River. All but Leo, anyway."

"Darling!" his mother cried, more amused this time than angry, perhaps because she shared his view. "After all the lovely presents they've given you, too."

Beebo watched her curiously. Venus was not dense or callow. But her glamour and her fortune obviously hadn't spared her the problems of raising a pubescent boy. Most mothers approached their kids with a mixture of love, common sense, and frazzled tempers. Venus approached hers with all the gorgeous razzle-dazzle, passion, and impatience that made obedient slaves of the older men in her life.

Toby, at fourteen, was supposed to react with the fascination of an adult male three times his age for a beautiful and tempestuous woman.

If he ever does, Venus will get the shock of her life, Beebo thought with amusement.

Instead, of course, Toby lashed out at her in frightened confusion. He loved her very much, but he was afraid and overawed, and bitter about the life she made him lead.

He wanted a mother comfortably middle-aged and unpretentious, like other people's mothers. Instead, he had what other people thought they wanted: a glittering courtesan who couldn't kiss him at night for fear of smudging her mouth, who took him on vacation trips with her lovers while her husband—and Toby's friend, Leo—stayed behind in Hollywood.

Beebo sensed much of this in the pointed wordplay between mother and son. Their mutual love stood aside, forlorn and unexpressed, while they took out their grievances against one another.

Beebo stood up to leave as soon as she decently could.

"Heavens, you're not going!" Venus protested.

"I have a heavy date," Beebo smiled. "Thanks very much, Miss Bogardus."

"You're welcome. Who's the lucky boy?"

Beebo frowned uncomprehendingly at first, till she realized Venus meant her date. "Oh," she said, humiliated to know she was blushing. "Just an old friend."

"Bring him around."

Beebo began to stammer excuses and Toby came to her rescue. "Let her go, Mom," he said, ashamed of Venus, as usual. He liked Beebo for taking his side; for making him laugh and getting one up on his mother. And it galled him to see Venus tease her. He was not too young to see how uncomfortable Beebo was. When Venus turned to him with a dangerous smile, he said, "I just wish you'd act like a mother now and then."

"Why, I act like a mother twenty-four hours a day," she said innocently. "I *am* a mother. There sits the proof, eating his pizza like an absolute boor." She turned elegantly to Beebo, who had just noticed her dainty bare feet under the table. "All right, darling, go. But do come again some time," Venus said.

Beebo smiled her thanks and got as far as the door before Venus called her again. Her voice, even though Beebo half expected it, sent a wave of shivers down her back.

"I forgot to ask," Venus said. "What's your name? I mean, so we'll know when we order peerless pasta again."

Toby had had it. Venus was practically flirting with Beebo. He clambered over Mrs. Sack and started out of the kitchen. Venus turned in her seat and said, "Damn it, Toby, you come back here!" Her eyes sparkled.

"What for?" he said blackly.

"To finish your dinner."

"I've lost my appetite, Mother." He glanced at Beebo and added, "I apologize for my mother. I hope you don't have a rotten impression of us."

"Not at all," Beebo said, moved by his distress, his anxious efforts to protect her opinion of them. She wondered if he had any friends at all up here in his gilded cage. A Manhattan apartment isn't the ideal place to raise a spirited boy.

Mrs. Sack rose to her feet clucking, but Venus waved her down. "Oh, the hell with him, Mrs. Sack," she said. "He'll be right back.... He's a lovely boy," she told Beebo. "He'll outgrow this rebellious stuff in another year or so." She spoke confidently but Beebo knew it was a cover-up for deep concern. "Now—what did you say your name was?"

Beebo answered in a low voice, "Beebo Brinker."

"You're kidding," said Venus.

"No." Beebo smiled.

"Lord, that's even worse than mine. Did your press agent dream it up? Or don't you delivery boys—excuse me, girls—have press agents?"

"I have dozens, but they're all starving," Beebo said.

"Mercy, we'll have to find you a job," Venus said. "Are you literate, by any chance?"

"No, I'm perfectly normal," Beebo said. She had learned not to get mad at the wild assortment of jibes people tossed at her. It was better to catch and toss back than to fall and lie as if dead; make a sideshow of your strangeness.

Venus put her head back and laughed, and Beebo felt suddenly very warm and nervous, looking at her. From across the room her face looked flawless. "Poor Beebo," Venus said, enjoying the name. "Came all the way up here in the rain to bring me a pizza, and I didn't even pay her for it."

"You fed me part of it," Beebo said.

"Well, I'll order spaghetti next time. When the sun is shining and I have a few nickels in my jeans," Venus promised. "I suppose you're in a mighty rush to get home to your heavy date?"

"If you don't mind," Beebo said politely.

"Of course I mind, but go anyway. I'll see you on spaghetti

day," Venus smiled, and Beebo slipped out the back door with her spine still prickling.

Beebo wondered, all the way downtown in the truck, what sort of kicks Venus got out of inviting a strange delivery girl in for an unpaid-for dinner. *She had a bad day and I amused her,* Beebo thought. *The cook cut out, Toby bugged her, and all six husbands are out of town.*

She approached Pasquini's wishing she could leave the truck somewhere else for the night, just to avoid seeing Pete. But he was out of sight, if not off the premises, and she parked and left without incident.

Under a streetlight she looked at her watch. She had been away three hours instead of one and she was anxious about the trusting girl she had left behind. She ran most of the way to Paula's place.

It surprised her when Paula left her waiting in the entry almost four minutes before she buzzed to open the door.

No one was in the living room when Beebo came in. She called, feeling her heart quicken with alarm.

"Paula, where are you? Are you all right?"

"In here." Paula's voice was faint and Beebo rushed into the bathroom to find her, standing quiet and sad in front of the mirror. A bottle full of pills, with the cap off, rested on the bowl. Paula had an empty glass in her hand.

Beebo looked at her face in the mirror and then saw the bottle.

"Sleeping pills?" she said, picking it up. Her eyes went dark and she grabbed Paula by the shoulders. "You didn't!" she said. "Good God, Paula!"

"No, I didn't," Paula murmured. "The bottle's still full."

Beebo emptied it into the toilet and flushed the pills away. She turned to Paula, trying to comfort her, but Paula averted her face and broke into tears. She flung her arms around Beebo. "Where have you *been?* You've been gone for hours," she wept.

"She wanted me to eat the damn pizza with them," Beebo said clumsily. "Come on, honey, lie down on the bed." She pulled a protesting and white-faced Paula toward the bedroom. "What's the matter?" Beebo said as Paula's resistance stiffened.

"I think she's afraid of a scene," came a cool, unexpected voice. Beebo whirled and saw Mona Petry sitting on Paula's bed, smoking calmly. "But she needn't worry. Will you please tell her I don't plan to stay more than a minute? I tried to tell her myself, but we don't seem to speak the same language."

Beebo looked back at Paula, who had covered her mouth and cheeks with tight-pressed hands while tears spilled out of her eyes. Beebo stood between the two jealous girls; one frightened and hurt, the other pleased to have her so. It was up to Beebo to restore peace.

Beebo walked into the bedroom, leaving Paula in the hall behind her. "All right, Mona, I'm sorry," she said briefly. "If you're angry about it, remember you're the one who stood me up." Her voice was sharper than she intended. She wanted to get it over with.

"I didn't stand you up at all, Beebo," Mona said. "I told you to call in one hour. If you had, we could have spent the night together. Instead, you walked out and disappeared."

"I called too soon," Beebo said, recalling the man's voice through Mona's door.

"Not on the phone," Mona said, and through her disdain, Beebo could see the flash of real anger. "Do you mean you eavesdropped?"

"I didn't have to, Mona. I went in to use the phone in the front hall, and you were throwing things and arguing with some guy. So I left. I just figured you had a taste for men that night."

"Did you really?" Mona said acidulously. "After the way I acted with you? Knowing that any man in my apartment must be an uninvited guest?"

"An uninvited guest doesn't get in with his own key," Beebo shot back. "I didn't like the idea of sharing you with a man, Mona."

"I fought with the man," Mona said, standing up. "I wouldn't have fought with you, ever. Now, it can't be helped." She crushed her cigarette on the floor under her shoe as a gesture of contempt for Paula's tidy bedroom, and smiled. "Or did you think we could all be buddies? We three?"

Beebo colored up with anger. "Three's a crowd, Mona. You make such a thing of it. Why didn't you call *me?* I waited for days. I wanted you to call."

"Wanted. Past tense," Mona said, looking at Paula. "Besides, Beebo, I was wronged, not you. The least you could have done was let me explain. Now you don't give a damn. Well, just know that I don't either. I wouldn't dream of taking you away from Paula. She needs somebody to count the sleeping pills for her." She hooked her sweater on her index finger, and swung it over her shoulder with an air of satisfaction. Paula was distracted and Beebo was exasperated with Mona. This was Trouble and it exhilarated her.

"Is that what you came here to say?" Beebo demanded.

"That's most of it," Mona said. "It's only fair to warn you, though…I may drop some more bricks before I'm through. You turn such a nice color when you're burned, Beebo." She sauntered deliberately through the hall, past Paula, who shrank from her, and to the front door, where she turned for one last shot.

Beebo had followed her and stood in the middle of the living room with her arms folded over her chest, the way she faced Pete when he crowded her.

Mona looked her over and then blew a poisonous kiss toward Paula. "I hope you two will be happy," she said. "It's obviously one of those marriages made in hell." She pulled the door shut very slowly till Beebo reached over and gave it a hard shove to.

Mona thumped against it on the outside, laughing at the show of temper.

Beebo turned to Paula, mystified. "What in hell was all that about?" she said.

Paula was leaning against the wall, still pale and quite exhausted. "You've heard of jealousy," she said tiredly.

"She had something more than that on her mind," Beebo said. "She looked like she wanted blood. You can be jealous without being plain mean."

"Mona can't. That's how she makes her life interesting. It's funny. You think of a *man* being sadistic, coldhearted, capable of evil just for kicks. But when a woman's that way, it shocks you. Mona just—enjoys it, I guess."

"Enjoys tormenting people?" Beebo said. She had known people like that back in Juniper Hill, but it was hard to believe about someone you had so recently admired.

Paula nodded. "I think she came here tonight because she's mad at Pete and she can't find him to give him hell. Pete sent you over to bug Mona, and it worked. And you and I went right along with his game and fell for each other. Mona likes to think she's a femme fatale, and I guess to Pete, she is. She jilted him once and he never got over it. She's always telling me I'm a 'goddamn milkmaid' and nobody wants a milkmaid these days. She must have really wanted you, Beebo, or she wouldn't have been so hurt to lose you."

"Pete told me he dumped Mona when he found out she was a Lesbian," Beebo frowned.

"He's lying, as usual. He only falls for gay girls," Paula said. She had gone to Beebo's side and put her arms around her for consolation. Beebo, reviewing Pete's behavior toward her in a new light, felt faintly nauseated. "And I thought he was just trying to get my goat," she said, returning Paula's embrace.

"Darling," Paula said, and Beebo thought how much warmer and truer the word was when Paula spoke it than when it bloomed on Venus's perfect lips like a gaudy rose.

"Beebo, I want to explain—about myself—" Paula said haltingly.

"You don't have to, I understand."

"No, you don't. I didn't myself. Beebo, I've always been such a steady, sensible girl. Even when I discovered I was gay, I didn't go all to pieces like so many kids. It shook me up, yes, but I did the reasonable thing. I went out and learned all I could about it. I'd never had special prejudices against other people's problems, and I hadn't any against my own.

"I tried to accept the fact, and after a while I got used to it. But all the time I was waiting for somebody wonderful to come along; for a beautiful love affair to make it all right. We'd live quietly together, we'd cherish each other, and life would be rosy.

"I didn't think it would be simple, but I thought it would be satisfying—and permanent. That's the kind of girl I am, Beebo.

"I found other girls while I was waiting so trustingly for this perfect love," she said, speaking with the disillusioned realism of hindsight. "And they taught me a lot. I thought this was necessary. You have to know the different kinds of love before you can recognize the kind you need. I met Mona during this period. She's mean as an old crow, but she's sharp and I learned a lot from her.

"And then the girl in the plaid pajamas came along. It wasn't beautiful, Beebo. Nothing I had learned before prepared me for what I went through.

"I lost my self-respect...my ideals. My efforts to please her rubbed her the wrong way. I did everything I thought would draw us close, even when it seemed like madness. I moved to the Village, I went with her fast crowd, I quit my job. I drank too much and played too hard, for fear if I didn't she'd think I was square. I did things that were downright degrading."

Beebo embraced her tightly. "Honey, you're the sweetest girl I ever knew," she said. "I won't believe anything bad about you." She guided her back to the bedroom.

"What I want you to know is," Paula whispered, lying down

107

on the bed, "that I'm not a kook. I don't usually fly off the handle emotionally. I never did it before my affair with the girl in the pajamas. I live an orderly life, I work hard, I care about people. Only, Beebo, you just couldn't have happened. You walked in here asking for Mona last night—was it only last night!—and I realized that all I'd suffered before was the dark before the dawn. Maybe it was a sort of price I had to pay for being gay. I paid it, and Heaven dropped you in my lap. I want to deserve you, Beebo."

Beebo was nonplused. She kissed Paula's white throat, holding her and frowning into the dim light where Paula couldn't see her face. It was disturbing to have such a strong emotion centered on her. She desired Paula passionately. Every endearment Beebo had spoken to her, she had spoken truthfully, but without once repeating, "I love you."

Paula had brought her out; something Paula herself couldn't believe. And no matter what other women might figure in Beebo's life, Paula would always be dear to her for that alone.

But Beebo was afraid of hurting her. There was more than a humble excuse in Paula's explanations; there was also that weapon of amorous women, a plea for sympathy. It was a hint to Beebo: *Don't hurt me like the girl in the plaid pajamas did, or you'll destroy me.* Beebo caught it and fretted over it in silence.

Paula began to worry that she had said too much. She raised up on one elbow, pressed her mouth against Beebo's cheek, and said, "I want you to know I'm as surprised as you are by this love-at-first-sight thing. I thought it was all rot till I met you. Darling, I'm well aware it didn't hit you as hard as it did me. I promise I won't be a nuisance. I'll love you very quietly like a good sensible girl. I won't shriek and weep in public, or chase you, or take pills. I'll just love you. So much and so well you'll have to love me back...someday. You will, won't you?"

Beebo felt suddenly cornered and couldn't answer. But when she finally glanced at Paula, Paula had found the courage to smile at her, to tuck her dismay out of sight. It gave Beebo an odd sort of pride in her, as if a child of hers had performed bravely in the face of a hard disappointment. It made Paula still sweeter and more attractive.

"Doesn't everybody love you, little Paula?"

"Almost everybody...except Miss Plaid Pajamas and Beebo Brinker." Paula gave her a wry grin that let Beebo relax. "But they don't count. All the intelligent, rich, beautiful people are insanely in love with me."

Beebo laughed and pulled her down on the bed. "Not hard to see why," she said. "You're adorable." She was still full of wonderment and fascination over the new role she was playing with Paula: lover, friend, protector. It felt so good, it fit so well, it rather astounded her. It was like picking up a violin for the first time and finding you could play a lilting tune with no practice at all.

Beebo's good humor rescued Paula from the dumps. She began to feel affectionate again. For Beebo, it was a delirious pleasure to act out on a real girl in a real bed all the intense love play that had filled her solitude. She fell asleep very late, very tired, with Paula in her arms.

Beebo got up early the next morning. She was in no hurry to face Pete Pasquini, knowing what she now knew about him, but she didn't want to lose her job till she could scout down another. She was not in a financial position to get hard-nosed with him yet, and besides she was confident that she could handle whatever he could dish out. They were nearly of a size, and he had never shown himself more than a brash nuisance. And anyway, a man who could fall in love with the likes of Mona Petry was not likely to find himself erotically interested in Beebo Brinker.

Paula was pensive throughout breakfast and when Beebo demanded to know why, she admitted, "It's Mona."

Beebo laughed, but Paula was serious. "She's one of those people with nothing to do. She has to make trouble to keep from going mad with the 'Flats'—that's what she calls it. She doesn't work—her men give her enough money to live on. She doesn't do a thing but amuse herself. If you know her at all, you have to be a lover or a hater. There's no middle ground with her."

"Shall I hire a bodyguard?" Beebo kidded.

"She'll try to punish you somehow. She's been stood up by you and tricked by Pete. She's not the kind who can tolerate being made a fool of. Pete doesn't count, he's only a man, and she can twist him around her finger if she's in the mood. But *you*..."

"What can Mona do to me?" Beebo said, still smiling.

"Mona is very inventive. She'll think of something," Paula said.

"Do you mean she'd hurt *you?*" Beebo's smile faded.

"Oh, I doubt it," Paula said. "It wouldn't be half as much fun as making an effigy of Beebo and sticking pins in it. If she does, you'll squirm, too. For heaven's sake, darling, don't do anything she could blackmail you for."

Beebo laughed and reassured her. Mona's jealousy seemed more silly to her than dangerous.

Beebo didn't see Pete Pasquini at work all day, and Marie had no idea where he was. "Out making babies with the *filles*," she said with offhand contempt.

Beebo had no wish to confront him and she finished out the day's work in relief. But when she got home that night, there was a new surprise for her.

Jack let her in, taking the bags of groceries from her. "Haven't seen you for two nights," he said. "Paula must have attractions I can't match."

"Oh, you're not bad," Beebo smiled. "For a man."

He started stowing things in the refrigerator, and Beebo

became aware of Pat, who had followed them into the kitchen. "Good news," Jack said. "Celebration tonight." He pulled a bottle of sparkling burgundy from the shelf.

Beebo glanced from one to the other. "Did you boys finally tie the knot?" she said, trying to make it sound light.

"Nothing formal yet," Jack grinned. "I believe in long engagements. No, little pal, we are festive tonight because Pat is no longer with the Sanitary Department."

"It was too unsanitary," Pat chuckled.

"I thought you were taking your vacation," Beebo said. Suddenly, her precarious place in this still-new city was menaced. The time to move out was coming fast.

"Vacation, hell. He quit," Jack said. "I asked him to."

"How come?"

"I don't want my betrothed to work," Jack said, pouring the champagne. It exploded into tiny fountains of fizz, and they each took a glass.

Jack lifted his. "Long life and health," he said, and added significantly, "and love all around."

They drank. Beebo nodded to Pat. "All I can say, Pat, is what they said to me when I left Juniper Hill: good riddance to bad rubbish."

"Beebo, you should have been a poet," Jack said.

She finished her drink and stood up. "I guess you two want to celebrate by yourselves," she said.

"Not at all. Have dinner with us," Jack said.

"I think Paula's waiting for me," Beebo said. After an awkward pause she added, "She asked me to move in with her."

"She doesn't waste time, does she?" said Jack. "Do you want to?"

"I don't know. It would give her the right to expect me to be faithful. I can't imagine a lovelier girl. But I hardly know her. And there are so damn many girls in the world."

"Which reminds me. How was La Bogardus?"

"If you mean the bosom, it's authentic."

Jack laughed. "You must have been a big hit, if you got that far."

"No. I just have good eyes. And she's allergic to underwear, which makes it pretty obvious." She sat down heavily for a moment on a kitchen chair across the table from Pat.

"You look tired, honey," Jack said concernedly.

"I haven't had much sleep the last two nights," she said and let them chortle at her, smiling a little.

"She's a doll, that Paula," Jack said. "If I were you, I'd keep a close eye on her." He waited a moment. "You don't have to go as far as moving in with her, though. Not if you're not ready."

Beebo looked up at him and reached out to squeeze his arm. "You're too damn good to me, Jack," she said. "I know it's getting crowded here."

"Nobody's complaining!" Jack said. "Besides, if you move out, Pat will probably go, too. You're still my biggest asset."

Pat smiled and Beebo laughed, but there was just enough truth in it to make them all a little uncomfortable.

"If only you could get your elbow in your ear," Pat said to her wistfully, making Jack hilarious. But despite the bantering tone, Pat had found a serious new interest in himself. He was staring and wondering at the many handsome, mannish, and somewhat authoritative girls around Greenwich Village. His crush on Beebo had the effect of opening his eyes to a new and quite fascinating possibility. But so far it was nothing to threaten his affection for Jack, and he said nothing.

Beebo lighted a cigarette, watching as Jack refilled her wine glass. "If I ask a hard question, will you boys tell me the truth?" she said at last. They nodded at her curiously in silent assent.

"When you want me to move out, will you, for God's sake, please say so? I feel bad enough about mooching from Jack as it is."

"Forget it," Jack said. "Stay as long as you want to, pal."

She sipped the drink. "It's not that I don't want Paula," she said. "I just don't want her enough to cut loose from all the rest of the women in the world yet. And I'm not earning enough to live alone."

"You should have met her five years from now," Jack said sagely. "You would have been ready then."

"Maybe we can make it together after a few months," Beebo said. She was musing guiltily about somebody else; someone who had nothing to do with Paula, and yet who affected Beebo's decision not to go live with the pretty little redhead. Beebo had been eager to stay with Paula, eager to be asked, throughout the first night and day of their acquaintance. It would have solved so many problems, economic and emotional.

Then she got away from Paula for a few hours. She met a woman of provocative beauty who stuck in her imagination, almost without her realizing it at first, and who roused her desire for variety: Venus. When she got back to Paula, she was made to see that Paula was urgently in love with her, and it scared her. She was flattered but afraid of the responsibility. And not at all sure she could return the love in full measure.

So she dodged the decision temporarily by volunteering to take Jack's sofa and leave the bed to the men. And for a while it worked out. Beebo spent most of her evenings with Paula—and sometimes the entire night—and Paula wisely refrained from pushing her any more on moving in.

There was a complete—and, Paula thought, ominous—silence from Mona. And another odd development was the disappearance of Pete Pasquini. For almost two weeks, nobody saw him. Marie kept saying she hoped to God he had deserted her at last. She was massively uninterested in finding him.

When he finally made a startling appearance, he touched off a howling family feud, with Marie vowing to drown him in spaghetti sauce and his mother promising to throw Marie in after him. The children lined up on the narrow stairs leading up from the kitchen and shrieked approval of the melee.

Beebo walked in on it at eight-thirty in the morning and brought a sudden stillness to the room. She stood there uncertainly with all eyes on her and finally said, "Don't let me stop you." Pete smiled at her.

Marie came to life, striding toward Beebo to plead her case with feminine ardor. "We find out this morning. He gets back last night, without telling nobody," she said, waving a steaming red spoon at her husband. The coating of sauce underlined her threats to drown him.

"We're all asleep, it's late. The phone rings twice and stops. We go back to sleep—they must've hung up. What we don't know," she hollered in a rising voice, "this piece of dung is in the shop and *he* answers it. Why is he in the shop in the middle of the night? It's dark, no customers, nothing to do. Nothing but tin cans and dry pasta. Is he making love to the tomato paste? Who knows what a crazy dago goes for?"

Pete laughed, and all the while his brilliant black eyes were fixed on Beebo, who refused to meet them, concentrating instead on Marie's theatrics.

"So who's on the phone? *Bogardus,*" Marie said.

Beebo gasped.

"Yeah, that's right," Marie said, hands on her hips, spoon dripping bloody sauce. "She wants spaghetti this time. It's the middle of the night—never mind. She got a taste for spaghetti. 'Send me that one with the funny name,' she says. And she don't mean Pasquini." She threw Pete a look of ferocious scorn. "So Hot Pants here, he says sure, he bring it right up, the stupid sonofabitch. No spaghetti, never mind, he makes up a leftover pizza." She rolled her eyes to Heaven for vengeance.

"What happened?" Beebo said, her mind suddenly full of the star's vivid face and sensual body.

"So I make the delivery," Pete said languidly, seating himself on a table amid the crunchy bread crumbs. "Bogardus opens the door herself and says, 'Where's Beebo?' Well, I'm surprised, I don't realize how popular you are with these actress types." He grinned and picked his teeth with neat nonchalance, while Beebo began to sweat nervously.

"So I tell her, you're sick, you can't make it, but it's okay, I got her spaghetti. She says, 'Thank you, darling—'" He rolled the endearment interminably off his tongue, always smiling directly at

Beebo. "—and opens it. I'm waiting for her to hand me some money, minding my own business—"

"For the first time in two weeks!" Marie interpolated. "Where was your hands all this time, Pete?"

"In my pockets," he replied coolly. "She wasn't in a mood for no man last night."

Beebo's whole face flushed a high red. She wanted to turn and rush out of the place, but the thought of his raucous laughter alone prevented her.

"So instead of the money," he went on leisurely, "she hands me back the pizza. In the face."

"I begin to respect this woman," Marie commented.

Pete continued, "She says, 'What do you mean spaghetti? This ain't spaghetti. And *you* ain't no Beebo Brinker, neither.' How do you like that, butch? You can write your own ticket with that one. Only you better make it a round trip. I understand you got a good reason for visiting back on McDonald Street these days."

"She got a good reason to spit in your face, you damn wop!" Marie declared, siding with Beebo.

Pete ignored her. "That Paula, she's a looker, hm? I wouldn't mind cracking that little nut myself," he said to Beebo, folding his arms and enjoying her alarm.

"I'll crack yours one of these days," Beebo said in a sudden fury. "Don't talk about Paula, you dirty her name."

"Don't mind him, Beebo," Marie said, sensing trouble. "It ain't just Paula, anyway. It ain't enough he runs after skirts all the time. He wants the girls who want other girls. Figure *that* one out. After all his big talk about fags."

"Fags go for other fags. I go for girls," Pete said, but Marie had finally rattled him. Any challenge to his manhood threw him into a panic. It was clear he drew a fine distinction between his own sexual preferences—"normal"—and everybody else's.

"You go for Lesbians," Marie said, silencing him with a wave of her gory spoon. She did him further insult by describing his desires to Beebo, as if Pete were not even in the room. "He's three-fourths fag and the rest sadist," she said. "That's why he don't chase real women. He has to hurt a girl—a girl who don't *want* it—before he can get it up." She glared at him like a cannibal.

Pete looked back with cold wrath. "I got five kids on those stairs says you're a liar," he said. "Or are you saying *you* ain't a real woman?"

"Don't fake with me, Pasquini. I know what you pretend in bed," Marie shouted. "You married me to prove you was a man, and once we left the church, you figure you proved it. Well, it ain't that simple."

Pete walked toward her and Marie paled and stiffened, ready for a blow. But he passed her and went to Beebo, who could only stand her ground like Marie and hope he'd go on by. But he stopped, putting a hand on her shoulder, and pulled her aside.

"Don't listen to her, she's cracked," he said softly. "I told Bogardus you'd be up with the spaghetti this afternoon. Does that make me your friend?"

"After your cracks about Paula?" she said, shaking his hand off roughly.

"I told you where to find Paula, too," he reminded her, and his eyes glittered. "I always say nice things about that one. She's a nice girl."

Beebo looked at him with revulsion. "You sent me there to even some secret score of yours with Mona. Don't act noble about it."

He chuckled. "Still, I sent you, butch. And you went. You tell me if you're sorry. You tell me if I ever done one thing you want to complain about."

"We'd be here all day," Beebo snapped. She turned to start working on the morning's orders, but he followed her into the store, leaving Marie and the others to understand he was through fighting. Beebo heard Marie say wearily to Mrs. Pasquini, "So how come your son looks so good in Bordeaux and so lousy in New York? Okay, don't yell, go see about the kids."

Pete and Beebo worked in silence but whenever she glanced at him he seemed to have glanced at her first and was waiting for her eyes with a smile. He got his orders packed ahead of her and loped out the back door at a jaunty pace. Beebo watched his retreating back with relief. Before he drove away he leaned in and called to her.

"Don't forget—Bogardus wants her pasta at five-thirty," he said. She straightened up and glowered at him till he laughed and withdrew.

Beebo finished the orders quickly, her mind teeming with ideas for another job. Anything would be preferable to Pete's endless leering. It was one thing for him to chase pretty Lesbians like Mona. But that he might desire Beebo—big and rangy, almost more boy than girl—seemed as utterly perverse and unnatural to her as that she might desire him.

She was surprised when the front bell rang and Pat Kynaston walked in. She was just ready to leave.

"What are you doing here!" she exclaimed.

"I brought Marie some goodies for her cockroaches," he said, shaking a colored cylinder full of powder. "The Last Supper. Going to make some deliveries?"

Beebo nodded.

"Take me along," he said pleasantly. "I haven't anything to do, and the heat in that apartment is godawful."

She relented after a moment's indecision, and gave him a smile. "Okay, bring those boxes and follow me," she said. "You can take my mind off things."

Late in the afternoon they arrived at Venus Bogardus's apartment on Park Avenue. Beebo parked in the service entrance, letting her hands drop between her knees with a sigh. Pat lighted her cigarette and they sat and smoked a minute.

"Kind of a stuck-up looking dump, isn't it?" she said, squinting up at the glistening windows, stacked with parallel nicety clear to the clouds. "Well, let's go do it."

She got the hot spaghetti and, on a sudden inspiration, included a jar of kosher dills intended for a different customer.

"Who are we going to see this time?" Pat yawned on the way up.

"Probably another maid," Beebo said.

"Whose?"

"Venus Bogardus's."

Pat straightened up and stared at her.

But it was Toby, Venus's problem child, who let them in. "Hi, Beebo," he said, pleased to see her.

"Hi, buddy. Where's your mama?" She was sorry at once she had asked. There was a cook by the stove this time, apparently the one who ditched Venus periodically, but always came back. She was thin and sticky with butter, and she looked inhospitable.

"I hear Venus threw some food around last night," Beebo smiled at Toby. "I brought her a peace offering. Sweets to the sweet," and she handed Toby the pickles. "This is a friend of mine, Toby—Pat Kynaston." They shook hands and a silence ensued. All Beebo had to do now was wait for her money and leave. But she heard herself asking again, "Is Venus here?"

"Come on in. I'll go see," Toby said unwillingly.

He left the kitchen briefly and returned, his hands jammed nervously in his pockets. "She's in her room," he reported. "In a goddamn peignoir. She only wants to see you, Beebo. I told her about Pat and she said she didn't want any peace offerings. She wouldn't even listen about the pickles."

"Oh, God," Pat whispered to Beebo. "I suppose I go to the cook as a consolation prize."

Toby walked over to them. "I have a good collection of records," he said diffidently. "And guns. That's one thing all those fathers are good for. I didn't go for the guns at first, but I've gotten kind of interested. If you'd like to see them…I mean, I think Mom is busy for a few minutes."

Beebo was touched by his loneliness, his eagerness for company. She had the feeling that he was choosy about his friends, and living a life where he could hardly meet any anyway. It made her seem quite important to him.

He grinned at her. "You're still on my side, aren't you?" he said.

"All the way," she laughed. "I just want to apologize to your mother for our delivery boy. I guess he got fresh."

"No," Toby said, his face lengthening. "She did."

The cook absorbed all this with silent disapproval. She was the type who disapproved of everything—even food.

"I wish you wouldn't see my mother," Toby confessed unexpectedly.

Beebo's mouth dropped open a little. "I thought somebody ought to ask her pardon for last night," she said, embarrassed. "The Pasquinis don't want to lose her."

"They don't need her," he said, looking at the floor.

"Hmp," said the cook to the spinach during the shocked pause that followed.

"That's no way to talk about your mother, Toby," Beebo said.

"You heard how she talks about me," he countered. "What am I supposed to do? Pretend I'm deaf?"

Beebo listened, full of compassion, but afraid of the big-eared cook. Toby spoke as if she were no more than another kitchen appliance, like her stove.

But he saw Beebo's glance, and pushed the kitchen door wide. "Come on in my room," he said. "We can talk there."

Beebo put the spaghetti on the counter and followed him, with Pat behind her. The apartment was richly decorated and unkempt.

In his room, Toby sat on the bed, and Beebo and Pat found places on chairs. He had his guns in two glass cases hung on the wall, and the rest of the room was a jumble of phonograph records, books, and school mementos.

Toby wanted to talk frankly to Beebo, and yet they were more strangers than friends. But he needed to talk, to melt the strangeness away and find the friend. At last he began, rather abruptly, "I just don't want my mother to turn you against me. I mean, you're a good kid and I want you to know me the way I am. Then you won't think I'm such a dumb baby when she starts talking about what a 'lovely child' I am, but she can hardly wait till I outgrow it."

Beebo heard this awkward speech with an ache of recognition. How it hurt to be so young, so at the mercy of your elders, and, often, lessers. So full of rainbows and music and romantic love...yet always cracking your head against the walls of reality.

"I know she says some silly things, Toby," she said seriously. "But you love her anyway, don't you?"

"I guess so. But I've seen her with so many guys it just about makes me sick," he said tiredly. "Until this year. Now, she says they all bore her and she's sworn off men forever. I hope she means it. It's been three months since she had a date. She's terrible to men. They make such fools of themselves for her. I don't know what she does to them, honest. And I'm not stupid!" he added quickly. "I mean, I know what she does—*technically.*" It was a toss-up whether his contempt was greater for his mother or her men.

Pat cleared his throat to camouflage a smile. Toby was conversant with sophisticated sex beyond his years; yet it was difficult and embarrassing for him to talk with friends his own age. Venus could take the blame for it, and Beebo felt a swell of righteous anger at her.

"You know what I think?" Toby said thoughtfully. "I think she's bored with me, too. Well, after all, I'm a male." He said it with pride and resentment, as if it were a fact not always respected in his family. "She needs somebody new to hurt and tease. If you make yourself available, I'll bet she picks on you. It's no fun, either."

"Me?" Beebo said incredulously.

"You see her today and *you'll* find out," he warned.

Beebo, conditioned by Venus's flirting and by the mood of her night with Paula, said incautiously, "You mean she's interested in me? I mean…" Her voice trailed off, giving her meaning away, and Toby's cheeks turned crimson. She realized she had shocked him, but he thought it was his fault for making the wrong implication.

"Not *that* way," he explained hastily. "She's not *sick*."

"Oh," Beebo said. "Excuse me."

Pat frowned at her, and she looked at her knees.

"She wants somebody around to admire her and say yes to her," Toby said. "Somebody whose feelings she can hurt. You have to be tough as Leo to get along with her. Leo doesn't have any feelings…at least, they never show."

"Leo—her husband?"

"Yes. He's the only man in her life who won't get down on his knees to her. But I think he's the only one who really loves her, too. The others love the glamour, but Leo knows her through and through, and he loves her." He shook his head as if it were incomprehensible.

"You love her too, Toby," Beebo said.

He hunched his shoulders. "She's my mother. What can you do?" he said with heartbreaking, youthful cynicism. "Even if the old bag did raise me."

"Who's the old bag?"

"Mrs. Sack. She's my—well, you might say, my nurse…she's been around so long, she's part of the family, even if I am too old for her now." The blush on his face deepened, but he needed terribly to share his burdens, and he felt safe with Beebo. She was a girl, so she couldn't fall in love with his mother. And she had spirit and humor, which she had used to defend him. Besides, his solitude weighed desperately on him.

"Mrs. Sack was there when Mom brought me home from the hospital, and she's done everything for me since then. Mom just sat around and blew kisses at me between lovers."

"She must have done more than that or you'd hate her," Beebo said.

"I do hate her!" he flared. "Leo hates her, too. That doesn't mean we don't love her, but she makes it awful hard." In a knowing voice he added, "There are two things in this world my mother really loves, and one of them is not *men*." Pat and Beebo stared at him. "She loves herself and money. Mostly herself. She'll tell you that if you ask her. She'll tell the whole damn world. That's how full of shit she is."

"Toby," Beebo said gently. "Maybe you just see all the bad things now. Maybe when you grow up and get away from her, you'll see her good side."

"If she *has* one," he said. "She calls me 'darling' all the time, and five minutes later she's calling a complete stranger 'darling.' I mean about as much to her as the stranger."

"I think it's just a habit with her," Beebo guessed. "Like some people calling everybody 'honey.'"

"And secretly hating them all," Toby said. "I wish just once in my life she'd call me Toby—when she wasn't mad at me, I mean. That *is* my name. She gave it to me."

Beebo wanted to pat him on the back, wanted to smile and say, "She will—I guarantee it." He was a perceptive boy and very appealing. But she had nothing to comfort him with. "Well, if it's any consolation, *I'll* call you Toby," she grinned, and was pleased to see him answer her smile.

There was a difficult silence until Pat said, getting to his feet, "That's quite a bunch of guns. Who gave you the Japanese bayonet?"

Toby followed him to the case and began an animated conversation. Beebo sat pensively listening. Evidently it never occurred to Toby that Beebo could be sexually attracted to his mother. All his precocious knowledge of sex was confined strictly to his mother's—admittedly free-wheeling—activities. And while Venus had done many things with many people, she had not, to Toby's knowledge, done everything.

Beebo was surprised to feel so concerned about the boy. She was better acquainted with him now. His descriptions of his mother's character were so youthfully lopsided they revealed more about him than they did about her. But it seemed certain that one thing he said was true: he did honestly both hate and love her very much.

The three of them were startled when Toby's bedroom door swung open and Venus stood in the hallway. "Well, darling, why didn't you send my visitor to me?" she demanded of her son.

Toby turned around, his chin jutting forward, ready for a tilt with her. But she merely inclined graciously all around, her smile flitting over Pat as though he were just another gun and settling on Beebo.

"Come in and talk with me," she told Beebo. "I had a dreadful experience last night and it's all your fault."

"I'm sorry, Miss Bogardus," Beebo said, standing up and feeling like a bumpkin dripping hayseeds in front of her.

"Don't go, Beebo, it's a trap," Toby said sardonically.

"Darling, what a lyrical sentiment," Venus fired at him. "Come on, Beebo." She turned and sailed down the hall, and Beebo felt angrily like a toy dog, expected to jump when Venus snapped her fingers.

Pat went to her and whispered, "If you feel yourself getting friendly, scream for help."

"Big help you'd be," Beebo said.

"Well, at least I won't be tempted to sin," he said. "I don't go for peignoirs."

"I hope you don't go for guns, either," she warned him in a whisper. And aloud, she said to Toby, "Don't worry, I won't turn traitor."

Then, with a sense of exasperation, shame, and excitement, she followed Venus to her room.

It was a real boudoir: a luxurious old-fashioned bower, a glamorous retreat where a coveted woman makes herself irresistible in perfumed privacy, receives the gifts of rich and handsome men, and strikes them helpless with adoration. At least, that was the general idea.

The rug was white, the walls pale blue, and the dressing table wore six silk chiffon petticoats.

"Well, darling?" Venus said. "Do you like my little nest?"

Beebo began to laugh in spite of herself. "If you'll forgive me, Miss Bogardus," she said. "It's one great big gorgeous cliché."

"Of course it is," Venus smiled. "I planned it that way to offend Leo.... You know, you sound like you've made it in more boudoirs than Errol Flynn."

"Oh, no," Beebo said, taken aback. "I've just read more bad novels. The sirens always have a boudoir like this."

Venus turned around and studied her with amusement in the oval mirror above her dressing table. "Come over here and tell me why they sent that ghastly man over with the pizza, when I asked for you with spaghetti."

Beebo stood her ground, suddenly aware that there was nothing under the "goddamn peignoir" but naked Venus. "That ghastly man owns the place," she said. "He sent himself."

You wouldn't look at Venus Bogardus without admiring her form. Even in her late thirties, it was fine: the kind men hope and dream all women will have, especially their wives. She was small-waisted, full-breasted, with a firmly swelling hipline and long shapely legs; the whole package wrapped up in mathematically right proportions that hadn't changed since Venus was a bouncing daisy of sixteen.

Venus scratched something on a piece of paper and swept across the room with it in a cloud of cologne and blue silk. "Here you are, darling," she said. It was her autograph. "Take this to your boss and tell him I hope he gets the sauce out of his ears."

"He'll be overcome, I'm sure," Beebo said, tucking it in her shirt pocket.

Venus stood a few feet from her, watching her and making up her mind to open a difficult subject. "You know, poor Toby is absolutely terrified we're going to like each other," she said restrainedly. "He's quite ashamed of me."

Beebo was far more embarrassed by Venus's admissions than by Toby's. Toby was still a child you could pity and help. But who could pity someone with the blinding assets of his mother? Who had enough crust to offer her any help?

"Miss Bogardus, I'm sorry about the pizza thing. I—" She hesitated, wanting only to duck out and avoid facing the new feelings taking shape inside her.

"I only threw it at him because he wasn't you," Venus said, and Beebo allowed herself one quick startled look at That Face. She felt perspiration under her arms and knew her face was damp, too.

"Sit down, darling, you look feverish," Venus said. And when Beebo stuttered something about going home, Venus laughed. "Why Beebo, I think I've got you going," she said. "I'll bet I'm not the first girl who ever did that to you." It was said in a light friendly tone intended to tease, but it made Beebo so intensely uncomfortable that she began to tremble. It became acutely clear to her that she desired that remote and laughing goddess very much; so much she suddenly lost her voice.

"You were full of beans the last time you were here," Venus said. "Don't be a square now. Tell me all the nice things you know about me. I promise not to take any of them seriously."

Beebo got her voice out finally by blasting on it like an auto horn. "I only know what everybody knows," she blurted.

"The gossip columns?" Venus said. "You can't be so naïve that you believe that crap, darling. I'll bet Toby's been talking to you. Telling you stories about his wicked mama." From the look on Beebo's face, she concluded he had.

Beebo didn't want to insult her. "Why should he?" she said, wishing all the while that she could open a window somewhere for fresh air.

"Oh, he thinks I'm dreadful. And of course I am. But I'm kind of sorry he realizes it already."

Beebo saw a real regret shadow her face, and all at once it seemed possible—almost—to feel sorry for her.

"If you don't want him to know it, you'll have to put blinkers on him," Beebo said quietly. "I was fourteen a few years ago. You don't miss seeing much at that age."

"When he was born," Venus said, "I was much too young and ambitious to give a damn about him. Now, when he matters, I find I've done everything wrong...everything I've bothered to do for him, that is. I haven't bothered to do very much."

"You don't need to tell me these things, Miss Bogardus," Beebo said, amazed to hear Venus speak such damaging truths about herself, to see the steel surface of her go-to-hell gaiety buckle and crack.

"He likes you," Venus said, somewhat self-conscious now. She lighted a cigarette and shrugged. "He's such a baby. I love him awfully, but he makes me so damn mad."

"He's a nice kid, Miss Bogardus," Beebo said. "Maybe if you could see his side now and then....It's so easy to ruin a kid that age."

"I'm a nice kid, too, darling," Venus flashed, and Beebo realized from her anger that she had spoken too bluntly. "And I'll do whatever I damn please with Toby. That includes ruining him if I feel like it." She sat down suddenly on a satin-topped stool, tired. "I—I ruined him anyway, and I never felt like it at all," she said, as if too weary to repress the truth.

"I don't want to bore you, Beebo. But I do want to know what he's been saying about me. I know he's been talking to you the last half hour." She looked across the room at Beebo. "Please," she said. Her voice was rough with fatigue.

Beebo shifted her weight and her legs felt almost boneless.

"Well," she said uneasily. "I don't suppose it's anything he hasn't already said to you." Venus looked directly at her, and Beebo wondered if it might not impress her more to hear these things from somebody other than Toby. "He loves you very much, Miss Bogardus," she said. "But I don't think he likes you."

Venus merely nodded. "That's no news," she said. "He's like all the other men I know." She looked disgusted.

"He said you didn't like men," Beebo said.

"I beg your pardon!" Venus exclaimed. "I absolutely *adore* men. All but Leo, anyway." She stood up and walked briskly back and forth for a moment, as if she intended to hear no more—at least not till her feathers settled.

"Tell me about yourself, Beebo," she said, and again Beebo was miffed by the offhand order.

"I'd bore you to tears," she said. "You don't want to hear about my daddy's cows and chickens down on the farm."

"I think I do," Venus said sincerely. "I never had a daddy. Or a chicken." Beebo began to protest about leaving again and Venus waved at her impatiently. "All right, all right, but before you go, tell me the rest about Toby."

Beebo didn't know what to make of her. Hadn't she heard it all from him herself? Venus glanced at her. "He's been chattering about you since you brought that pizza over," she explained. "He *likes* you. That means he'll talk to you. He only shouts at me.... Sit down, Beebo."

Beebo obeyed her out of growing curiosity. It seemed clear to her now that she had inadvertently become a line of communication between mother and son; that perhaps Toby did say things to Beebo he refused to mention to Venus—or at least, said them more candidly.

"There isn't much to tell," Beebo said, trying to squirm out of it. Venus looked very worried. "He just seems lonesome. I think it was a relief to him to spout off at me." She smiled.

Venus sighed. "He's a bewildering little devil," she said, "but I guess he's the only human being I've ever loved. Or ever will love.

I loathed him when I was carrying him. I thought he'd ruin my waist. I scarcely looked at him till he was nine or ten. Mrs. Sack brought him up. He grumbles about her, but there are times when I'd give anything if he'd grumble about me the same way...times when I actually hate that woman!" Beebo watched her blow her nose on a tissue on the dressing table and realized with a twinge that she was crying.

"He calls her 'the old bag,'" Beebo said kindly.

"And I'm 'the old bitch,'" Venus said. Her voice was unsteady. "I should never have let him slip away from me. But he scared me, to tell the truth. Not just that he was a baby, and I resented him and didn't know where to begin caring for him. But he...he had convulsions and things. Terrifying things that absolutely paralyzed me. And Mrs. Sack was so efficient and reassuring. Oh, hell, it's no excuse. But it seemed like one then."

"Convulsions?" Beebo repeated, surprised.

"Yes. He has epilepsy. The *grand mal* kind. Big stuff." There was a shocked silence and Venus added sharply, "Well, it's not a one-way pass to the bughouse."

"No, no. I know," Beebo replied. "I—I'm just so sorry."

"Well, I'm sorry, too," Venus said, and she had control of herself now. The tears had stopped. "Most of the time he's perfectly normal—whatever *that* is for boys of fourteen. But every so often, when he's especially tired or nervous, he gets these...seizures. He gets rigid as a post." She faced Beebo. "Have you ever seen it?" she said.

Beebo shook her head. "But I've heard about such things. It's like a muscle spasm, isn't it?"

Venus's eyes drifted away, seeing it in her mind. "He shoots up from a chair like a jack-in-the-box, and falls straight and stiff as a pole. His saliva foams. We have to be careful that he doesn't swallow his tongue." She took a breath. "It's frightening to see your own child like that.... Well, then he goes to sleep, a stone-dead sleep, and when he wakes up he usually can't even remember it.

He just wants to be quiet for a while, by himself. Read books and stare out the window, sometimes for a couple of days."

"What do you do for it?" Beebo said. "Is there anything?"

"There are treatments," Venus said. "Shock therapy, chemotherapy. He hates it but it helps. He hates to talk to me about it. Mrs. Sack always rescued him while I ran screaming from the room. He thinks it makes him repulsive to me. I've tried and tried to explain—I'm just a coward!—but he's so jittery about it now, I don't dare bring it up."

Beebo sat looking at her linked fingers, young enough to wonder why the fair and fortunate of this world are afflicted with sorrows as humbling and frustrating as those of the poor. Venus, whom men feared and worshipped, women feared and disliked, and children simply feared; Venus, herself afraid.

"Toby said some hard things about you, Miss Bogardus," she said at last, "but he also said he loved you, and you don't get that kind of mush out of fourteen-year-old boys unless they mean it."

"I wish he'd say it to me!" Venus cried. "I love him so terribly, but all I do is drive him nuts. I can't talk to him and he clams up with me." She came and put a perfumed hand on Beebo's shoulder. "He hasn't made a new friend in years," she said. Her hand was tight and warm and busy, twisting Beebo's cotton shirt. "I haven't made much sense, I'm afraid," she said. "I'm trying to be honest and I'm not used to it." She gave a clumsy little laugh. "He seems so impressed with you. That was half the reason I wanted you to come back. I thought if you could draw him out somehow.... Did he say anything else?"

Beebo was worried about that expensive and beautiful hand on her shoulder. About that "half the reason I wanted you back"— what was the other half? About Toby's opinion of his mother's beaux?

Venus guessed the last part. "My admirers?" she said. "I know he can't stand them. Neither can I."

"He thinks you're too fond of..." Beebo stopped and cleared her throat.

"Don't get scared off all of a sudden," Venus pleaded. "I couldn't take it. I'm too fond of *what?*"

"Money. And yourself."

"He's wrong," Venus said, frowning. "I know it looks that way. And I do like money. But myself I hate. I hate, hate, hate!" Her voice broke and her hand held tight to Beebo's shoulder, steadying her. "Money and my career. That's all I have in the world. That's why I hang on so hard to them both."

"You have Toby," Beebo ventured, wishing she dared to look up at Venus's face, knowing it was kinder not to.

"Toby isn't mine," Venus whispered bitterly. "He just lives here. He won't let himself be loved. I gave birth to him, but Mrs. Sack is his mother." She was weeping again.

Beebo reached up and touched her hand, her eyes still down. The whole mess was so sad and ugly; sadder still for having been preventable. Beebo was moved and hurt by Venus's words because she was moved by Toby: his loneliness, his hopeful trust in her, and now the revelation of his illness.

"You've reached him, Beebo," Venus said. "He wants to be friends with you. You could help me." She came around the divan and sat down next to Beebo. The swift drum-bump of her heart was visible under the gauzy blue silk and it made Beebo want to touch her there; hold her and say something wise and therapeutic. But she hadn't the wisdom to manage her own life yet, let alone someone else's.

"I don't know much about love, Miss Bogardus," she said shyly. "I just know if you love somebody, he can't stop you. All you have to do is keep loving him till he believes in it, I guess."

"That's not enough, or he'd be happy," Venus said.

"Maybe if you did things with him," Beebo said. "My dad used to spend a lot of time with me. We walked, we talked things over, we played chess."

"I don't know the black from the white," Venus said miserably.

"Toby's pretty big on guns right now."

"I don't even know which end the bullet's supposed to come out," Venus said. But after a pause full of self-examination she added, "But I guess I could learn...guns. God."

"It might make all the difference," Beebo said.

"Will you come back and see him?" Venus said. "That would help."

"Sure," Beebo said, but she looked away. Venus had touched her arm again. "He could drive around with me while I make the deliveries tomorrow. Would he like that?"

"He'd probably die of joy. Anything with a motor in it sends him into rhapsodies."

Beebo stood up, her own heart beating so fast now that she felt near suffocating. "It's getting late," she said. Venus followed her to the door.

"He might resent it if I start sticking my nose into his guns all of a sudden," she mused.

"Not if you're really interested," Beebo said. "He won't hold it against you, Venus...beautiful Venus." It was an unpremeditated explosion of admiration. Beebo clamped her mouth shut suddenly, mortified.

But Venus was restored by the slip to good humor. She laughed, and this time it was a pretty sound, a charming answer to a compliment.

"Maybe Toby will turn out all right," Venus said. "You're bound to be a good influence."

Beebo smiled in embarrassment. "He'll probably disgrace you by turning into a model citizen," she said.

"I hope he does." Venus walked the rest of the short distance between them and put her hands on Beebo's shoulders. She looked very solemn and a bit surprised at herself. "Thanks," she said.

"For nothing." Beebo shook her head. She had a wild impulse to pull Venus's hands off and run.

"Beebo," Venus said thoughtfully. "Do you want to kiss me?" In the electrified pause that followed, Beebo heard Toby's voice echoing in her ears: "Not *that* way. She's not *sick*." It pounded through her like a pulse and she knew the answer was obvious to Venus. She reached down and touched Venus's waist. "Yes," she murmured. Venus seemed reassured, almost pleased. She was on home ground again. She lifted her face and gave Beebo her lovely mouth.

It was an astonishing kiss, long and warm. And after it they stood with their arms around each other a while, faces averted. Beebo didn't realize how hard her embrace was until Venus began to giggle. "Darling, you're crushing me," she said. Beebo released her and backed off hastily, mumbling apologies.

"Here," Venus said, handing her a hanky. "Take the lipstick off, or Toby will think I've perverted you and come after me with one of those damn guns." She watched Beebo dab at her chin ineffectually, and then did it for her. Beebo stood still and let her work, watching her face intently. It was classically beautiful still, though lacking the pearly perfection of a twenty-year-old's. But the bone structure beneath was superb. Beebo admired her ardently. "Think of all the poor girls who have to go homely in the world to make one Venus Bogardus," she said.

Venus smiled. "I don't think it works that way, darling," she said. "Besides, a face is a temporary thing. After a while you find it doesn't work the same old spell any more." She spoke soberly. "Then you have to depend on what's behind it...if anything. Know who told me that?"

Beebo shook her head.

"Leo. My louse of a spouse," Venus said, blinking. "He told me that when I was seventeen, and I didn't believe him. I do now." She stepped back and transformed the mood with a smile. "There, you look completely innocent."

"Thank you," Beebo said.

"What for? The mop-up? Or the kiss?"

Beebo swallowed. "Both," she said.

"Do you have to go, Beebo? Really?" Venus swirled away a few steps, making Beebo want to dash after her. But she stood resolutely with her hand on the door, still too unnerved to know how to behave. "Another heavy date?" Venus asked.

"You might say," Beebo said.

"Tell me the truth," Venus said, looking at Beebo over her shoulder. "Was it an 'old friend' last time? Or was it a girl?"

Beebo looked up at her slowly, her hand so hot and damp it slipped on the knob. "A girl," she said finally.

Venus took this shattering intelligence with serenity. "I thought so," she said. "I warn you, darling, I'm going to order spaghetti all week. You'd better teach her to play solitaire."

Beebo bridled at the teasing certainty of Venus's attitude. "Then Pasquini will have to make the deliveries," she said flatly.

"All I can do is invite you," Venus said. "I can't make you come."

The double meaning was not lost on Beebo. "I don't think it would be the best approach to Toby if you and I got involved," she said edgily. She was seeing more than Toby, however; she was seeing Paula. Gentle, sympathetic, pretty Paula, so in love with her. Paula for whom she felt such affection and desire. Paula, who told her to run from Milady Bogardus. She wanted to be safe in Paula's arms, not here in this silk-lined trap where so many lovers were so neatly netted.

Beebo was deeply suspicious of Venus, anyway. What could such a woman want but transient amusement? Was she gay at all, or just bored and curious?

"Toby is the only human being I'll ever love." Venus said it. It would be madness for Beebo to fall in love with her, knowing that. But she had already learned from Paula that falling in love is not a deliberate act at all. Sometimes the only way to fight it is to do as Paula said: run.

"I wish you'd stay a while," Venus said.

Beebo gazed steadily at her, and then she opened the door and strode out.

The boys looked up from the living-room TV, Toby catching Beebo with worried eyes and wondering what humiliations Venus had invented for her. But the sight of his beautiful mother swishing after Beebo with her face screwed into a scowl consoled him and his heart rose. He wanted Beebo to teach him nonchalance; teach him to laugh and take Venus less seriously, before Venus scared her off.

"Are you going already?" Toby said.

"How would you like to drive the route with me tomorrow, Toby?" Beebo asked with a smile.

Toby threw his mother an uncertain glance, but she said, "Go on, darling. Learn something about the mysterious pasta business."

Toby grinned at her. He hadn't smiled at her in so long that Venus merely gazed at him with her mouth open, unable to answer until he had turned back to Beebo.

"I'll pick you up after lunch," Beebo said. "Come on, Pat."

"Just a moment," Venus said. She caught Pat and put her arms around him, boarding him like an empress her barge, and kissed him soundly on the mouth. "There, darling," she said alluringly. "Don't wash your mouth for days. Everybody will die of envy."

Pat touched his lips and said a startled, "Thank you."

"Mother, that's repulsive," Tony muttered.

"Just wait a year, dear, and it will all come crystal clear," Venus told him.

Beebo took Pat by the arm and propelled him into the kitchen. She was dismayed at the effort of will it took to leave Venus behind.

"What a spectacular female," Pat said, scrambling through the door with her. "If I weren't already in love with you, I'd fall for her."

"And Jack would be best man," Beebo quipped.

"You know, something tells me I *could* fall for a girl," he said, hoping Beebo would pay attention.

But she only said, "Well, fall outside, will you?" She was afraid if she didn't get out fast, inertia would set in. The back door latch eluded her skittery fingers.

"Turn it all the way right," said a crisp female voice.

They saw the cook, still stirring her witch's brew.

"Thanks," Beebo said, and they got out at last with a grateful gasp. Pat began to laugh, until he saw Beebo put her head in her hands while they waited for an elevator.

"What's the matter, honey?" he said. "Was Venus bitchy? I'll go back and throw something at her."

"After the bussing you got?" Beebo said.

"How about you?" Pat asked softly. And when she didn't answer, he put his arms around her, enjoying the contact, standing with her till the elevator arrived.

The wicked witch peered at them through the glass in the kitchen door.

Beebo was gloomy all the way home, answering Pat laconically.

"I didn't even leave a note," Pat lamented. "Jack will snatch me bald-headed."

"Never. He's too fond of those blond curls."

"Not so fond he won't clobber me when we get home. It's late."

"You've got Jack and I've got Paula," Beebo said, and they brooded about it.

Beebo parked in front of Jack's apartment. Pat looked up at his windows. "The lights are blazing," he reported. "And so is Jack, you can bet on it."

"I never saw him mad before," Beebo said, looking at him quizzically. Pat's apprehension seemed silly to her.

"He's not in love with you, my friend," Pat said, and made her wonder at the distortions—some good, some bad—that love could work in the lover.

"He probably called Marie. She'll tell him you're with me," she said.

"That'll only make him frantic. He thinks we're a couple of lambs in the lion's den."

"Maybe he's right," Beebo said. She had never felt so exhilarated and confused and afraid and eager for God-knew-what in her life.

They hesitated with a common reluctance before the apartment door. "You go first," Pat said. "You're the bravest. If he throws anything, so help me, I'm going to run for it."

Beebo chuckled at him, and then turned the cold brass handle. She opened the door with a quick swing that revealed only the empty living room. They walked in. "Jack?" they said together, and a pile of newspapers on the sofa rolled over and sat up. Jack was very drunk.

"Hello, you two beautiful dolls," he said. They looked at one another. "Paula was here," he told Beebo. "We got loaded together. If you don't want her, I'm going to marry her."

Beebo picked up Jack's empty glass and the bottle on the coffee table and poured herself a shot. She gave the Scotch to Pat. "Have some. Jack won't mind, will you, *darling?*" She imitated the famous Bogardus inflection.

"Why should I?" he said, eyes on Pat. "Did you run into Venus while you were lunching at 21?"

"We went up to her apartment. She threw a pizza at Pasquini last night."

"I heard all about it. Marie was celebrating when I dropped in. Well, it must have been a jolly reunion." He saw the smudge on Pat's lips. "Looks like the goddess and the gay boy are starting a new trend. You're solid lipstick from the nose down."

Pat reproached Beebo instantly. "My God, why didn't you tell me?" he demanded.

"I wasn't looking at you. I'm sorry."

"Where's yours?" Jack said, turning to her. "Or wasn't this ladies' day?"

"I wiped it off," Beebo said touchingly, and Jack didn't know whether to believe her or not.

"Something for everyone," he said. "She must be a Democrat. And what was Patrick doing while you and Venus occupied the loveseat? Taking notes?"

"Watching TV," Pat said casually. "With Toby. Her son."

"I hope he was friendly," Jack said.

"Very," Pat replied, irritated by Jack's jealousy.

"I'll bet. Especially if you curled up in his lap."

"He's a nice little kid, Jackson," Beebo said, surprised at him. Jack was usually so patient and gentle and funny. "He's just fourteen, very mixed-up and very straight." Jack's spite amused her a bit and made her sorry for him. She had never seen him hurt before. He was comical, but the pain showed too and roused her affection for him.

"He's a baby, and I don't go for babies," Pat said. "It's illicit."

"Oh, let's be licit, by all means," Jack said. "I can see the both of you, sitting there watching Captain Kangaroo together. Just a pair of Babes in Boyland."

"Honest to God, Mann, you just bug the hell out of me!" Pat exploded in sudden wrath.

"With pleasure. Till you scream for mercy," Jack snapped.

"Jack, it was your idea that Pat give up his job," Beebo said. "I took him with me today for fun. It's better than having him cruise the streets all day. Admit it."

After a pause, Jack said, "Okay. You're a pair of worms...but I'm a dirty bird. I'm sorry. Call Paula, she's frantic."

Beebo hesitated so long that Jack looked at her and added, "In case you've forgotten, the phone's in the kitchen."

"I know where it is.... I can't call her. I don't know what to say," Beebo said, and took down another shot like cough medicine.

Jack noticed her unsteady hands and brooding eyes. "Say, 'Hello, Paula. It's me, Beebo. I'm home,'" he suggested. While his attention was on Beebo, Pat went over and sat down quietly beside him on the couch. He took care not to touch him.

Beebo folded dejectedly onto the floor. "I'm just not sure how I feel, all of a sudden," she said, letting her forehead drop into her hand.

"You didn't fall for Toby, did you?" Jack said, ignoring the tentative hand Pat put on his knee. "This seems to be the night to go straight."

"Don't make lousy jokes, Jack."

"All right, pal. What happened with Venus? Did she really kiss you? Was it that great?" True to form, he pushed his own chagrin aside a while to worry about her.

"She hates everybody but Toby. She can't even like herself, and Toby's the only human being she'll ever love. How can such a lovely woman be so messed up?" Beebo mourned.

"I see she's messed you up a bit, too. Beebo, was it you who was cheating tonight, and not Pat? Are you falling for Venus? Because if you're not, you'd go call Paula and laugh this off with her. You wouldn't care who Venus loved or why."

"I don't know. Don't ask me," Beebo said, crushed almost to despair by the shame of it—of being a pushover for a professional temptress, and too mesmerized by her even to phone Paula, whose love for her had become a torment to them both.

Pat leaned against Jack cautiously and said, "Toby has seven yo-yos. We watched the Lone Ranger."

"Okay," Jack said, smiling into space. "Hey, Beebo. Hey!"

She had rolled over suddenly on her stomach to cry, her face in the scratchy rug. She shook her head to show she heard him but couldn't stop.

Pat clucked softly at her. "She couldn't have cared less about that woman till she checked out the boudoir. They were in there an hour. Beebo came out transformed."

Beebo wept into the stiff wool pile. "I thought I wanted to apologize. But I really wanted...oh, God help me, I'm wild for her. She's fabulous."

Jack lighted a cigarette and blew a stream of smoke over

Beebo's back. "Well, that's two nuts in the family: you and me. We fall in love with the wrong ones as if it were in the by-laws."

Pat turned to stare at him. "Who's in love?" he said.

"I am. With you."

Pat began to smile. "Why the hell didn't you *say* so?" he exclaimed. "You never said so."

"I was waiting for Beebo to go first. Misery loves company."

"Come on, you nut, you know I'm crazy about you," Pat said, smiling at him. He leaned over. "Stick out your tongue," he said. Jack obeyed. "It's black. You're lying, you don't love me at all."

Jack began to laugh. Suddenly they forgot Beebo. It was the wonderful selfishness of love that swept them out of her world into their own; the selfishness that friends can only envy and forgive.

Beebo stood up after a while and wandered into the bedroom, wanting to give them some privacy and herself some relief from their pleasure. She lay down on the bed and saw Venus on the ceiling; shut her eyes and saw Paula and felt the tears start again. She stuffed her face into the pillow, beating it and crying Paula's name. But when the fit passed, it was still Venus for whom her limbs ached and body burned; Venus whose face flamed in her brain and made her heart race.

Before she slept she thought of Jack and Pat, facing up to their love at last, and knew she had to move out. Yesterday she could have gone to Paula, even if it was premature. Today, there was again no place to go.

Beebo drove the truck to work with a thundering headache. She felt cut off from home and help; cut out—halfway at least—from Jack's life. Venus wanted her to come back but only, Beebo was sure, to entertain herself. Paula wanted her, but to smother her with a love she couldn't honestly accept, much as she respected and even wanted it.

At the shop she handed Venus's autograph to Pete Pasquini. "Something for your memory book," she said darkly.

He looked at it disinterestedly. "So how come you're so cheerful this morning? Didn't she throw nothing at you last night? She got a good right hand, that one."

"She said to tell you she's sorry," Beebo said, refusing to look at him while she worked.

"Yeah? I think you're the one was sorry. You didn't do so good, hm?"

Beebo lifted a heavy can of peeled tomatoes, almost persuaded to heave it, when Marie's voice broke in. "Beebo—a visitor. A young lady."

Beebo put the can down, and a hand to her head. Paula. *Holy God! I can't face her.* But she had to. She walked slowly to the front of the store, aware that Pete was trailing her at a discreet distance.

A tall dark-haired girl wheeled around and took off a pair of showy sunglasses. "Hello, Beebo," she said. It was Mona.

Beebo could find nothing to say. Even "hello" was too much of a courtesy.

"I want some groceries. Over there on the counter—I've got most of them. I'm taking them to Paula. She didn't feel much like going out today…for some reason."

The thought of Paula, defenseless against Mona, was enough to crowd Beebo's reluctance to see her little redhead right out of her mind. "I'll take them over. I was going to see her at lunchtime anyway," she said.

"I'm sure it'll come as a surprise to Paula," Mona observed, smiling at a display of spinach noodles.

Pete heard it and laughed his oily mirth to the canned fruits in the next aisle. Beebo wanted to strangle him. She shoved Mona's five-dollar bill back at her and put the food for Paula on a shelf behind the counter. Mona had that high color on her face brought up by the excitement of willful malevolence. "I hear you and Pete are getting to be regular cronies," she said in a syrupy voice. "Isn't he a ray of sunshine, though?"

"You ought to know. He's your sunshine, not mine," Beebo said briefly.

"Pretty noble of you to pay for the groceries," Mona said, sliding the bill back into her purse. "On your salary." She gave Beebo a provocative stare that reminded them both of the night they met at the Colophon. A warm feeling arose in Beebo that was strictly physical and angered her.

Mona slunk down Pete's aisle and Beebo heard them murmuring together. From the back of the shop she could see Pete making animated gestures as he told Mona something. Marie came out of the kitchen a minute to glance at them. "Ain't that a pretty sight?" she said in a caustic whisper to Beebo. "The 'Happiness Kids,' Jack calls 'em. They was made for each other, them two."

Beebo had to grin at the spunky little Frenchwoman.

Pete didn't let Mona leave till he heard the motor of Beebo's truck starting in the delivery yard. Beebo was backing out when he caught her. He put his head in the cab, forcing her to stop.

"Well?" she said impatiently.

"Bogardus just calls in," he said. "For tonight—lasagna. You can deliver; I want no more in the face." He waited for her reply, but she was gazing through the windshield, seeing nothing but that face, that face. So fair. So unfair! Pete slapped her knee and made her start. "You alive?" he said.

"I hear you."

Pete squeezed her knee—the kind of grip known as a horse bite. It hurts and it tickles at the same time. Beebo wrenched her leg away and the truck lurched backward. Pete leaped agilely out of the way, laughing at her disgusted curse.

She drove off fuming, wondering what it was about him that made her think, when they met, that he never laughed. She would damn well quit, whether she had another job or not. But then she saw herself, jobless and homeless at one stroke. Everything had seemed so right and easy just a few weeks ago. Everything now seemed bewilderingly bleak.

She spent an hour with Paula at lunchtime, trying to explain by fits and starts how she had made friends with Toby, talked to Venus about him, and got home late, too tired to call.

"I'm sorry," Beebo said, her voice soft with embarrassment. "That was plain selfishness. Please eat, honey; I brought you all this good food."

"Because Mona Petry told you I was staying at home today." Paula put a bite in her mouth as if it were a ball of cotton. There was little more said, and the silences between words became unbearable. They did not make love, they didn't laugh. Beebo's lapse of the previous night hung between them like a fog. She was almost too inhibited when it was time to go to kiss Paula. At last she leaned over and gave her a shy peck on the cheek. Paula accepted it with solemn dignity, but would not return it.

"May I see you tonight?" Beebo said.

"If you think you can put up with my mood."

"I'm afraid the mood is my fault. Let me come over, please, Paula."

Paula gave her a faint smile. "I won't be very nice to you," she said.

It was the first of many quiet cool nights, when Paula's intense desire for Beebo, and Beebo's unadmitted desire for Venus, kept them restrained and doubtful with each other.

Beebo picked Toby up the next day and spent the afternoon with him. He turned into a handy helper, carrying orders with her and keeping her busy with his talk. He was interested, as a child five years younger might have been, in the panorama of the city, especially the areas that were new to him. Though he lived there much of the time, he saw very little of New York.

He would fire a broadside of questions at Beebo and leave her wallowing in his wake, searching for answers, while he hurried on to set up the next bunch. Fortunately, it seemed more important to him to be able to ask than to get answers. Beebo didn't want to disappoint him with her ignorance.

They became quite good friends in the following few weeks, and to Beebo's surprise, they accomplished it without any sideline coaching from Venus. Venus, in fact, stayed out of sight, though she kept on ordering from Marie Pasquini. And Beebo, knowing, as Toby did not, that Venus was sacrificing her pleasure for his sake, was grateful to her.

Beebo dreaded facing her, even though it seemed inevitable sooner or later. And when it happened, Beebo foresaw her relationship with Paula going down the drain; her friendship with Toby smashed; and her self-respect, already dipping, destroyed completely.

It was something to be spared the encounter for a while. Everything in Beebo's life felt very temporary and precarious to her. But at least she had a breathing space, a time to test her feelings before they were exposed to others.

Alone, she was miserable with the problems of where to live, who to live with, how to control her urgent new emotions. But with Toby, she forgot a little and studied his troubles instead. They kidded each other and they laughed a lot. And they talked. At first it was mostly about guns—Toby's forte; or horses—Beebo's. Boy talk. Getting-to-know-you talk. The necessary preliminaries to a heart-to-heart. And it did Beebo as much good as it did Toby.

When they first met, Toby had blurted some awkward and ugly things to Beebo about his life with Venus. He seized upon her empathy for him and used it brashly because for all he knew he would see her once and never again. And it might be years before somebody else came along who seemed able to understand it. It had to be someone Toby instinctively liked and respected or it wouldn't ease his troubled young heart to bare it. So Beebo was special and he had grabbed her and said too much too fast.

So he back-pedaled into gun-talk, horse-talk, horseplay, and finally friendship, now that he could approach it more slowly. A little at a time, he unbent with her. He told her about the girls he knew in Bel-Air, California, where they lived when Venus was working in a film.

"I love it out there," he said. "We have five horses. Leo rides with me. You'd love it. Say, maybe you could come out and take care of them for us. You know all about it from your dad. It's too bad other girls are so square. You know, I took one riding once, and she was scared to death."

"You just got the wrong one," Beebo said. "Lots of girls like to ride."

"Not the ones I know," he said. "Or if they like to ride, they don't like me."

"You haven't looked around enough."

"It's embarrassing," Toby said. "The dumb ones can't talk to you about anything. And if you find a decent one, you can't talk to *her*. It's awful." He smiled ruefully while Beebo laughed at him, and then added, "Why can a guy talk to other guys but not to girls?"

"You talk to me," she said.

"You're different," Toby said, with no inkling that he might have scraped a sore spot. He meant it as a compliment and she took it that way. "I don't think I'll ever love a girl, Beebo. You can't trust them."

"You think they're all like your mother," Beebo told him.

"They are."

"No more than all men are the same."

"According to my mother, all men are dirty dogs. That includes me. Sometimes I think the reason she named me Toby was because it makes me sound like an alley cat. Toby the Cat, and Leo the Lion. What a zoo she lives with. I wonder why she didn't name me Fido. She treats me like a hound most of the time."

"Hey, buddy," Beebo said. "Maybe she's mixed up but she's still your mother. You know what we talked about that day when I was there? How much she loves you. She cried because you don't believe her."

Toby pressed his lips together, unwilling to concede a single virtue to Venus. "My name isn't Bogardus," he said finally. "It's Henderson."

"Your mother loves you, Toby Henderson."

"My father lives in Chicago. Were you ever there? He runs a dairy processing plant in Gary, Indiana. I've never met him and I never want to."

Beebo was shocked. After a moment she said, "Well, maybe you can't love somebody you don't know, even if he is your father. But aren't you curious?"

"Oh, he's probably a dirty dog like the rest of us. At least if I never meet him, I can pretend he's something better."

Beebo felt a stinging sympathy for him. "My father means a lot to me," she said.

"How come you don't live with him, then? You said he lived in Wisconsin. Did you run away, Beebo? You're awful young to be on your own here. How come?"

He had scored a bull's eye. She wondered how many years of lonely introspection it had cost Toby to become that perceptive; that quick to see the truth beneath the social tricks.

"I had some tough problems, Toby," she said. She was suddenly so grave that he retreated from the subject, afraid of hurting her. Beebo was thinking what it would do to him to know that she was a Lesbian; how desperately he would worry about her and his mother.

"I'm not the dope Mom thinks I am," he declared. "You can talk to me."

"No, you're no dope, but I am, for running away. And I'll tell you something, buddy. Fathers are something special. Even yours."

"Sure. He and Mom got together and manufactured me. Something special. A gorilla could have done the job better, Mom

145

says. Or a test tube. Sometimes I think that'd be okay—a test tube. Then I'd never even have to know his name."

Beebo felt a little like crying. But it would ruin her prestige with him. She swallowed and said, "He must write to you. Send you birthday presents, and things."

"The only present he ever gave me was epilepsy," Toby said in a flinty voice. "Mom says it came from his side of the family. So I haven't much to thank him for. Do you know what that is— epilepsy?" He had said the word so many times there was no longer any drama in it for him.

"Your mom told me," Beebo said. "Does it…make things rough for you? Like at school, with the other kids?"

"Not too bad," he said. But she looked at his face and thought differently. It had made him shy and apologetic about himself, and, consequently, fiercely defensive. At any time, he might become a major source of inconvenience or even panic to his schoolmates, though the seizures hit him infrequently in their presence. Still, it was those times he remembered better than any others.

"Leo is good about it," Toby said. "He's a pretty good guy. I'd rather have him around than Mrs. Sack, even."

"What's Leo like?" Beebo said, suddenly afire to know.

"He stands up to Mom, if that's what you mean. She hates him, naturally, but she respects him. Leo gave her her name. He knew her before anybody else in Hollywood. He was her agent, and he got her started."

"What's her real name?"

"Jean Jacoby."

"That's pretty…. Why won't Leo divorce her?"

"He really loves her, I guess. Boy, what a glutton for punishment," Toby marveled.

"If she hates him, why did she marry him?"

"Oh, she talked herself into a crush on all her husbands," Toby said, and Beebo wondered who had explained it all to him with such authority…. Leo? Mrs. Sack? "They were all rich and good looking and married to somebody else till she came along. I think it was sort of a challenge."

Beebo absorbed this in silence, disapproving and yet oddly amused. "What does Leo do?" She pictured him as a sort of legitimatized gigolo for his stunning wife.

"He's a director now. He directs all her films. That's why people think she's an actress. He can get a performance out of her nobody else can. She hates to admit it, but she loves her reviews. If they ever did get divorced, she'd have to let him keep on directing." His words made Leo Bogardus seem like more of a man than Beebo would have liked. She lighted a cigarette.

"Hey, can I have one too?" Toby said, with the light of friendly collusion in his eyes. "It's okay, I've smoked before."

She handed him her pack. "I'm contributing to the delinquency of a minor, you know," she grinned. "It's your fault, buddy. You'd better kick the habit before they haul me in."

He did not inhale the smoke, but he was very pleased with himself, and with Beebo. He held the cigarette in a self-conscious imitation of a man's gesture, taking a cautious mouthful occasionally and blowing it out with dreamy satisfaction.

"Do you get along with Leo, Toby?" Beebo asked.

"He's been real decent to me. He does things with me, even when they're things I don't want to do. It's nice of him...you know? And sometimes I end up liking the things I didn't think I would. It's funny...he tries to make them interesting. I guess you could say I like him."

Beebo grinned at him, impressed by his adolescent acuity; and aware, despite his wary phrasing, that Leo was quite an influence in his life. "You're pretty grown up for your age, aren't you?" she said seriously, and made him smile at the flattery.

But his answer startled her. "I had to grow up," he said, "with men climbing in and out of Mom's bed while I played on the floor with my blocks."

"God! Was it that bad?" Beebo said.

"They all thought I'd be the best adjusted kid for miles around," he said with psychological detachment into a cloud of very grown-up smoke. "I don't know why all that stuff should embarrass me now that I'm nearly fifteen. I used to sit there and watch the whole show when I was little." His face lengthened. "It never got to me then."

Beebo saw the resentment on his face flash and alternate with confusion, even love, for Venus. She wondered how much Venus was trying to show her love for him these days, and if it was making Toby all the more suspicious of her.

"Toby," Beebo said. "Do you know that Venus is kind of afraid of you?"

He turned his face away.

"She wants you to know she loves you, but she's afraid you'll think she's kidding after all these years."

"She's right."

"Maybe now that she's trying to say it, you could listen," Beebo suggested casually.

Toby gave a deep sigh. "I guess that's what she's been doing all week," he said. "She keeps saying she has something to say but she never says anything." He returned Beebo's gaze, his blue eyes, so like his mother's, pained and puzzled. "I don't care how she says it, if only she means it. I was lousy to her because whenever I try to tell her something, she's lousy to me. I wanted to get back at her."

"You've only got one mother, Toby. You've got to make the best of her. I wouldn't care so much what my mother was like, if I'd only known her. She died when I was young."

Toby pondered this a while, and then said, "If you ever run away again, I'll go with you." It was not an offer, it was a request—a plea.

"You're welcome aboard," she smiled.

Venus was waiting for them outside the elevator door in the service entrance, one early evening in the first week of September. Strangely,

Beebo wasn't surprised. It had been coming for weeks, and now she had to face it.

Toby grimaced at his mother, and Beebo handed her the carton of home-cooked food. "Here's your dinner," she said. "Mrs. Pasquini appreciates all the orders."

"You might as well keep it, she never eats it," Toby revealed. "She just orders it to keep you coming over."

"Sh!" Venus exclaimed at him. She was wearing a bright-blue knit dress, into which her famous frame was smoothly slipped; a glowing target for the eyes.

"Toby says you're a good driver," Venus said. "Now I suppose he'll pester Leo to teach him when we get home."

"You know I can't drive, Mom," he said wearily. "They don't give licenses to epileptics."

"Well, we'll talk to the governor, darling," she said.

"Besides, what do you mean, 'home'? California?" He looked at her suddenly, brightening. "I thought we were going to be here all winter."

Beebo felt almost dizzy at the thought of losing Venus before she had won her. It was too much to bear. Everything went wrong in bunches. "Home?" she repeated, frowning at Venus.

"Well, you both look as if I had dropped a bomb," Venus declared. "I just thought, with Toby's friends in California, and all those miserable horses and sunshine and ocean…I guess I can put up with the smog."

"Mom, that's great," he said, surprise all over his face. "Are you doing a new picture?"

"No, darling. I'm turning over a new leaf," she said.

They looked at each other and Beebo sensed an awkward rapport between them. After a decent pause she said, "Well—have a good trip, you two. I guess I won't be seeing you again, Toby."

He turned to her in consternation, and Venus said, "Don't be silly, darling. I have some lovely martinis all ready upstairs and a perfectly irresistible business proposition for you."

"Business?" Beebo said.

Toby made a face. "Monkey business," he said. "Can you walk on your hands, Beebo?"

"Hush, darling," Venus said, pulling them both into the elevator. "Not until she's had her martini."

Toby had a distant look on his face on the way up. "I'll have to write to everybody," he said. "So they'll know I'm coming."

Beebo let herself be led into the living room, full of sharp doubts that made her jumpy. Venus watched Toby go with a smile. "He'll be busy for hours," she told Beebo. "He rewrites all his letters two or three times. You'd think he was going to publish them someday."

Beebo sat down on a long white sofa and accepted a martini with an unsteady hand. The trembling had started already, and it seemed impossible to talk or act like a normal human being.

But Venus, who was more of a sorceress than a goddess, talked softly to her for half an hour, letting the drinks and her own silvery charm relax her guest. Even then, Beebo looked so gloomy that Venus began to chuckle at her. She refilled their glasses and asked her, "Do you hate yourself for coming up tonight?"

"Not as much as I hate you for asking me," Beebo said.

"Be fair now, darling," Venus chided. "I'm not responsible for your weakness, am I?"

"You know damn well you are," Beebo said. And in the pause that followed she felt that if she didn't escape now, she never would. "I'm sorry, it's not your fault," she said, trying to sound matter-of-fact. "I guess you were born with—all that." She couldn't look at "all that" while she spoke of it.

"No, I had to grow it, darling. Took me fifteen years, and it was a hell of a wait."

Beebo moved to the edge of the sofa when Venus joined her. "Were you a poor proud orphan till some movie scout discovered you?"

"Oh, God no!" Venus laughed. "My family was solid apple pie. The trouble was, I was always so damn beautiful I never had a chance to be normal." She spoke dispassionately, as if she were analyzing a friend. It wasn't snobbish. "I was supposed to be fast and loose because I looked it. At first the attention spoiled me. I was cocky. A candy-box valentine brat with corkscrew curls—my mother's pride and joy. Until I drove her frantic, and my friends out of my life. Nobody could stand me. *Honestly.* You laugh, but I cried when it happened. I couldn't understand why I was alone all of a sudden.

"I got shy and scared. Went my own way and told the world to go to hell. After a while, when my figure caught up with my face, I made some new friends: boys. It was so easy to give in. So hard to be anything but what people thought you were," she said, and Beebo responded with a startled swell of sympathy. "Well, in a phrase, they made me what I am today: a conniving bitch." Venus spoke defiantly…and regretfully.

"I'm not proud of it, but I want to be truthful with you. You're a sweetheart, Beebo. And very young, and maybe not too experienced. Tell me why you've made Toby come up alone with the food all these weeks. Did you think I'd throw spaghetti at you?"

Beebo took a swallow of her drink. "I don't want to crawl, Venus. I don't want to be hurt," she said harshly, defending herself with painful honesty in lieu of a worldly white lie.

"Nobody does," Venus said. "Were you expecting to be?"

"Isn't that what you want?" Beebo said, looking deep into her ice cubes. "To play games?"

Venus touched a finger to Beebo's cheek. "You're not crawling," she said. "You're being difficult. That's new for me."

"Is playing around with girls new for you, too?" Beebo asked, afraid to know the answer.

"Depends on how you mean it," Venus said. "You don't trust me, do you?" She smiled.

Beebo caught Venus's hand as it caressed her cheek and kissed it warmly. And remembered with sudden sadness the way

151

Paula had done that to her when they met. She put Venus's hand down gingerly on the sofa.

Venus let her sit and stew for a minute and then slipped across the cushion toward her. Their faces were very near and Venus put her rejected hand on Beebo's leg. "I'm trying to give myself to you and you won't have me," she said. "Now who's crawling?" She let her other hand, cool and questing, touch Beebo's neck and slip over her shoulder, drawing fire with it.

"You're putting me on," Beebo said, determinedly suspicious as only the young and uncertain can be. She took a deep breath. "But I don't care," she cried suddenly. "I don't care. I'll have you any way I can." She put her head down and kissed Venus's throat, putting her arms around her and grasping her firmly. Venus leaned against her, warm and willow-supple.

"You want to know how it feels, don't you?" Beebo said, trying to hurt her feelings, so sure Venus would hurt Beebo first if she could. "You want to know what it's like for a girl to hold you instead of a man. Any time you get bored, let me know." She bent to kiss her again but Venus stopped her. She was dismayed, and Beebo was ashamed to see it.

"You really *do* hate me, don't you?" Venus said.

Beebo closed her eyes for a minute. "I'm sorry," she whispered. She felt Venus moving in her arms. "I thought you were bored and frigid. Taking me like a prescription, or something. The way you talked—"

"The way I talked about *men,* not women. Beebo, do you know something? I was scared to death you'd take one look at this face of mine, panic, and run out." Her hands slid around Beebo's back and into her short dark hair.

Beebo's face turned hot while those hands trailed softly through her hair and over her eyes. "You're superb, Beebo," Venus said. "I think I'm the one who's afraid. I wouldn't be if I knew you better. And myself."

"You know more than I know," Beebo said. "Is this all a joke, Venus?"

Venus hushed her by pulling her down and kissing her mouth, and her tenderness was no pleasantry. Beebo kissed back: Venus's face, her ears, her pale throat, till Venus made her stop, shaking her curls to be let loose, and laughing.

"Who the hell am I," Beebo exclaimed, "that you should kiss me like this?"

Venus caught her breath. "You talk to me as if I were a woman," she said at last, gratefully. "Not a goddess, or a bitch. It hurts a little, but it feels good to hurt like that. Like when you're awfully young and you have a beautiful dreamy pain to cry over."

Beebo rubbed her head back and forth in the cradle of Venus's shoulder. "Did you cry over your dreams like other girls, Venus?"

"I cried, but not like other girls. I never did anything like other girls. I never even looked like them."

"Would you rather be plain?" Beebo asked.

Venus looked away and found the dignity to be honest. "No," she said. "It's a funny thing about women and me. Half the time I want to make them weep with despair over my beauty. And the other half I ache to be friends with them. Accepted. All the things I wasn't when I was growing up. My whole world is men. They're the only friends I have, and they aren't really friends at all. Not with a woman like me. The women close to me are either fat and old, like Mrs. Sack, or homely and heartless, like Miss Pinch."

"The cook? Is that her name?" Beebo gave in to laughter that relieved her tenseness a little.

"I know, it's too good to be true," Venus said. "Leo started calling her that, and it caught on. I fire her regularly but she comes back like a bad dream. She's devoted to Leo."

Beebo put her head down so she could talk without exposing her emotions to Venus's eyes. "Do you miss having a woman in your life?" she asked.

"Yes. The right kind. Somebody cultured and intelligent and well-educated. Somebody to teach me things. I'm so damned stupid."

Beebo gave a short wry laugh. "Venus? I think there's something you should know."

"What?"

"I didn't finish high school."

Venus laughed, a charming sound, full of pleasure. "I thought you meant, did I want a secretary, or something," she said.

"I'll bet you did." Beebo sat up and lowered herself to the floor, where she leaned back on the sofa, locking her fingers around her knees. She felt Venus's hand come down to play with her ear.

"Did I say something wrong, darling?" Venus said.

"Not a thing. Just that for a girl who likes girls, you did a damn queer thing marrying six men," Beebo said.

Venus answered pensively. "I kept thinking one of the six would set me straight somehow," she said.

Beebo felt those lovely hands in her hair, and she looked over at the kitchen door. It was about thirty feet away...thirty miles, it seemed.

"You've got such soft hair, Beebo," Venus said, and she leaned down and kissed the crown of Beebo's head, and then lifted her face and kissed everything upside-down from her perch on the couch. "You kiss me so gently," she said. "I never knew a lover so gentle before. There isn't a man alive who could come near you." And she kissed Beebo again till Beebo reached up from the floor and caught Venus's breasts in her hands, returning the kiss with a young warmth that struck sparks in Venus. Beebo held her hard and groaned, "Don't, don't, you don't know what it's doing to me. Oh, God...oh, please..."

"Do you still think I don't know?" Venus said. "Don't you understand by now I'm not doing this for kicks? Or to hurt you? Or God knows what other medieval torments you imagined? I think you're amazing. Exciting. Adorable. Did you think I'd never tried it before with a woman? I've tried everything, darling. Everything but corpses, anyway."

"Oh, Venus, Venus—"

"Hush, I'll explain. You see, it was always so rotten with men. It was as good as it ever got with a girl. But never this good." Her directness threw Beebo emotionally offstride. "I kept thinking it should be. If men were so bad there had to be something else worth living for. So I kept looking. But I have to be so damn careful. Whatever I do is news."

Beebo looked at her and saw tears on her cheeks. "My daydreams were always better than my life," Venus whispered, "and when you reach that point, you're in trouble. All the money in the world can't make those dreams real." She brushed lightly at the tears, embarrassed by them.

"I was wild when that dreadful Pasquini came up here," she said. "I'd been looking forward to seeing you all day. After he left, I began to think maybe his coming was a sign that I should give you up while I still could. An affair between us would seem like the world's worst cliché: the jaded vamp seducing the innocent girl for the sake of a few cheap kicks." She sat silent a moment and then she smiled at Beebo.

"Do you know what Miss Pinch said after you left? She came marching in and announced that you were a dyke and Pat was a queen."

"Miss *Pinch* said that?" Beebo said, and laughed at the incongruity of it.

"Well, she put it a little differently. She said, 'The dark young gentleman was a female and the blond young gentleman was a lady, if you know what I mean, ma'am.'"

They laughed together and Beebo felt suddenly close to Venus; her fear had vanished. "The only thing I worry about is, Miss Pinch might tell Leo," Venus said. "It makes him simply wild when I take up with a girl."

"Do you take them up often?" Beebo asked, looking down.

Venus shook her head without answering. It was a wordless admission of her loneliness and frustration; as great, in its way, as Toby's. Beebo got up on her knees and encircled Venus's waist. "Venus, darling," she said softly, hesitantly. "I love you so much.

I can't understand this thing. I thought you were—all glittery and cold. I thought we'd finally climb into bed, and you'd kill me with your laughter. And then to have you like this! God, I don't know what I'm doing. It's so crazy. Venus, Venus, I adore you." She began to kiss her again and Venus let herself be pulled off the sofa and into Beebo's arms, giving in a bit at a time, so that Beebo was trembling and wild-eyed one moment, and overwhelming Venus the next.

She had just enough sense to pick Venus up moments later and carry her to the bedroom, through the overstated boudoir, and out of the sight of Toby and the women. She laid Venus down on the blue silk coverlet of her bed, leaning over her with her fists planted in the mattress.

"This is where I do my dreaming," Venus told her. "I take off my clothes and lie down here and tell myself beautiful crazy stories. I've been doing it for years."

"Who do you dream about?" Beebo asked.

"Who do you think?" Venus smiled. "God, you're so tall for a girl. So tanned and strong. Like a boy."

"I hate to think of you all alone on that blue silk, wanting me," Beebo said. "And me out delivering salami."

"And talking to Toby," Venus said.

"That means a lot to you, doesn't it?"

"Everything," Venus admitted. "I can't tell you how much. I can talk to him now without screaming at him. I owe that to you, Beebo."

Instead of accepting the compliment gracefully, Beebo stared moodily out the window. "Are you keeping me around so you won't lose Toby again? I don't want to find myself pounding on your locked door the day you learn you can talk to him without me."

"What does it take to make you trust a girl, Beebo?" Venus teased.

"I guess I never will trust you—quite," Beebo said truthfully. "You're too good to be true."

Venus pulled her head down on the pillow and asked seriously, "How many people know you have a crush on me? Don't fib, darling. I have a special reason for wanting to know."

Beebo gritted her teeth together a moment before she answered. "My roommate. His name is Jack Mann. He's gay, too. He's the best friend I ever had and I trust him more than I trust myself."

"Who else? Pasquini?"

"No," Beebo said, lying forcefully with the sudden knowledge that Venus was trying to decide how dangerous their affair could be. The safer it seemed to her, the better the chances she would keep Beebo with her...perhaps even take her to the West Coast.

"How about this girl who's in love with you?" Venus said.

"She's not in love with me. It's a crush," Beebo said, ashamed of the betrayal but unable to help herself. "She'll get over it."

"Do girls ever get over their crushes on you?" Venus said.

"Every day," Beebo protested. "Venus...would you ever lock me out...if people knew?"

Venus rolled away from her, sitting halfway up. Her face was dark. "I'd have to," she said. "For Toby, if for no other reason. And even without him, there's my career. It's my life, my anchor. I can't afford to jeopardize it, especially now that I'm thirty-eight." She glanced at Beebo. "Is that unforgivably selfish of me? Don't answer. It is, of course. I want you, and all the rest, too. And that means you're the one who'd have to sacrifice. It's just that...for some people a job is a job. For me, it's self-respect. Acting is about the only thing I've done in my life I'm not ashamed of. Is it too much to ask, Beebo—secrecy?"

"Is it possible?" Beebo said.

Venus nodded. "There are ways. I've had to learn them."

"With the other girls," Beebo said resentfully.

Venus stroked her shoulder. "You don't have to be jealous," she said. "I do."

"I'm jealous of all your husbands. All your lovers, male and female. Every slob who ever saw you in a movie."

Venus chuckled, letting her tripping voice twist her body back and forth on the blue silk, and Beebo suddenly forgot everything in her life that had preceded this moment. She lunged across the bed and caught Venus by the wrist, whirling her around just as Venus got to her feet.

For an instant they stayed as they were, breathless: Beebo stretched out the length of the bed, looking at Venus with her blue eyes shining like a cat's. Venus could feel the avalanche of passionate force trapped inside Beebo, ready to burst free at the flip of a finger. Already it was near exploding.

Venus stood there pulling against Beebo; warm, even hot to the point of perspiring. The light sweat excited Beebo far more than the perfume Venus usually wore. Her body was a soft pearly peach and between her breasts Beebo could see the quivering lift and fall of her sternum.

Beebo gave a swift tug on Venus's arm and brought her tumbling down on the bed, laughing. That laugh sprang the switch in Beebo. She stopped it with her mouth pressed on Venus's. And at last Venus submitted, all the twisting and teasing melting out of her. She let herself be kissed all over.

Beebo looked at her, stripped of the tinseled make-believe and the wisecracks; her lips parted and her eyes shut and her fine dark hair spilling pins over the pillow, coming down almost deliberately to work its witchery. Beebo kissed handfuls of it.

She fell asleep a long time later, still murmuring to Venus, still holding her possessively close, still wondering what she had done—or would have to do—to deserve it.

They were shaken out of sleep by the shrill ringing of the blue phone by Venus's bed. Venus answered sleepily, pulling the receiver onto the pillow by her ear where she lay across Beebo's chest.

But she came awake fast.

It was Leo Bogardus, calling from Hollywood. Beebo opened her eyes and watched while Venus flushed with wrath and suddenly burst into furious tears, threatening to hitchhike for Reno if she had to.

When she had slammed the phone down she told Beebo angrily that Leo had signed her to a television special series called *Million Dollar Baby*.

"I'm the Baby, but I'll never see the million bucks," she cried. "God, I hate TV! You get overexposed, underpaid, and worked to death. And all the lousy profit goes to the lousy sponsors."

Beebo stroked her and tried to calm her. After a while Venus sat still, her head in her hands. "Will you really go to Reno?" Beebo asked.

"No," she sighed. "He won't give me a divorce. I've tried everything.... I'll go to Hollywood. I have no choice, Beebo. That's where they're going to film this little horror."

"Well, you were going anyway, for Toby."

"But not *this* soon! God damn that Leo! Well, at least I asked Toby first. I tried to do it—right."

"How soon is *this* soon?" Beebo asked disconsolately.

"Tonight, if I can get reservations."

Beebo sat up in a mood of defiance. "Venus, you can't—"

"I have to, darling. Leo has ways of forcing me. Besides, I knew he'd been talking about this for months. But I didn't think it would come so soon." She glanced at Beebo and suddenly turned halfway around to kiss her mouth, startling Beebo.

"Is that goodbye?" Beebo said, so coldly that Venus smiled at her.

"I told you I had a business proposition for you, you wicked child," she said. "And it's a damn good thing, or I could never explain to Toby why you spent the night. I'm going in right now and mess up the guest room. Bring your clothes."

Beebo pulled some of them on en route to the guest room. "What proposition?" she demanded, full of new hopes.

"Would you like to work for me?" Venus said, turning down the covers of the extra bed. She had thrown her negligee around herself.

"As what?" Beebo said. "Your companion?"

"No. Toby's. He says you know horses. Maybe you could work in the stables." She spiraled the sheets around on the bed and dumped a pillow on the floor. "That should do it…. Well, don't stand there, darling, go home and pack," she said, glancing up at her astonished guest. "I want you back here before six tonight. There's a flight at eight I can usually get seats on. What's the matter, don't you want to go?"

"I—yes—I do," Beebo stammered.

"Well, go, darling. Go, go, go!" Venus said, clapping her hands under Beebo's nose and laughing. "And don't talk about it!" she hissed at Beebo's retreating back. *"To anybody!"*

Beebo drove downtown in a fog of confusion. After the first shock of flattered pleasure died away, she found herself preoccupied with Paula; so concerned, so anxious, that there were tears in her eyes she had to keep squeezing away, just to see the traffic ahead of her.

She would stop at Paula's apartment before she left. She had to. It was one thing to hurt somebody, but to do it like a snake, striking and slipping away before the victim knows what hit her— or who, or how—was beyond Beebo. She would tell Paula the truth herself, however much it cost them both in sorrow and resentment.

Beebo returned the Pasquinis' truck, hoping to escape unnoticed. But Pete was lying in wait for her.

"So, you brought it back!" he said, grinning at her like a slick little fox. "We thought maybe you was taking a vacation in it."

"It's your truck," she said, getting down. "I don't want the damn thing." She turned to look at him. "I—uh…I'm quitting, Pete. I got another job."

"No kidding." He picked his teeth without disturbing the leer on his face. "Walking the dog for some swell lady?"

"I've had it with dogs," Beebo shot back. "I've been working for one all summer."

Pete left the pick in his teeth in order to fold his arms over his chest in imitation of Beebo when she was insulted. "So, Beebo," he said softly. "You don't like it here with us no more?"

"You tell Marie I'm sorry," Beebo said. "I like her fine."

"Sure you do, sweetheart. She wears a skirt," he said, rocking back and forth on his heels, needling her skillfully.

Beebo felt her temper expanding in her like hot air. It would have relieved her hugely to have punched him where it would hurt the worst. But that was no way to solve any problems—especially not with this covert, twisted young man who was trying to provoke the punch out of her on purpose.

"Marie is a friend of mine," Beebo said stiffly.

"Meaning I ain't? Ain't I been friendly to you, Beebo?" he said, sauntering toward her. "Well, I can fix that up right now." And with one abrupt movement he reached her side and threw her hard against the door of the truck, pulling her left arm up high in the back in a wrenchingly painful hammer lock. Beebo gave a gasp of shock and tried to break free. But for all her size and strength, she was still a girl, and no match for an angry, jealous man who had been wanting her and wanting to hurt her since he first saw her.

He forced his mouth on hers and when she struggled he bit her. She tried to knee him, and he pulled her arm up so hard they both thought for a moment he had broken it. Beebo went white with the pain, and leaned weakly against the door. Pete kissed her again, taking his time and not trying to unhinge her arm any more. The rough scratch of his whiskers and smell of his winy breath, the push of his hard hips, almost made her faint.

"Now why do you make me hurt you, Beebo? Why do you do that?" he said in a tense whisper, as if it were all her fault. "I don't want to hurt you. I want to be friends." He kissed her again. "Don't that prove it?"

Beebo knew she was crying with pain and fury and sickness. "Let me go," she said hoarsely. She would have screamed if she had had any strength, but her heart was pounding and she was clammy pale, very near to toppling over.

Pete released her suddenly, caught her as she stumbled, and seated her on the running board. He shoved her head down between her knees till the blood flow revived her. "You don't got to put on a show," he said irritably. "I know you don't want it from a man. I know you're gay, for chrissakes. That's one thing I can spot a mile off. I like gay girls, Beebo, in case you ain't noticed. I'm on your side. Jesus God, you'd think I hated you, or something."

She looked at him sideways, when she thought she was strong enough to stomach him. "Get out of my sight, you rotten little creep," she said. "Go find Mona. She plays both sides of the street."

"Ah, Mona's a drag," he said. "She's got this big thing about putting you down on account of Paula. And you standing her up that night. I'm sorry about that, Beebo, it was kind of my fault. It was me at her place that night."

"Oh, God," Beebo said, and let her head drop into her hands again. "I should have known."

"Well, how am I supposed to know she's bringing somebody home? I know this girl for years. I drop in on her when I feel like it."

"If you're so goddamn big with Mona, you call on *her* when you feel like it, not me. Don't you come tomcatting around to me, Pasquini." She stood up, weaving slightly, and put a hand on the fender to steady herself.

He stood beside her, and she saw that her angry disgust with him was beginning to annoy him. He wanted a fight—that was part of the build-up for him. But he wanted an eventual surrender, on his terms. Beebo showed no signs of yielding and her revulsion for him was plain enough to anger him.

"Maybe Mona was right," he said, his voice getting thin and mean. "Maybe you need a lesson before you learn what's good for you."

"I don't need any from you," Beebo spat at him. "I'm getting out of here right now, and you'll never see me again."

"I'll catch up with you one of these days," he said. "No matter where you go."

"The hell you will. You're not going to chase me all the way to California just to kick my can," Beebo said hotly. But when Pete began to smile, she rethought her words in sudden panic.

"California?" Pete grinned. "Well, that'd almost be worth the trip. I think I'd like it out there. Maybe get another autograph from Venus. Huh, butch? You could work it for me."

Beebo looked at him, her face a mask but her heart dismayed. "You believe it if you want to," she said. "If you think I'd work anything for you, you're more of a fool than a creep."

She turned and ran out of the delivery yard while he watched her. He didn't like to let her go. But at least she was leaving a trail behind her; one that shouldn't be hard to follow. Pete smiled.

Beebo and Pat drank a few parting shots while Beebo packed her strap-fastened wicker bag and waited for Jack to get home. She was ready to go and a little tight when he rolled in at five.

"Having a party?" he asked.

"A goodbye party. I'm getting off your back, Jackson," Beebo said. "I'm going to Hollywood."

"They were bound to call you sooner or later," Jack said. "Anyone can see you've got talent."

Beebo looked at the floor. "I'm going with Venus," she said, humiliated by it. "I didn't know what else to do, Jack," she added vehemently. "I couldn't live with Paula. I couldn't live with you, not if I wanted to keep your friendship. I had to quit the Pasquini job— Pete's been helling after me since I started. And besides—besides…" She stopped, throwing her arms out and letting them drop against her sides.

"And besides, Venus asked you to go?" Jack said. Beebo

nodded. Jack made no comment, but she knew he thought it was asinine of her. "Did you ever write to tell your father where you are?"

"I thought about it, but I didn't know what to say."

"Have you told Paula?"

"Not yet. I was waiting till you got home."

"Paula's more important."

"Jack, damn it, Paula doesn't own me!" she cried, angry because she knew he was right. "My father doesn't own me. I don't have to tell them every move I make, just because they—"

"They love you," he finished for her. "Listen to me, little pal. You came to this town to grow up and find yourself. You can do that without breaking hearts. And so help me, Beebo, the first one you're going to break is your own."

Beebo sat down on the bed. "Jack, I didn't ask Paula Ash to love me," she said. "I never said I loved *her.*"

"Well, that makes it all swell."

"She's a sweet, fine girl. I wouldn't hurt her for anything. But what can I do?"

"Should I give her that message?" Jack asked.

"I'll tell her myself!" Beebo said, stung. But she wished, with all the force of shame and indecision, that she didn't have to.

Jack lighted a cigarette thoughtfully. "I've gotten to know her a lot better the last few weeks. She was over last night, when you didn't show again. There's a new girl in her life, Beebo." He tossed his match in an ash tray, scrutinizing Beebo's startled face. "Miss Plaid Pajamas. You know her?"

Beebo was shaken. "I know about her," she said. "Oh, Paula…" She recalled the sleeping pills, the tears. Paula's red hair, her scent, her green eyes luminous with love. She pressed a hand over her mouth, half to control a sob, half in recollection of Paula's first gesture of love.

"Regrets?" Jack said gently.

Beebo took a deep breath. "It's Venus I love," she said softly, but it was strangely hard to say.

"Well, that's that," Jack said. "Off you go to follow your star."

"I can't help myself," Beebo said, and that, at least, was true. "I'd rather cut my arm off than hurt Paula, believe me."

Jack smiled and lifted a hand to show he would not sermonize. "I wish you well, pal. I wish you love," he said. "I only wish—"

The phone rang. They all looked at each other. Finally Pat answered it, while Jack and Beebo watched him. "It's for you, Beebo," Pat said, holding out the receiver. She took it, looking apprehensively at him, and he mouthed the word, "Paula."

She shut her eyes. "Hello?" she said.

"Hello, Beebo."

"Paula, I was just coming over. I—I wanted to tell you..." Her voice trailed off.

"I know. I called to wish you Godspeed."

"You what?" Beebo wheeled around to look at the two men.

"Pete called me," Paula said. "He likes to play town crier."

"God damn him!" Beebo exploded. "Paula, I'm so sorry. I wanted to tell you myself, at least. I—what did he say?"

"He said you were going to California with Venus Bogardus," Paula said simply.

"Is that all?"

"It doesn't matter about the rest, Beebo. Pete always exaggerates. I just wanted to tell you, it's all right. I think you should go. It'll be a great experience." Her voice faltered ever so slightly, and Beebo wanted desperately to hold her, to be able to say, "No, I'll stay with you," and somehow still be able to go with Venus. She felt as if she were being physically ripped in half.

"I'm not being melodramatic, honest!" Paula said and she managed a small laugh. "I'm a hopeless optimist. I think you'll be back. Or I couldn't be such a good sport. Mona says 'good sport' is just another word for 'sucker.' She's wrong, isn't she? Beebo?"

"Yes, Paula. She's wrong, honey." Beebo felt her own voice break and Paula said quickly, "Don't come over, there's no need. It's much easier on the phone. Write to me now and then."

"Paula? Is that girl in the plaid pajamas pestering you again?" Beebo said anxiously. "Jack said—"

"Jack is my knight in shining armor. If things get bad, he'll come rescue me. He has before." There was a pause. Beebo glanced gratefully at Jack and then she heard Paula saying, "Goodbye, Beebo. Good luck. No, *bad* luck, and come home soon. I love you, you know. You worm."

"I know." Beebo swallowed. "Goodbye, Paula." She let the receiver drop into its cradle and stood with her head against the wall for a minute.

"You look like you're set for a real pleasure cruise," Jack said, noting her wan face and full eyes.

Beebo picked up her bag in a brusque motion and strode to the door. But she couldn't turn the handle. "Thanks for everything, Jack," she said, full of fears at cutting loose from her only friend in the new world.

"Come back when Venus shows you out," he said kindly. "Our bunk is your bunk," and he put an arm over Pat's shoulder.

"She won't show me out," Beebo said with what pride she still had. "Jackson, take care of that Paula for me." She caught his shoulders in a hard grip. "I don't know if I can stand to do this to her."

"You're doing it," Jack commented.

Beebo looked at her bag, then grabbed it and ran down the hall and front steps without daring to look back.

Jack shut the door softly and gazed at Pat. "You're tanked," he said indulgently. His thoughts were elsewhere.

"You didn't tell her about Pete and Mona," Pat said. "Why?"

"She's going three thousand miles from here. Let's hope she doesn't need to worry about those two twerps any more."

"I've heard some of their sickening stories about Beebo around the bars lately," Pat brooded.

"Well, don't give Pete and Mona all the credit," Jack said shrewdly. "Not that they ever say anything nice about anybody. But it helps to have someone else feeding them information.... Somebody whose initials are Pat Kynaston." It was as sharp a reproof as Jack had given him.

"I only say *good* things about Beebo!" Pat protested, instantly wounded. "I adore that girl!"

"I know. Good things. That's all they need. Somebody in the Cellar heard you carrying on Tuesday afternoon: Beebo's father, her home town, even that thing at the livestock exhibition. You want Pete to hear that, Pat? Think what he could do with it, if he wanted to."

Pat sank dismally to the living room floor. "Lord, I didn't realize. I thought I was telling them how great she is. I thought Pete and Mona were inventing their stuff."

"They are, but not all of it. The nearer the truth they can get, the louder they'll shout it—screwed around just enough to make Beebo look like the type of witch decent citizens should spend their Sundays burning."

Pat's chin trembled. "I could strike myself dumb," he said bitterly.

Jack sat down and put an arm around him. "Just watch it, lover. She's put herself in a spot to be crucified, if Pete has anything against her...and Mona already has, or thinks she has. All that girl needs is a whim, anyway."

The Bogardus home was located in a lush and secluded area of Mandeville Canyon Road in Bel-Air. It was huge, elegant, well-staffed and maintained. The grounds were a glowing sweep of hand-tailored grass, tropical palms exploding against the sky like green rockets, swimming pools—two—and the noisy brilliance of equatorial blooms.

Toby showed Beebo around. They walked over the lawns in bare feet, and Beebo marveled at it. It dazzled her eyes enough to take her mind off her sore heart a while. "Every time you push a button, somebody runs up with a martini," she said. "It's fantastic, Toby."

"I wish it weren't," Toby said. "I wish I had an ordinary house to live in."

"Poor little rich boy," she grinned. "Wants an ordinary mama and papa, too, no doubt. Maybe when you're older you'll be glad you're different."

"How would you know? You didn't have to grow up this way."

"No, but I had to grow up," Beebo said. "I would have traded my problems for yours any day."

"That's what Leo says. His family didn't have a dime," Toby told her as they picked their way over the manufactured rustic rocks circling one of the pools.

"Where is that guy, anyway?" Beebo said. Leo worried her, like a family ghost: much was made of him, yet he was rarely seen.

"He's in S.F.," Toby said. "The servants expect him back the end of the week. He's talking to a sponsor for Mom's show."

"What's he like? How do you talk to him?" Beebo said.

"Oh, you don't have to worry. He likes kids. Beside, he's been talking about getting somebody to help with the horses for years." Beebo felt a sudden wave of relief. She had not brought up the reason for her presence here, and it seemed odd to her that Toby hadn't either—till she realized how Venus had explained it to him. "Besides," Toby added, "it'll be nice to have you around. You can help me with my homework. You ought to be good with the biology. For once, Mom didn't get a square for me."

Beebo wondered how many other young people had preceded her in this household; how many synthetic friendships with young tutors, horsemen, and valets Venus had tried to promote for Toby, hoping he would turn into the easy-mannered socialite she somehow pictured him being when he was grown.

At least it was reassuring to have a job, something legitimate to do to explain her membership on the family staff.

Toby sat down at the pool's edge and put his legs in the cool water. He was well-developed for his age, though still only five-feet-six. Beebo looked at his young male body, so carelessly normal, and she envied him painfully.

"Leo's jealous, but he's tolerant, too," Toby said. "I mean, he's put up with so damn many men tailing Mom, he knows how to outsmart or outlast all of them. He doesn't like it much, but he knows she needs them. At least, that's what *she* says. I don't know why a woman can't be happy with one man…especially if he's a good one."

"Some women can," Beebo said. But she was thinking that a man of Leo's knowledge and well-founded suspicions would doubtless take one look at Beebo and know good and damn well what his beautiful wife was up to. There was nothing to do but wait till he got home for the showdown.

She confronted Venus with her misgivings about Leo. "He won't hurt you, darling," Venus said. "Don't offend him and don't defy him. He's nervous as hell with a girl around the house."

"If he puts up with your men, why not with your women?" Beebo said gloomily.

"I never cared much for the other girls," Venus said circuitously. "Only for you."

"Well, that ought to ingratiate me with Leo for good," Beebo said.

"Leo's afraid for my career. I guess that's the only thing we agree on. My 'normal' affairs have scandalized enough people as it is. A gay love—if it got out—would finish me, Beebo." She looked at her apologetically. "It's hard for me to fight Leo. He—sort of—owns me. Economically, I mean, like he owns this house."

"Do you really hate him, Venus?"

Venus picked at a nonexistent thread on her skirt. "I guess he's a kindly man at heart. I think I've ruined his temperament." She put her arms around Beebo as they lounged on her private sun porch. "Beebo, are you sorry you're gay? Are you bitter about it?"

"Yes," Beebo said, and Venus frowned. "All day long, when you go off to the studio, I'm sorry as hell. At night, I get down on my knees and give thanks."

"There must have been bad times before I came along."

Beebo surfaced from a kiss on Venus's golden shoulder. "When I was younger, I used to look out my bedroom window on summer nights," she said, "and the brightest star in the sky was Venus. I wanted to reach out and take it in my hand. Put it in a box and make it mine forever."

Venus chuckled. "I'm not in a box yet, thank God. And I'm a lot handier than that dreadful planet."

Beebo settled closer to her and said with comfortable intimacy, "I want to share so many things with you, Venus. I want to see you sparkling at parties...take you shopping...watch you at rehearsals..."

"You can't," Venus said, putting a finger on Beebo's nose. Beebo brushed it off, protesting. "There won't be time, for one thing," Venus explained. "Not while we're filming. And besides, Leo won't let you. You're too young, you're too noticeable, and you're too—well, female. I'll have all I can do to keep him from putting *you* in a box."

"Well, of all the goddamn nonsense!" Beebo said, clouding up. "I just want to drive you places and wait. Watch you from a distance. I'm willing to be a servant, Venus, but not a dog on a leash."

"Darling, use your head. What if we were seen together, and it was common knowledge you lived here and went everywhere with me and—oh, Beebo, don't look so crushed. I don't like it either."

"You don't want me around where you have to look at me all the time," Beebo sulked.

"Darling, I can't look at you enough!" Venus said, half-amused and half-concerned at the outburst. "You're the handsomest thing I ever saw."

"Is that what I am? A thing?" Beebo said, swinging her legs to the ground. She was surprised at herself for being pettish. But the moment she questioned herself about it, her thoughts flew to Paula. *Paula would never talk to me this way.*

"That's not what I meant and you know it," Venus said.

"You don't want your *things* following you around in public."

"Beebo!" Venus cried, hurt. "I love you!" Her words made Beebo turn back and take Venus in her arms.

"I'm sorry," she said, realizing all at once that Venus was crying.

"I adore you," Venus wept. "I feel so free with you. Able to do the things that used to terrify me. Able to *think* about them without shame. I never let go like this with anybody in my life, Beebo." She clung to her. "Darling, don't shout at me for the things we can't have. Be glad with me for the things we *can*. I'm trying to look at the world more charitably, Beebo—for you and for Toby. You try to look at me that way. Don't just love me, understand me. I need it so." She wiped her tears on Beebo's shirt and glanced up at her.

"You know something silly? I want to dress up for you. I want to sit and hear you talk. I don't care whether I say a word. I want to be a real actress, not an obedient puppet. I even want to mother my son. When you tell me to do a thing, I fret for the chance to try."

Beebo stared at her, amazed at this oddly touching admission. "I even got a bunch of pamphlets from the Department of Agriculture," Venus said, "on how to raise chickens and wean calves."

Beebo succumbed to laughter. "All you had to do was ask me," she said.

"I'll show them to you," Venus offered, trying to get up, but Beebo pulled her down again, her fit of pique soothed away.

"I'll take your word for it," she said. "Besides, I've got you half undressed. What would the servants say?"

"They'd say Venus is in love," Venus answered, letting Beebo hold her. "And they'd be right."

Beebo made love to her with a new tenderness. And yet, again, when they fell asleep, she dreamed restlessly of Paula Ash.

Venus began to spend all the daylight hours, and some of the night, with the production staff of *Million Dollar Baby*. Leo returned from San Francisco, but Beebo would not have known it if Toby hadn't pointed it out.

They had been all day riding Leo's horses in the boulder meadow surrounding the Bogardus estate, and when they got in, Toby announced, "Leo's back."

"How do you know?" Beebo asked, suddenly on her guard.

"Orange juice glass," Toby said, pointing to a brandy snifter with an orange puddle at the bottom, sitting on an end table. "That's all Leo ever drinks. He says we've got orange trees in the yard and the juice is free. He likes things that are free. Besides, he's always on a health kick. Right now it's citric acid. When he's home there's always a mess of sticky glasses around."

"He's not going to like seeing *me* around," Beebo said glumly.

"Why not?" Toby looked at her curiously. "The stables are cleaned up for the first time in a year. And Mom is getting so nice to be around…. Gee, Beebo, he'll probably hang a medal on you."

Beebo understood from his answer how little aware he was of his mother's relationship with her. He had grown to trust Beebo, as well as like her, and as far as he knew, she was there only to help out with the horses during the day and look over his homework at night. The fact that she had been able to encourage Venus and Toby to try to know and respect each other at last was the frosting on the cake.

But after he went to bed, Beebo would go to Venus's room. They were lovers at night, but during the day, if Venus was home, she had to be as breezy and casual with Beebo as she was with everybody else.

As for Leo, Beebo didn't meet him for nearly a week. He got up at six A.M. and left the house by seven, before Beebo was stirring. He looked in on her with Venus once. Beebo was awakened early by the click of the bedroom door shutting behind him. But when she asked Venus about it, Venus only said, "I told him you were a farm kid. He likes that it makes you a sort of walking health exhibit."

"Does he like the fact that I'm a girl?"

"Not a bit," Venus said with a grin, refusing to spoil the moment by elaborating.

Beebo dodged around squads of empty orange-juice glasses for several days with the eerie feeling that the ghost who emptied them would come cackling out of the rafters at her before long.

The night they finally met, Beebo had been living under Leo's roof for over two weeks, using his hospitality without ever having seen or spoken to him.

She was sitting in the huge recreation room with Venus and Toby, watching TV and listening to Venus tell about the casting problems, wardrobe, scripts she had read.

Beebo commented quietly, "It takes up your whole life, doesn't it?"

Venus looked at her anxiously. "You're lonesome during the day, aren't you, darling?" She threw a guarded glance at Toby, but he spoke without taking his eyes off the TV screen: "What do you mean, lonesome, Mom? She's busy all day. Besides, I get home from school at four, and I'm better company than you are."

Venus smiled and reached out to hug him. She startled herself as much as Toby, but he endured the embrace with less embarrassment than he would have felt the month before in New York.

"When is that PTA thing at school?" Venus said. "I want to go with you, Toby." *Toby.* His name. The first time in memory she had called him that when she wasn't in a rage. Beebo saw the smile in his eyes.

"You can go if you promise not to call anybody 'darling' or wear a knit dress," he said.

Venus gasped and Beebo laughed at him, looking behind his back at Venus. "All right, darling, I promise," Venus said wryly. "If *you* promise not to ditch me this year, and tell lies to your friends about how I do the dishes every night, like all the other mothers."

Toby smiled without looking at her, and it was a bargain. Beebo felt her own satisfaction at this bashful honesty between mother and son. And then Venus surprised her by saying, "Beebo, I'm going to get you a car. It isn't fair to make you shovel manure all day."

"What would I do with a car?" Beebo said, mystified at the sudden generosity.

"You could ferry Toby around. Pick up the groceries for Miss Pinch. Maybe we'll get something to eat that isn't poisonous for a change."

"Miss Pinch doesn't use poison," said a gravelly voice. "Just too much paprika. It's her Hungarian heritage."

Beebo turned around with a start to see, at long last, Leo Bogardus coming down the wide steps to join them.

"Well, darling, you should know," Venus said. "You and Miss Pinch have such a beautiful thing together."

Leo strode across the room, a solid, rather squarely built man; gray hair and gray suit; neat and natty and silver-eyed behind his black French-framed glasses. He was about Beebo's height and attractive without being handsome.

Beebo stood up to greet him, somewhat subdued. "Mr. Bogardus? I'm Beebo," she said and held out her hand.

Leo put a just-drained orange-juice glass on a table. "I know," he said. "I hope you'll be comfortable with us for as long as you stay, Beebo." He shook her hand briefly.

Beebo wasn't sure if he meant to be sarcastic or not. She let her hand drop awkwardly and sat down again as Bogardus settled in a chair, trying to size him up. His face was clean-lined and his manner decisive. She imagined him quick to anger, stubborn, and hard to handle when he was mad.

"You're picking them younger every year, Venus," Leo said five minutes later, without once having looked at Beebo in the meantime.

Venus grimaced a warning at him over Toby's head to shut up. Leo nodded wearily.

"I don't pick them, darling; they pick me," she said in a pointed whisper.

To Beebo's discomfiture, Leo gazed straight at her then and laughed with a honk of mirth. Moments later he got up and left as abruptly as he came, and Beebo spoke not another word to him for several more days. She had just begun to hope she wouldn't have to at all. It would have suited her, not because she disliked him— she didn't. Considering her position in his house, he was more than decent. But he scared her. He was no ghost, but he was still the unknown quantity.

Fortunately, the next few times they saw each other there was only time for small talk, and no more.

Venus got her the car before the end of the week—a silver sport coupé—and Beebo and Toby cruised around Hollywood and the coastal communities when he got home from school in the afternoons.

Toby kept on talking, confiding in her, and she began to see how much he respected and liked Leo; how strongly he sided with his step-father in any argument between Leo and Venus; what a source of strength Leo was to him. Here was no dirty dog like the rest of the boys. Here was a man to admire and emulate, and Toby did. Leo was good for him, and Beebo was glad they had each other.

Beebo felt conspicuous, even though they rarely stopped the car or got out. She was afraid somebody would recognize Toby, and she hated to be stared at, with her short hair and slacks and casual cotton shirts. Skirts looked wrong on her and men's pants looked fake.

She looked the best in riding wear: a formal tight-waisted jacket and white stock, hard velvet cap, smooth leather boots, jodhpurs. The kind of clothes she used to wear at shows around Juniper Hill, when she won ribbons for jumping other people's horses. She had a lithe elegance that the riding clothes dramatized.

But you can't walk into Schwab's drugstore in formal riding clothes. At least not if you have orders to make yourself invisible. Beebo began to feel hemmed in. The only safe place in the county of Los Angeles was the Bogardus estate, and even there she worried about guests and servants.

Miss Pinch disapproved sniffily of her, but she'd probably hold her tongue for Leo's sake. Mrs. Sack was as plump and amiable as a currant bun, and about as perceptive. The others were a shadowy and obsequious crew whom Beebo rarely saw, yet she distrusted them all.

In the evenings, when she was alone, Beebo started writing to Paula and Jack. They were short letters at first, though the ones to Jack were longer and franker. To Paula, she described the flash of October across the southern California landscape; the whipped-cream weather, the purple hills, the flowers.

To Jack she said, "Venus is wonderful. She's working so hard I hardly ever see her, though. But she says she'd spend every minute with me if she could. Nobody else exists but me. It's funny—that looks so made-up on paper. But she really said it, and I believe her.

"I almost never see Leo, either. When I run into him, I ask about his diet and he asks me about the horses. I think he's a good man—good for Toby—but I'd hate like hell to have him mad at me.

"I guess the one thing I don't like about it here is being alone so much. Even Toby's gone till late in the day. What a nice kid he is, underneath the shell. He wants to be somebody in his own right, and I'll bet he makes it.

"How is that doll you room with? Please write and tell me *everything* about Paula. Best—Beebo."

There was no trouble between Leo and Beebo until the day she and Toby picked Venus up at the studio in Television City. They knew she was coming home early to prepare for a party, and they talked one another into it like a pair of school boys ditching class for a day to have a ball. It seemed quite innocuous, and yet rather worldly and exciting when they discussed it, tooling around in the silver car.

But when they actually arrived in that principality of a parking lot, they were rather abashed.

"What if she doesn't see us?" Toby said.

"That'd probably be all for the best," Beebo said.

But Venus saw them plain and clear when she emerged from the building, surrounded by aides and admirers. She walked briskly to the car, surprising the crowd, which began to straggle after her, opened the door, and pulled Toby out by his collar.

"Darling," she said smoothly, "I want you to meet Mr. Wilkins and Mr. Klein. Boys, will you introduce him around for me?" She smiled at one of the men, who quickly obliged her.

Venus thrust her head into the car. "Beebo, what the hell!" she hissed.

"I'm sorry—we thought it would be fun," Beebo faltered.

"You thought—" Venus shut her eyes a minute and swallowed her temper. "Oh, balls. I'm not going to get mad at you. I can't, I'm too much in love with you. But oh! you fool, *Leo* can. I hope to God he doesn't hear about it." She withdrew, collared Toby again, and popped him into the front seat, sitting down beside him to wave and smile at the group of people so charmingly that no one but herself was likely to be noticed as they pulled away.

The sponsors for *Million Dollar Baby* were openhanded, despite long rehearsal hours and high rents and salaries, because they figured that with Venus in the show, it had to be a smash. So Leo, anxious to live up to their expectations, worked her unremittingly day and night throughout October.

Venus not only had to act, she had to dance and sing. The big number for the second show, then in production, was "I'm Putting My All on You."

"I never sang before in my life!" Venus yelled at Leo.

"Marilyn Monroe can do it," he said softly, infuriating her.

"Leo, *I can't sing!*" she cried, trying to explain fundamentals to him as if he were retarded.

"Well, don't," Beebo said, surprising both of them. She was watching the scene in the Bogardus rec room. Leo threw her an irritated look, and Beebo explained quickly, *"Talk* the song. Whisper and wiggle like Marlene Dietrich. Venus, Leo's right. You have to live up to the title. *Million Dollar Baby.* God, you ought to be able to do anything for that price, including grand opera."

Leo laughed, a clattering jangle of a sound, while Venus salved her wounds in prim silence, peeved at Beebo for backing up her husband.

"Now, you see?" Leo told her, waving at Beebo. "That's it. Beebo can see it. Why can't you? I tell you the same damn thing and you squawk at me like a fishwife. Okay, I'm not young and handsome, but I'm smart. That's how you got where we are today. You do this right, and you'll get more than that million."

Beebo watched him with interest as he directed Venus. He was electrically alive, cunning in the way he teased and bullied and loved the song out of her. Beebo could almost feel the tune, the words, Venus herself, coming to life. Leo was a good seat-of-the-pants psychologist.

After several run-throughs he turned to Beebo. "You're helping," he said laconically. "She sings better for you than for me. I show her what to do. You make her feel it." He scratched his head, then let his shirt-sleeved arms drop. "That's okay, as long as she doesn't lose it at the studio," he decided. "Maybe we'll let you watch some other scenes at home, Beebo."

Beebo grinned. It was a relief to participate at last in the paramount sphere of Venus's life.

"It helps to have her in love again," Leo observed candidly. "Makes her much more responsive."

"Don't talk about me as if I were a machine," Venus flashed at him. "And don't laugh at me. I know how silly you think it is. I *know* Beebo's too young."

Leo sat down on a leather-topped bar stool. "You're happy, Beebo?" he asked.

Beebo nodded, wondering where he was going.

"It's rough, isn't it? Venus isn't home much these days. And you have nothing to do but goof around in that car."

"I get along," Beebo said cautiously. "Are you against the car, Leo?"

"No, just the taxi service." There was a deadly pause, and Leo's face folded into a heavy frown. Beebo was lost for a moment, till Venus sighed and lighted a cigarette with angry movements. "Who squealed?" she said.

"It doesn't matter," Leo said crisply. "I don't like the idea of you two ladies consorting in public."

"Leo, don't pull that solemn face on me," Venus said. "She and Toby came together. They picked me up at work. Nobody saw her face—"

"Nobody had to," Leo said, taking a drag on his cigarette.

"Look, Leo, let's not fight over it," Beebo said. "Be reasonable. Things are working out all right. I'm discreet and I swear I'll never—"

"I know, you'll never do anything to hurt darling Venus," Leo said acidly. His eyes narrowed, and he began to pace the room. When either of the women tried to speak he silenced them with a gesture.

Finally Venus said, "That poor kid never goes anywhere. She deserves—"

"She deserves to torpedo your career, just to alleviate her ennui?"

"Well, damn it, Leo, if you turn her out, I'm going with her. I happen to be in love with Beebo and I don't give a damn what you think of it."

"Venus, go upstairs," Leo said. He lighted a cigar—a concession to his mental distress. When Venus objected he said, "Will you please go?" as if she were a naughty child. He was almost fatherly with her. "I can't talk to Beebo with such a distraction as you around." He made her hope he and Beebo would understand each other. She left slowly, telling Beebo not to believe a word Leo said.

Leo stopped his pacing and sat down to face Beebo. "There's too much at stake, Beebo," he said at once. "I can't tolerate even small slip-ups. Venus is silly, but that's no excuse for you. You're a sensible kid."

"But Leo, such a little thing—"

"Nothing is little, Beebo," he said. "Let's be frank with each other. It worries me enough that you're so young. At least her other lovers were nearer her own age. But to have you a girl..." He puffed rapidly on the cigar. "I won't disguise the fact that I find you rather...well, unsympathetic. I think most normal men would. Partly from masculine resentment, I guess. A natural revulsion for women who parade as poor imitations of men, but—"

"You liked me well enough when you got home and found Venus acting like a lovable human being," Beebo interrupted him heatedly. "I'm the same person now as then. I just happened to pick her up in a parking lot and drive her home."

"The guy who told me about it," Leo said thoughtfully, "said Venus was picked up by a good-looking boy. A friend of Toby's he supposed. Of course, you were hard to see inside the car. But Venus had told him, when she saw you pull up, that you were one of the servants. So he was a little surprised to see her jump in the front seat with you...and you didn't have a uniform on, either. He was giving me the old elbow-in-the-ribs-treatment." He blew cigar smoke at the ceiling without looking at her.

Beebo cleared her throat. "It was so innocent," she said.

"Nothing is innocent," Leo said flatly. "Especially a classy young butch on the make."

"Damn it, Leo!" she said. "I'm clean, I'm healthy, I've worked hard all my life. And so help me God, I'm not ashamed of being what I can't *help* being. That's the road to madness." Her cheeks were crimson.

"Well said, Beebo," he acknowledged calmly. "You're right—but so am I. You might as well face up to the world's opinion. I speak for the ordinary prejudiced guy, too busy to learn tolerance, too uninformed to give a damn. We are in the majority. I admire your guts but not your person. As for the intolerance, it's mostly emotional and illogical. I can't help it and neither can most men. I apologize. I warn you that it's there. I add: it's beside the point.

"What I think of you is less important than what the people in Venus's world think. I don't care what you say, somebody in this world besides the Bogardus family knows you're living here and laying my wife. It's no secret from the servants, you know."

Beebo caught her breath and Leo looked at her piercingly. "I've heard them laughing about it," he said. "And our servants bat the breeze with the other stars' servants. They know more guff about us—what we eat, when we pee, who our lovers are—than all the gossip columnists rolled into one and stashed behind the keyhole. All I can say is, I pay them and most of them like me. Not Venus, not you. But *me.* I hope they respect my privacy, but I know human nature. Sooner or later they'll blab."

Beebo rubbed a hand over her eyes, angry and frightened. "Well, if it's so bad, why the hell did Venus bring me out here? She must have known how it would be."

"Venus isn't very big for denying herself what she wants," Leo said. "Besides, there's a lot to be said in your favor. Venus is more stable. She means it when she says she loves you. I believe that, Beebo, and I hope you do. Her love is a unique gift, and I tell you honestly that I envy you it. It has transformed her."

Beebo was flattered and surprised to hear this coming from Leo. She felt suddenly sorry for him. He seemed gray all over, from his damp shirt to his strained face.

"I struggled for years to win her love...my God, just to win her attention. I finally decided there was no love in her, not even for poor Toby. You proved me wrong, and in a way I'm grateful to you. Venus will never be an easy woman to live with, but she's improved measurably with you, and I think some of it will last long after you've left us."

"Left you?" Beebo opened her mouth to protest but was bull-dozed by his rush of words.

"Her tantrums now are kid stuff compared to the blasts we used to get. Now, I get a sort of half-assed cooperation. Toby gets some affection. The servants get some peace. And that's a lot when you're starting from zero."

Beebo was taken aback by it.

"I thank you for that, Beebo. I thank you for being discreet most of the time, when it's boring and humiliating. But I have to look at the other side of the coin. Venus has survived some potentially filthy scandals because she has the smartest director and press agent in the world: me. But it took all I've got and more to keep them out of the papers. Sometimes the only way was to jump in front of her and take the crap meant for Venus on my own kisser, just to keep her clean. I'd do it again if I had to, but I don't want to do it for you. If it gets out she's sleeping with a girl, we're dead. All of us.

"Venus makes a touching speech about walking out of here with you if anything goes wrong, but she won't, Beebo. Don't kid yourself. Don't get hurt worse than you have to be when the end comes."

Beebo was too mad at him and too proud to admit any such thing. "The end won't come, Leo," she flared. "She's in love with me and that makes her a different woman from the one you've always known. You can't make predictions about her."

"I can predict anything about that woman, Beebo," he said in a sad voice that mourned the passing of mystery in his love. "I wish there were something left in her for me to worship. You forget that there was a great love in her life before Beebo Brinker came along and that love will last to the end, long after Beebo falls by the wayside. That's self-love. She loves herself more than she loves you."

"You're unjust, Leo. She's told me—"

"Sure—that she only loves the money, the career. Why, Beebo? Because they glorify the *woman*. The woman she loves—herself."

Beebo stared at him, silenced.

"You flatter her, you kid her, you make a good try at understanding her, despite your blind spots. And you're also nuts about her, which she finds very ingratiating. Plus the fact of your femininity...something I will never understand. You know, she's tried this Lesbian stuff before."

"She said you objected pretty violently."

"Hell, yes. It's much more dangerous than a normal affair. I'm no blue-stocking. I'm for falling in love and making it work, as long as it doesn't hurt other people. It has nothing to do with my emotional prejudices. Intellectually, I'm damned fair. The only two people Venus hurts are me and Toby. I give her hell about Toby; I try to protect him. But letting Venus hurt me is the abiding condition of my life. The rock on which our marriage is built."

Beebo listened, rooted with fascination, shock, pity, distaste. He was making an accomplice of her by revealing the secrets of his life with Venus; putting her in a spot where she would be virtually obligated to help him, if only to save all their skins.

"But when I see disaster coming," Leo went on, "that will crush our son, destroy her career, ruin all our lives—I have to act. Beebo, you're eighteen. You're among the adults. I lay this on the line to you. I'd ask you to leave of your own free will, if I thought you had any left. But you're too infatuated for that. All I'll say now is, stay out of sight, watch the servants, and do as I say."

"Look, Leo, I know you're bending over backwards for me," Beebo said. "I appreciate it. Since I've been here you've been just a face to me, but a kind enough face. Now I see you're not just an operator—you're an intelligent and honest man. And it's too bad Venus won't admit it. I think she could have loved you if she had.

"But if you're working up to telling me that no matter how good a kid I am, I'm going to have to pack up one of these days and blow, I'm sorry. I can't go." *Unless,* she thought, *I go for Paula. I'll never go because I'm pushed.*

"No," he said. "I'll tell you precisely what the situation is. I should have talked to you about this before. You should know where I stand. It must never—under any circumstances—get out that you're queer, much less involved with Venus." He spoke without self-consciousness, his voice coming sharp and sure. Beebo wondered if his long experience with "artistic" types had made him a little wiser than other men.

"I found Venus when she was about your age: just plain Jeanie Jacoby from Fostoria, Ohio," Leo said. "She wrote me a letter saying she was beautiful, available, and hated her family, and would I please make her a star. She enclosed a snapshot. And she added that she was writing me because I was the biggest agent in Hollywood. It was pure guff, but her picture got me.

"Later I found out she wrote the same letter to twenty other guys. But I was the one who fell for it and sent her a ticket for L.A. I figured if only half of what I saw in the pic was for real, I could still sell her and make a fortune. Well, she came. I saw. She conquered. I named her Venus for the obvious reason, and Bogardus because I guessed I'd never have the chance to give her my own name any other way. I never thought we'd marry.

"I loved her the day we met, for all the wrong reasons, and I love her still. My reasons haven't improved any.

"I was just an agent, but I went out and worked my ass off and got her going. I launched her. She would have sunk after a couple of the flops she made if they hadn't let me direct her finally. I made an actress out of her and saved her career.

"When her star rose, so did mine. Her success was the only thing we loved together and cried over and cherished—together. I watched her run through five lousy marriages in ten years. And when she was weary and demoralized, I stepped in like Sir Galahad, thinking I could make her happy. I was delirious when she said yes, and I think even Venus was pleased. Till the honeymoon was over.

"I suppose she's told you what it was like. Things have been more peaceful with you around. But we've driven each other to mayhem in years past. She thinks she wants her freedom. But she'd come back to me, Beebo, even if she got it. She needs me as much as I need her. (Don't tell her that, she won't believe it.) I'll never divorce her. I love her enough to prefer the torment of living with her to the torment of living without her."

He stopped a moment, fixing Beebo with his silver eyes to impress his next words on her. "That is one hell of a terrible lot of love, Beebo," he said slowly. "I doubt if you could top it. There's one thing Venus and I agree on: I made her and I'm keeping her on top. If she didn't care about that, she wouldn't care about me, either.

"Listen, Beebo. I don't want her ever to love you more than herself. And if I see it coming, I'll fight you. I'll bring out every drop of self-love and self-pity and money-lust in her system—and she's got more of it than she has blood. Because if she drops her career, she'll drop me with it." He paused and they looked at each other.

"That's it, Beebo," Leo said at last. "I'm sorry if it sounds egotistic to you. You just mind me, and maybe we'll make it for a while. I don't know what you can do about Toby. He doesn't get the picture about you and his mother yet, but he will. He's a bright kid. But don't go out of your way to tell him. It's going to stagger him. I'll try to explain when he catches on.

"If anything comes up, deny it. I give you this chance because of what you've done for Venus. Don't make me regret it."

"I don't know whether to thank you or kick you in the slats," Beebo said sourly. "You make it sound like a great life."

"Did anyone tell you to expect something else?" Leo said. "You've been living it the last two months. You should be used to it."

"Used to it but not fond of it," she said.

"But fond of Venus…enough to put up with it? Because if you aren't, say so. I've been honest enough with you to hurt myself, Beebo. You be that honest with me."

Beebo's gaze fell. "I'll put up with it," she said, but her voice was rough with resentment.

"I'm sorry, Beebo," Leo said, and though his masculine aversion to her was as real as he declared, he was still capable of a restrained sympathy for her. "The world wasn't made for dykes, you know."

"No," she flashed. "It was made for movie queens and their tyrannical husbands."

Leo hunched his shoulders, unoffended. "The world was made for normal people," he said. "The abnormal in this world have a tough go. If they keep their abnormality secret, they're damnably lonely. If they broadcast it, they're damnably hurt. You were born with that, and you'll have to live with it, the way I have to live with Venus's faults."

Beebo was impressed with his sensitivity. But she answered moodily, "I don't feel so damned abnormal, thanks. I feel as normal as you do. I eat three meals a day, I pay my bills, I respect the other guy."

"Well, I can tell you, society doesn't give a hoot in hell how normal you *feel,* Beebo. You *look* queer, and that's enough. People are waiting around to throw some crap your way."

"What about the queers who look normal?" Beebo demanded.

"They have a chance," he said. "They can hide. You can't. And when the stuff hits the fan, I don't want Venus anywhere near you. You can have it all to yourself."

"You're a pretty goddamn infuriating individual, Leo," Beebo said.

"Sure," he agreed, getting up and stamping the cigar butt into the tile floor. "An honest man always is. I've said some harsh things to you, but they were true. And I've permitted you to stay on—conditionally. You know the conditions, my friend, and if you feel like ignoring them, you'd better feel like saying goodbye, too. You dig?"

"I dig," Beebo said, glowering at him from the sofa.

She wrote to Jack that night, sitting in one of the unused spare rooms, where she was shunted when Venus was out. She recounted a little of what Leo had said.

"God, Jack, it makes you want to go out and convert the whole damn world to homosexuality," she told him. "Just so you can walk down the street with your head up.

"Maybe I grew up too fast, maybe that's my trouble. I feel so lost out here...hung up between two worlds; half-kid and half-adult, half-boy and half-girl. And sometimes it seems like I get the dirty side of both. Leo's whole life is one long compromise...maybe that's what he was trying to tell me about mine.

"I wanted Venus and I got her, but I'm not sure having her is worth the shame and secrecy of it. I'm strong and tall as a boy, but I'm not free as a man. I wanted to be gentle and loving with women, but I can't be feminine.

"Venus tries to make it better for me. She argues with Leo to let me out more. She gives me things all the time—money, clothes, anything—and it makes me realize how much she thinks about me when she's working. She's even been going to Toby's PTA meetings.

"And damn it, Jack, I know she loves me. She proves it to me whenever she's home. But that's the catch—that whenever. It gets later every day, and she's so tired. She never says no, but I feel like a dog.

"You know something? I wish all this had happened to me ten years from now. You said that about Paula, but you were wrong. Paula was just what I needed. I miss that girl, Jack. I sit here on these long empty days and dream about her. My letters to her are awful, I don't know what to say. Say I love her for me, will you?

"No—better not. Because I don't know how I can leave Venus, and I'm still not sure I want to. God, what a mess!"

Leo confronted her one morning two days later and said, "Lay off Venus a little, Beebo. She has circles under her eyes."

Beebo, still half-asleep by herself in Venus's bed, mumbled at him and sat up.

"Her eyes don't photograph well. She looks her age and that's no good," Leo said. "She gets home at midnight, pooped, and you light into her for another couple of hours. She's too crazy about you to say no, but she has to get up at six-thirty next day, while you lie around till noon."

Beebo rubbed her eyes. "Leo, I don't force her to make love to me," she said, trying to clear her head. "She *wants* to."

"Well, she can't. Not till next Tuesday. That's the première showing and we're all under a hell of a strain till then."

"My God," Beebo whispered, almost to herself. "I have to give that up, too? Leo, what else is there?" She turned to him, scowling.

"After Tuesday night, whether we sink or swim, the whole cast and crew get a week off, and you can make up for lost time," he said, gazing at her long form with curiosity; wondering how it could appeal to anybody, yet respecting his wife's intense admiration. "I'm sorry, Beebo. It's either continence, or I take her to a hotel. You choose."

"I have so little of her, Leo. You're asking me to do without even the little I have." She put her head down on her knees.

"Just for a few days."

She lay down on the bed, turning her back to him, and Leo watched her a moment before he shut the door.

In the half week before *Million Dollar Baby* showed, a one-liner appeared in a trade gossip column. It said, "Who's been picking Venus Bogardus up at TV City in a silver sport coupé these days?"

Leo spotted it, underlined it in red, and left it on Venus's dresser, where Beebo picked it up the next morning and read it with round-eyed shock.

The next day, another columnist asked, "What's this about Venus Bogardus taking a personal interest in her son's friends? Especially one near and dear to the family?" Leo underlined that one, too. Beebo read it while she was sitting alone in the spare room again. She was sleeping there till Tuesday night.

Leo made no comments in the margins. He didn't have to. Beebo was scared enough at the unembellished print. She hadn't seen Venus for a couple of days. Venus was too busy and after the hints in the papers, she and Leo removed to a hotel. Beebo was afraid for Venus, afraid for their love affair, and afraid for herself. If only Jack were there to help her. If only it had been possible to tell all to her father long ago and run to him now.

Toby saw how blue she was later in the day and tried to cheer her up. "Hey, don't look so gloomy," he said. "What's got you down?"

Beebo looked at him. "Toby," she said, almost hoping he wouldn't hear. "Did you read the newspapers today?"

Toby's face reddened and she wished immediately that she hadn't brought it up. "I don't read them," he said. "I heard about it at school. Everybody wants to know which friend of mine they're talking about. But they all think it's a boy, naturally. I—I mean..." He paused, flustered, unwilling to hurt her. "There was a thing like this once before, Beebo, and it just wasn't true. Leo proved it. He'll get Mom out of this, he always does. There's always some jerk waiting around to throw a scandal at the movie stars." He sneaked a look at her to see if he was helping any.

"*I* know it's not true, Beebo, so don't worry," he said putting his hand on her arm "You know I don't believe that junk. You kid around, but you wouldn't do anything like that."

Beebo looked away from him. "I wouldn't hurt your mother—" she began.

"I know," he said, with surprising warmth and sympathy. "She'll be okay, don't worry. The thing that scares me is…well, I don't want you to leave us, Beebo. You've done so much for us. Besides, who'd help me with my biology? Honest—these gossipers—they'll say anything about anybody."

Beebo was touched by his anxiety. "I'm not going anywhere, buddy," she said. But she meant, *Not right now. Tomorrow, I may have no choice.* And Toby realized it.

Beebo was a thin line away from despair. All the charmingly confessed selfishness that had seemed adorable in Venus at first had become Beebo's prison.

And having nothing else to do, Beebo studied Venus's faults as never before. The self-love, the endless clichés. Venus might laugh at them, but she couldn't abandon them. People said there was only one great glamour queen left in Hollywood: Venus Bogardus. And Venus thought they meant her trimmings—her velvet-paved boudoirs and flashy conceits; not her Self.

Beebo loved her with excited fascination still. And Venus loved Beebo as well and truly as she knew how. More, certainly, than anyone but Toby. And yet…was that enough?

Beebo stood looking out the window of her room at twilight, taking in the grounds of the estate and the evening star. Venus. So high and bright and beautiful. And as far out of reach at that moment as ever it was when she was growing up back in Juniper Hill.

That night, when she tried to write to Jack again, she spoiled her page twice with tears and gave it up. She was trying not to admit that Venus had no room in her life for a gay lover; that theirs was a time-bomb romance, set to explode in their faces. The papers had lighted the fuse. And Beebo, looking at that perfect point of light in the black sky, knew in her heart that her days with Venus were numbered.

The morning of that crucial Tuesday, a nationally syndicated columnist who wielded huge power in Hollywood said she was checking a New York source for verification of a shocking news item about one of the town's greatest stars...a woman, currently headlining a TV series.

Two other columnists pretended special information on the same subject, but all refused to reveal their information or describe the scandal till it was authenticated.

Venus was on trial that night. One columnist had snickered, "If Leo doesn't mind, I don't know why I should. After all, he's been through this a dozen times."

Even at that they had let her off pretty easily. But the atmosphere around her crackled. Fortunately, advance notices on *Baby* were good. They had had a good schedule and an extravagant budget. And Leo, with bench-coaching from Beebo, had wheedled a radiant performance out of his wife.

Venus and Leo watched the broadcast on monitors at Television City with the whole *Baby* company, and went on afterwards to a baroque party on the famous Restaurant Row of LaCienega Boulevard. They hit most of the eateries, picking up celebrities en route, and capping the bash at the home of a popular singer who had guest-starred on the opener.

The party was noisy and crazy, and Venus, a showstopper in silver sequins, took Hollywood under her thumb, with the subtly effective aid of her husband. She had her arms around every man present at least once, as graceful and captivating as any lovely woman aware of her success. When she was twitted about the dark secrets mentioned in the papers, she laughed and told everyone she was screwing her cat, and the whole subject was swept away in the laughter that followed. Only Leo remained grave, smiling slightly and talking, but inwardly seething.

And Venus, if the truth were known, was even more disturbed than he.

❧

Beebo saw the show in the Bogardus rec room with Toby. The house was eerily quiet. All the servants had been given the night off, except Venus's correspondence secretary, a fussily officious young man; and Mrs. Sack, who never went anywhere anyway.

The show had hardly started before the phone began to ring: telegrams, roses at the front gate, long distance rhapsodies. The secretary took the calls, but Beebo and Toby picked up the red wall-phone and listened in to some.

At the station break, the secretary put his head in and said, "Beebo? Telegram for you." He handed her the yellow envelope.

Beebo felt the bottom of her stomach sink southward. She was sure it couldn't be good news. Not when she had left so much angry confusion behind in New York.

The wire was from Jack: "Get home, pal. N.Y. safer than L.A. Couple of people want your scalp. Jack."

What does he want me to do, go back and give it to them? she wondered, taking her worry out on Jack.

"Was it bad news?" Toby said, looking at her face. Beebo pursed her lips and nodded.

"A friend in New York. He says my enemies want me dead."

Toby paled, started to ask about it, and suddenly turned back to the TV screen as if afraid to know the truth.

When the show was over, Toby and Beebo went for a walk on the lawn, meandering side by side and speaking little. Beebo was full of the shadow-image of Venus on the screen; glittering, gorgeous, inaccessible. Finally Toby stopped in a garden path, standing stiff-legged and staring back at the lighted windows of the empty living room. "Beebo," he said. "You're not going to leave, are you?" It was not just Beebo he feared to lose. It was his mother as well.

Beebo's hands curled into fists. "I don't know," she said, so softly it was hard to hear her. She knew she was going to have to, that she was way beyond herself here. And yet not even the discouragements of boredom, shame, and abstinence had completely crushed her. She kept thinking of how it might have been.

"I feel so bad about it all," Toby said. "They have no right to say those things about you. It makes me sick. Stay with us, Beebo. Leo will take care of you."

His faith in Leo moved her. She wished she could risk the truth with him, without destroying him. She wished he could know somehow what she was, and that the knowledge would not make him loathe her.

Beebo stood beside him, silent in the night, letting him rant against the cruel accusations in the papers with youthful outrage, protesting his trust and affection, and she felt a terrible sob coming up in her throat.

Leo had forbidden her to tell him she was his mother's lover. But it was the meanest sort of cowardice to let him stand there and thank her, and beg her to stay on, when all the while she was betraying his gratitude.

"Nobody in this world ever did so much for Mom and me," he was saying. "Honest, Beebo. If you go now, it would ruin everything. I don't see—"

"Toby, stop it! Please! Oh, God," Beebo cried. The sob broke and her voice went hoarse. "Stop it, stop it, stop it!" She covered her face with her hands for a few agonized moments. Toby stared at her as if she had taken leave of her senses, very much distressed at her sudden explosion. He tried clumsily to calm her.

"Did I say something wrong?" he asked apologetically.

"It's no use, Toby," Beebo cried, so brokenhearted that he was stunned. "I have to go."

"Go where?"

"New York."

"You said there were people back there who want to hurt you," he objected, turning white again. "Beebo, if that's true, you *can't* go. I won't let you."

"Anything would be better than here," she said, looking at him in torment. "They'll flay me alive out here—if not tomorrow, then the next day. Oh, Toby, I'm sorry, I'm so sorry." The sobs silenced her for a minute. "Please believe me. I wouldn't do this to you for the world, only—"

Toby turned and walked away.

She pursued him, calling anxiously, "Toby! Toby, wait!" She caught up as he was letting himself down gingerly on a stone bench, moving for all the world like an old man with bursitis. Beebo joined him, reaching out to touch him, then pulling back when he turned away.

"I don't understand," she heard him murmur. "I told you—Leo—don't you believe me? He can help—if it were true, but it's not—"

He frightened her. The words were so breathless and disjointed, the voice so small and hurt. He was rocking back and forth, as if shaken with sobs, but there was not the slightest sound audible now from his throat. "Toby? Are you all right?" Beebo said.

He moved around, again with that strange parody of crippled age, and seemed about to answer her, when all of a sudden he startled her by springing straight into the air with a weird howl. In the elapsed time of less than a second, Beebo realized he hadn't sprung at all; he had been thrown upright by the abruptly powerful tensing of his entire muscular system. He was having an epileptic seizure.

And before she could move to help, he had fallen forward, rigid as a cigar store Indian. He struck his head on a decorative rock across the path when he hit the ground. Beebo cried out, horrified, and then dashed to his side, lifting him carefully off the gravel and onto the soft grass.

Her years of experienced with sick animals and illness steadied her a little. She knew he mustn't swallow his tongue but it was too late to put anything between his teeth. His jaws were locked shut. She rolled him gently on his side, thinking that he could breathe better and would be less likely to choke on his own saliva, which came foaming out of his clenched jaws. He was quivering like a vibrator machine and groaning uncontrollably while the white suds oozed from his mouth. It was a ghostly wail that made Beebo shiver. And yet she knew that a seizure—even one as alarming to see as this one—shouldn't be a cause for panic. Aside from his contortions, it was the blow on his head that worried her, but she couldn't get a look at it.

Toby's feet were pointed downward, tight and hard as a toe dancer's, and his arms were glued to his sides. Beebo was relieved when finally she felt him go limp. But it was then that she saw his forehead and gasped. There was a gash in it, deep and ragged. She began to tremble with alarm. Now that Toby was relaxed, the wound opened like a fountain. Such quantities of blood flowed over his face and onto Beebo and the ground beneath them that she felt almost sick.

She tried to pick him up, but her legs failed her momentarily and she collapsed beside him, sweating frantically.

"This won't help him, idiot!" she berated himself. "Get up!" She tried again and made it, desperate to get him in the house and clean the wound. She wanted help, anybody, a doctor—Mrs. Sack. "Mrs. Sack!" she shouted suddenly, but there was no sound from the house. Mrs. Sack's room was on the other side on the top floor and she would never hear Beebo calling from the lawn below.

Beebo lifted Toby and carried him into the house. She put him down on a satin-upholstered sofa, watching with pity and fear as the red blood soaked into the pink silk. She pressed her bare hand down hard on the wound and the flow abated slightly. Nearby was one of the house intercom phones, and Beebo reached it with her free hand.

"Mrs. Sack," she said breathlessly. "I'm in the living room with Toby. He had an attack and hit his head. Call the doctor and then get down here—fast!"

Mrs. Sack rushed into the living room moments later, armed with rolls of gauze and tape and disinfectants. She stopped at the sight of Toby, so limp and colorless, except for the scarlet stains on his face and the sofa.

"I've been waiting for something like this all my life," she said grimly. Beebo was astonished to see how firm and fearless she was; not at all the comfortable muffin she seemed when all was well with her boy. "We've had some bad falls before, but not like this."

"Is the doctor coming?" Beebo asked.

"Yes, in ten minutes." She knelt by Toby, washing the wound while Beebo watched.

"Shall I call Venus?" Beebo said.

"No," said Mrs. Sack emphatically. "She's worse than nothing in a crisis. She goes all to pieces. It doesn't help Toby and it certainly doesn't help the doctor."

Beebo thought, *I should be grateful she's here—she knows just what to do.* And yet she was distressed to think that Venus should be playing goddess at a party while her son lay hurt and bleeding—and no one was making a move to tell her.

"She has to be told, Mrs. Sack," Beebo said.

"Go and tell her, if you must," Mrs. Sack said. "She can meet us at the hospital. At least over there they can give her a sedative."

Beebo stood uncertainly by the phone, trying to picture herself walking in on the fancy party in her bloody slacks; infinitely preferring to call.

Mrs. Sack looked around. "Beebo, this boy is more my child than hers—she says so herself," she said unexpectedly. "All his life he's come to me when he was hurt, and I'm the one who knows how to care for him. Not her. It's my job. My life." She was as proud and strong in her words as a soldier bristling with defense.

To Beebo, staring at her, it became clear that Venus didn't just give Toby up. Toby was deftly taken from her by this plump, kind-hearted woman who never had a child of her own, but was obviously made to mother one. She believed Toby was truly her child because Venus had forfeited her right to him, even the right to be there to comfort him and patch his wounds.

"Mrs. Bogardus could have had him when he was born," Mrs. Sack went on, ministering to Toby. "But she practically threw him at me. And I was overjoyed to have a little son to raise and love. She can't walk in here like a queen and demand him back, just because he cuts himself and scares her."

Beebo went over and patted Mrs. Sack's shoulders. "I'm sorry," she said gently. "Nobody's criticizing you, Mrs. Sack. But Venus is his mother, no matter how much you've done for him or how much you love him."

"If you call that woman," Mrs. Sack said, turning around and standing up to italicize her words, "*I will not be responsible* for the condition of this boy. Beebo, you're a nice youngster and you're his friend. It'll be bad enough for Venus to see him at the hospital, but if she comes racing in here shrieking bloody murder, she's likely to make Toby believe it. Do you want a sick boy or a dead one on your conscience?"

Beebo ran a distraught hand through her hair. "But Mrs. Sack, I *can't* go get her."

"Nonsense. Just change your clothes and drive over. It should take you about half an hour, and by that time the doctor will be with us and Toby will be at the hospital."

"But the papers…" Beebo muttered.

"I don't read the papers, Beebo. But I'm quite sure they'll forgive you for getting the mother of a sick boy from a party." She had turned back to Toby. "It's an emergency and there's no one else to go."

"What about Rod—her secretary?"

"He doesn't drive. And besides, he overdramatizes everything. He'd really fix Mrs. Bogardus." Mrs. Sack didn't seem to care whether Beebo ever got there. But Beebo knew Venus had to be told at once. Venus herself had admitted to hysterical behavior in the face of Toby's attacks. Perhaps the only way then was to pick her up and drive her to the hospital, as Mrs. Sack suggested.

Beebo put on some clean clothes in her room, and as she ran down the stairs again, headed for her car, she heard the newly arrived doctor saying on the phone, "Yes, a concussion. Get an ambulance over here." He looked up and saw Beebo.

"Are you Miss Brinker? Get his mother, will you? Tell her not to worry—I don't want two patients on my hands tonight. Better not say much about the wound. Just tell her it's a bump. We're hospitalizing him till the risk of hemorrhage is passed."

"Yes, sir," Beebo said, and ran out to the garage.

She left her car directly in front of the main entrance to the house where the party was, and went in.

"Excuse me, this is a private party—" said a doorman, but Beebo, with that peculiar air of authority that came to rescue her from various crises, interrupted him calmly.

"Where's Miss Bogardus?" she said, scanning the living room. "It's an emergency."

The butler, who read the gossip columns like everyone else, gazed at her with new interest. "I believe she's occupied," he said with a venal smile. Beebo gave him a twenty-dollar bill, too worried even to begrudge it.

"You'll find her in the back gardens. Out the French doors," he said, gesturing toward them.

Beebo strode through the champagne-stained living room. Many a famous face glanced at her, and a columnist whispered to his scribe to take notes.

She slipped through the heavy shadows bordering the spotlighted garden. Venus was at the farthest corner. Beebo simply looked for the heaviest concentration of men. In the center, slim and straight in her coruscating sequins, stood Venus Bogardus: a silver exclamation point in the purple dark.

Too much shivaree had followed Beebo out of the house for

Venus to be unaware of it. Leo alerted her at almost the exact moment her eyes fell on her lover. There was a half-second of undressed fury visible in her eyes, flashing brighter than her dazzling gown. And then she pulled her pride across her face like a veil.

Beebo walked toward her, her mission making her impossibly sure of herself. The two women eyed each other as Beebo approached down an aisle of staring men, like an infernal bridegroom passing through an honor guard of devils. Luckily, neither Beebo nor Venus were people to collapse in the face of public shock.

Silence fell, except from Leo, who said clearly, "I'll tell you just once, Beebo. *Leave.* You're fired, and I never want to see you again." He spoke softly but in the hushed garden his voice carried to the audience of Hollywood topnotchers.

"Fired? I never worked for you, Leo," Beebo said.

"Venus, tell her to go," Leo ordered his wife.

But Venus, watching Beebo, loved her enough to feel instinctively that Beebo would not come to humiliate her in public without a drastic reason. With her characteristic public calm, so different from the histrionics she indulged in private, she walked boldly to Beebo and said, "All right, what is it?"

Beebo hadn't even time to take a breath before she heard Leo say, "By God, you get that kid out of here or I will."

Venus ignored him, walking toward the house with Beebo coming close in her wake. But this was once that Leo would not let himself be flouted in front of his friends. He had to bring Venus to heel as a matter of pride, and not only because he considered her action self-destructive. It seemed as if Venus were making a donkey of him before God and the world as payment for the years of tolerance and love and patience he had spent on her. It was too much for him. He caught up with her, spun her around, and brushed Beebo aside.

"Tell her to get out of our lives, or I'll take her apart," he said. He so rarely threatened Venus that he scared her. But Beebo faced him. "Leo, why in hell do you think I'm here? I came—"

He didn't let her finish. "You cocky little bitch, you want it all, don't you? Even her ruination! After all I told you."

"Let me explain!" Beebo said, alarmed now like Venus. But Leo reached out with icy rage and slapped her face. A red storm swirled up suddenly in Beebo, and she lit into him so hard that for several amazed seconds, he let himself be punched. But when he got his bearings he was after her with all the tornado fury of a cuckolded husband. Every man who had ever shared a bed with Venus Bogardus got a souvenir sock that night—and every girl. Only it was Beebo who took the blows.

She fought well enough, but Leo came on with a wild single-minded lust for vengeance that had her back in the grass before long, heaving for breath, cut and bruised. She would never surrender, and Leo, possessed by years of bitter grievances and pent-up vengeance, was in no mood to be merciful.

Beebo, sinking beneath his punishment, became aware at last that the blows had ceased. She heard Leo give a cry and opened her eyes to see Venus, shoe in hand, glaring at him. She turned to Beebo and her face softened. "Can you get up?" she asked. "I'll take you home."

Leo put a hand to the back of his head where the sharp heel had cut his scalp. He brought his fingers away, wet and red, and turned to look at his wife. But Venus, taking advantage of his brief confusion, had pulled Beebo to her feet and rushed her through the house toward the car.

The crowd surging after them deterred Leo's chase just enough to prevent him from catching them as they drove away. An uneasy silence settled on the party as the silver coupé sped off. Nobody knew what to say to Leo. But he left almost at once, making brusque apologies to his host.

"Well," said the smug voice of a Hollywood observer, who wrote for one of the trades, "I guess it's true, after all. I wasn't going to print it."

"Print what? What?" the crowd chorused eagerly.

"The tip I got from New York last week."

"I got it, too," a woman reporter piped up. "I thought it was sour grapes, but I have my people checking it."

The guests began to rumble for enlightenment, but the first gossipist said, "Read it in the morning paper, friends." And he left with several other members of the movie press, all chattering as they walked down the drive.

Beebo slumped in the front seat, her head against the window, mute with pain for several moments.

"We'll take you home and clean up those cuts, darling," Venus said, wincing at the sight of them when she stopped for a light.

Beebo shook her head. "Dr. Pitman has Toby at the hospital," she said. "That's what I came about."

"What?" Venus was so shaken she almost lost control of the car. Beebo had to grab the wheel from her. "It's okay, honey, he's going to be all right," she said quickly. "He had a seizure, that's all."

"God, I knew it was something awful the minute I saw your face," Venus cried as the car moved erratically down the street. "And that sonofabitch husband of mine had to pound you to pieces—"

"Don't blame Leo," Beebo said, her voice soft and drained. "I don't. It wasn't me he was hitting so much as all the people who came before me."

Venus was crying and Beebo tried to make her stop the car. "Toby's had dozens of seizures in his life, but they didn't put him in the hospital. What aren't you telling me?" Venus said.

"He fell," Beebo said. "We were walking in the garden after the show. He had a seizure and fell, and his head struck a rock. He has a cut on the forehead, but—"

"Oh, dear God!" Venus gasped, and Beebo said, "Stop the car. Damn it, Venus!"

"But we have to get to the hospital—"

"In one piece," Beebo said. "I'll drive."

"You're in no shape—" Venus began, but Beebo broke in, "I'm in better shape than you are." She made Venus slide over on the front seat while Beebo walked painfully around the car. Her wounds were the sharp residue of Leo's wrath—but her head was clear. She started the motor, and told Venus firmly, "Toby's going to live, and so am I."

Venus looked down at her sparkling knees, trying to control her weeping.

"Look, honey, if you have any ideas about running to Toby with tears streaming down your face, and carrying on as if the end were near, so help me, I'm going to join Mrs. Sack's team. She said that's exactly what you'd do."

"She's wrong," Venus said. It was just enough to prick her conscience into action, and she wiped her eyes while they were still flowing.

Neither of them said anything more about Toby or the coming storm with Leo and the papers till they reached the hospital. Venus insisted that Beebo accompany her inside, and Beebo acceded to keep her from getting frantic.

Toby had a concussion, all right. They were making a spinal tap to determine the extent of pressure, if any, on the brain, and to relieve it surgically if necessary. It was urgent to do this as promptly as possible, to avoid brain damage.

"The blow was pretty hard," Dr. Pitman told them while a nurse dressed Beebo's wounds in Toby's room, at Venus's request. No one dared to question Beebo about them. Venus said imperiously, "She's hurt. Can you help her?" But her eyes were wild and her thoughts all with Toby.

"Fortunately," the doctor went on, while Venus bent over her son, peaked and scarcely conscious on the hospital bed, "the skull is thick and tough in the front, with heavier bone than in the back. A blow to the back, of the same force as the one Toby sustained, might have done serious damage. As it is, I'm as concerned about the blood loss as the concussion. We're preparing a transfusion. He'll feel a good deal stronger after that than he does now."

Dr. Pitman looked curiously at Venus. "I must say, Miss Bogardus, you're taking this better than I expected."

"Mama?" Toby whispered, and Venus clutched one of his hands in both of hers.

"Yes, Toby," she said.

"Am I going to be all right?" He looked at her. "I feel so punk."

"Yes, darling, you are," she said.

He shut his eyes, reassured, and Venus turned away to cover a sob. The doctor gave her an "I-should-have-known" look and helped her to the door.

"You're very tired," he said. "Do you still have some of those yellow pills I gave you at home? All right, I want you to take one and try to rest. You can do Toby more good in the morning, when both of you are feeling better."

Venus tried to object, but Pitman pulled Beebo aside and said hastily, "I've been treating her for years. I know how she can be. If she doesn't sleep tonight, we'll see real fireworks, and that will set Toby back if she gets at him."

Beebo looked at the boy, resting now as the nurses prepared his arm for the blood transfusion, his head neatly bandaged. "Is he really going to be okay, doctor?" she said. "You convince me, and I'll convince Venus."

"I think so," Dr. Pitman said, but his concern was still plain on his face. "To be honest, there is always some risk with any head injury—especially with an epilepsy patient. He needs absolute peace and quiet and as little movement as possible, until the danger of internal hemorrhage is past…but he's young and sturdy, and we'll have a twenty-four-hour watch on him. I do believe, Miss Brinker, that his mother will only be in our way tonight. We'll call immediately if there's any change for the worse, but I don't anticipate one now."

Beebo took Venus out of the hospital in stages, letting her fold up and rest on chairs in the hall on their way, till she had her in the car and could drive her home.

Venus was forced to expend her frustrated maternal impulses on her hurt lover instead of her hurt child. She investigated and re-dressed all of Beebo's bruises, making small noises of reproof and pity.

"Thanks for braving that party, darling," Venus told her. "I'd have died of self-contempt if you hadn't let me know."

"Toby would have been all right."

"Maybe. But I wouldn't. It would have killed me to let Mrs. Sack do it all again. Especially now when Toby and I are getting so close."

"Where do you suppose Leo is?" Beebo said, touching a cut with careful fingers.

"I'll be damned if I know. Or care," Venus said harshly. "I thought for sure he'd be here, waiting to skin both of us alive. He'll be around sooner or later, you can bet on that." She sighed, leaving Beebo to turn on the radio by her bed. "I wish they had let me stay with Toby," she said. "I'm ashamed that they couldn't."

"You can see him first thing in the morning," Beebo comforted her.

Venus unzipped her sequins and dropped them in a starry heap on a chair. Fifteen hundred dollars' worth of dress and she treated it like a dishcloth. There was nothing underneath it but her shoes, which she kicked off.

Beebo put a hand gently on Venus's neck, massaging it a little. "Maybe this is a poor time to bring it up," she said softly. "But we have to talk, Venus. I—I love you, but I can't stand living this way, honey. I realized something in front of those people at the party: I was on trial. My life, my love for you, my self. I can never love you openly, like a human being. They don't give me credit for being human."

"Beebo!" Venus said, looking at her with a shocked face. "Don't say such ugly things. You're talking about the girl I adore."

Beebo looked away. "I'm not the kind of person I want to be, Venus. Not the kind I want you to love. I'd rather die than hurt you, but I feel as if I'm dying anyway...of shame and...well, doubt about us. I want to love you somehow without it torturing us both. And I can't."

"I know," Venus said, and Beebo sensed their mutual hopelessness. She embraced her and Venus began to cry. "When I saw him beating you tonight, I could have killed him," she said, her voice rusty with tears. "It took all the meanness out of me. I just wanted to console you. Beebo, whatever happens to us, always believe that I loved you—I *love* you."

"I promise," Beebo said, but the past tense gave her a premonition of what was coming. "What do you mean, whatever happens?"

"I mean, the papers, and the rest of it. I have to deny everything, Beebo. I have to pretend you're nothing to me. Oh, darling, understand why!" It was a declaration of love that struck Beebo's heart.

"I understand," Beebo said, and thought she did. But she didn't get quite all of it. For Venus was saying goodbye to her. Beebo didn't know that this loveliest night they would spend together would be the last. She had thought all along that when the end came, she would pick her own time and day to go; not that the whole thing would be out of her control.

Venus said nothing, did nothing, to spoil the night. She was silent about Toby, even though her heart contracted at the thought of him, and she ached to be beside him. She spoke only words of love to Beebo.

Beebo, surprised at Venus's ardor, gave in at first to humor her, and finally found herself forgetting even the bruises and cuts on her body.

The night was mild and the stars were sprinkled thick as spilled soapflakes across the sky. Venus pushed aside the sliding door to her patio, and they danced out there a while on a rug of cool grass, moving with the music and the air and the three o'clock mocking bird, arch-deep in the tickling soft grass.

Beebo felt as if she could have held and loved her fabulous lady forever. When she leaned down to kiss Venus's face, her cheek was wet.

"Oh, it's nothing, darling," Venus assured her. "I'm just a sentimental idiot. Say you love me and I'll recover."

"I love you," Beebo said. "I love you, Venus." And to her surprise, her mind was with Paula Ash for a moment. It staggered her a little. Venus stopped dancing and looked up at her in the moonlight. "Do you? Really?" she asked. It wasn't just a woman's endless need to be told over and over. It was the knowledge that she wouldn't hear it again after this night had passed.

Venus loved her enough to hope that when she sent her away in the morning—for she would have to—Beebo's wounds would heal and she would be able to think back on their love without the regret that rots so many sweet memories.

"Beebo, promise me one last thing, darling, and then I'll shut up."

Beebo squeezed her, turning her tenderly to the rhythm of a waltz. "I'll promise you that moon on a platter if you want it."

"Promise me you'll remember this night as long as you live. Everything about it. The stars inches over our heads, and the music, and the grass, and..." The famous voice broke and she cried again.

Beebo picked her up and sat with her on a bamboo garden chair. "Darling, what's the matter?" she demanded.

"Oh, Toby and—the damn gossipists. I don't know. It'll never be the same for us, Beebo."

Beebo, full of apprehensions, had no comfort to offer her now, except to hold her tight. Then Venus slipped from her arms to the feathery grass and Beebo followed her down, and there were no more questions or tears or promises. Nothing but beautiful oblivion till the trespassing sun announced the morning.

Beebo awoke, a head-to-toe bouquet of blue bruises from the jolting Leo had given her. But it hardly bothered her. Venus had loved her so warmly all night that she was half-ready to hope they could work out some sort of compromise; half-ready to give in to more months of demoralizing secrecy, if it could be like that every night.

Venus called the hospital the moment she awakened, and they reassured her that Toby was no worse; in fact, seemed better.

She hung up, looking as blue as before her call. "Now we have to face Leo," she said.

"He won't eat you alive, honey," Beebo said.

Venus paled suddenly. "Look!" she said, pointing at her dresser. Beebo saw the telltale glass, still coated with orange juice. "He's already been in looking for trouble." Venus stole a glance at Beebo, so young and handsome, so vulnerable to the worst ostracism society could offer; and her heart swelled. *I can't hurt her,* she thought in anguish.

I've had twenty years of adulation and I've got more money than I'll ever use. She began to wonder if she had the guts to go with Beebo after all. *What the hell, I've never loved anybody like this before. Am I afraid to stick to the one person who knows how to make me happy?*

It gave her the courage to try, at least, to defend Beebo against her formidable and stubborn husband.

While she was preoccupied with these thoughts the bedroom door opened. Beebo was just pulling her shoes on, sitting on the edge of the bed in her clothes of the night before. She stiffened, expecting Leo, but it was the corresponding secretary again. "Another telegram," he said to her. "For you."

"Thanks, Rod." Beebo got up to take it and was about to open it when she heard him say, "Good morning, Mr. Bogardus," and there was Leo. He dismissed Rod with a wave of his hand and Beebo stepped aside wordlessly to let him enter the bedroom. He had a lighted cigar—a bad sign—and another glass of orange juice in his hand. Beebo thrust the telegram in her pocket and followed him in, shutting the door.

"All right," Leo said. "We're adults, and we aren't going to scream at each other. Let me talk first if you please. Beebo, are you all right?"

His board-meeting tone, typical though it was of him, offended her more than an explosion of fury would have. "Relax, Leo, you won't have to pay any more doctor bills," she said. She was pleased to see that she had given him a shiner.

"I've been to the hospital. I was there all night. I can understand your concern at the party, Beebo. But let me remind you that this house is full of telephones, any one of which would have got a call through to Venus."

"Leo, Mrs. Sack told me Venus would—"

"But you preferred to repay my kindness to you by shaming me in public."

"The doctor said it, too: Venus would get hysterical if she heard over the phone that Toby was hurt and had to be hospitalized."

"You know it's true, Leo," Venus said softly.

"I didn't go there to shame you, Leo," Beebo said. "It's bad enough being holed up in this fort like a prisoner of war, but not so bad I'd do that to you. I just want you to believe one thing: I was really scared about Toby, and I never thought of anything but getting you and Venus to him as fast as I could."

Leo finished his glass of juice while she talked. "I believe you," he said. "I also believe you could have sent somebody else and spared us what we're about to go through—all of us. I've been tolerant about Venus's lovers in the past because they were vital to her existence. But none of them ever treated me like a sucker."

"Beebo has always treated you respectfully, Leo," Venus interrupted heatedly. "It isn't you she's rebelling against; it's the way we've made her live."

"What other way is there? Did she think she'd be your escort at parties? Meet all your friends? I think I've had to put up with a hell of a lot more than Beebo has. All the worry of this queer situation has been on my shoulders. Christ, I never could understand why a woman would want anything to do with another woman that way, anyway. And if she did, why love a woman who does everything possible to make herself look like a boy? Why not love a real woman? Or a real man? If you want a lover in pants, Venus, I'm available. I have been for years, and I still love you, though God alone knows why.

"If you want to love a female, don't run after a mistake of Nature like Beebo Brinker."

"Leo, that's brutal!" Venus cried. "Beebo can't help how she was born. Good God, do you think any human being would deliberately choose to live with a problem like this? Leo, there are homosexuals in this world—I'm one myself—emotional strays of one kind or another, who at least have the comfort and privacy of an inconspicuous body to live in. The shelter of a normal sex on one side of the fence or the other."

"Are you trying to stir my pity for her?" Leo said.

"I don't want your lousy pity!" Beebo said.

"I'm trying to make you see how it feels," Venus said urgently. "Leo, what if you'd been raised as a boy and learned to be a man, and had to do it all inside a female body? What if you had all your masculine feelings incarcerated under a pair of breasts? What would you do with yourself? How could you live? Who would be your lover?"

Leo nodded, answering slowly. "That's what I'm saying: it's not an easy life, nor a desirable one, no matter where Beebo lives it. And I know she didn't pick it out. But whether you two like it or not, she is a freak. And I am sorry for her. Now, Venus—do you want me to sit by and watch that kid wreck the career I've spent twenty years of my life to build? Yours, my dear—all yours!"

"I don't want it!" Venus shouted stridently, wanting to hurt and frighten Leo.

But Beebo was recalling Leo's words: "If you ever mean more to her than her career, I'll lose her. I won't let that happen. I'll fight you—I'm warning you, Beebo." When she thought of leaving Venus, she meant to leave a path open behind her for an occasional meeting, a correspondence, a night together now and then when Venus was in New York. But Leo was about to sabotage even that small hope. She looked at him and caught her own thoughts in his eyes.

"That shellacking I gave you was only the opening round, Beebo. Unless you're ready and willing right now to walk out of here and never come back. Never call, never write, never speak to Venus or see her again. *Never.*"

"Leo, I love this girl!" Venus said. "If you insist on kicking her out of my home, you can kick me out with her." It was not what she had thought she would say when the time came. She felt a sort of amazed pride in her foolish bravery.

Beebo, too, was overcome with gratitude, yet wondering at the same time what recriminations Venus would vent on her as the weeks and months went by, if they did leave together. Where would they go, with Venus as notorious as she was? The thought of running away with her—of being tied to her for life—alarmed Beebo in spite of herself.

Leo walked to his wife and spoke straight in her face. "Fine," he said. "Go with her, Venus. Never mind losing your money, your name...and your son. Not to mention me. The things that have sustained you all these years. Ditch them all.

"What for? For your bargain, here: Beebo. She'll love and protect you better than I can, no doubt. You're thirty-eight years old and you won't have that face of yours so damn much longer. If you quit now, it'll go to hell in a hurry. By the time Beebo's twenty-eight, you'll be nudging fifty. Probably a grandmother with a face full of charming crow's feet. Every night you and Beebo will sit by the TV and watch old Bogardus movies on the late late show."

Beebo and Venus stared at him.

"You won't have your face or your fortune or your home, or me to fight your battles, or Toby to love and respect you at last. You won't have Toby at all, for that matter. Do this, Venus, and you've lost him forever. No state board in its right mind would give custody of a child to an infamous Lesbian who'd surround him with scandal and expose him to homosexual obscenities—even if the child himself wanted to be with her, which he damn well would not.

"And what do you trade Toby for? A big, overgrown, penniless butch with no job and no prospects for one, who'll dump you the minute that face and body begin to sag."

"You bastard!" Beebo shot at him, appalled.

"Shut up, Beebo," he said coolly. "Do you have a job?"

"No, but—"

"Do you deny you're gay?"

"No, but—"

"Do you deny Venus would lose everything if she went with you? Do you love her so much you can't wait to destroy her?"

"Leo, for the love of God—"

"For the love of my wife I say these hard things!" he shouted at Beebo. "You were warned. You have no business standing there now with a slack jaw. What will you do, take a cold-water flat in Greenwich Village and live on love till you get hungry and cold? Do you think Venus Bogardus can go anywhere in the world right now with the papers headlining her lewd romance with another woman? 'Venus Bogardus, queen of hearts, has found a queen of her own.'" He was quoting, unknown to the two women, the morning's gossip columns.

Venus, thinking he had made it up, turned all her famous fury on him. "Get out of this house, you stinking dog!" she cried. "I never want to see you or hear your filth again!"

"I'll be over at Sam's when you're ready to call me," Leo said, referring to the friend who took him in whenever Venus turned him out.

"I'll never call you!" she screamed at his retreating back. It was always her parting shot. Later in the day she would pick up the phone and tell him that even though he was a sonofabitch, she guessed he'd better come home. Miss Pinch had just squeezed a batch of fresh orange juice.

At the door Leo picked up a stack of newspaper columns, torn from the morning papers, and held them out to Venus. "These will pass the time while Beebo is packing," he said, but Venus refused to glance at them. Beebo, in the grip of a spiraling alarm, took them instead.

Leo looked at her. "I'm sorry I had to hurt you," he said. "If you weren't so young you might have handled things better. I got hurt too, Beebo. The most I can hope for now is to save Venus and Toby. It'll take all my ingenuity—and maybe all my money. And I have to start at once. Just like you have to get gone."

She didn't answer him, but she felt moved, realizing slowly that he needed her pity as much as she needed his. She could never forgive him for calling her a freak, and yet it had been a valuable lesson in the prevailing attitude toward mannish women.

Jack had been sympathetic and patient with her. Pat, himself quite feminine, had responded to her much the way that the Lesbians who liked her did. Even the people back in Juniper Hill had been pretty used to her most of her life. They watched her grow up and while they laughed unkindly and sometimes lied about her, still they had never said to her face the things Leo Bogardus had said. Beebo damned well had to stand up and fight back, or lose her self-respect forever.

Her gaze fell on the pile of columns in her hand, as Leo left them alone. Venus tried to throw them all in the wastebasket, till she saw the spreading shock on Beebo's face. She read over Beebo's shoulder, holding her breath:

"Venus Bogardus, ruler of the heart of men the world over, is ruled herself, it seems: by a WOMAN! Is this true, or just vicious gossip? Readers of my column know I never use any but the most carefully validated tips from reliable sources. This one has been double-checked and we can say positively: the handsome youngster sharing the Bogardus manse as companion to Venus's son is really the apple of the movie star's eye. Is Venus Bogardus really one of those unfortunate misfits, a LESBIAN? Leo, do you know about this? Does your stepson know it? Our hearts are with you in this difficult situation.

"Readers who doubt me may ask themselves if I would dare to print such an accusation under the threat of legal action from Miss Bogardus, if it were false. No! I would never, etc., etc...."

Beebo shuffled through the others quickly. It was the top story in all the trades and made full columns in the big L.A. dailies. She looked at Venus and saw such a pallor on her face that she was afraid Venus would drop where she stood. Beebo helped her to her satin-draped bed, where Venus deflated in a heap.

Beebo stood beside her, her hands crammed into her pockets, afraid to touch her. At last she asked, "Does this mean I have to go right now? Alone?" She knew it did; she had known all along it was coming. Yet here they were, and the time was upon them, and it was abysmally hard to do. Strangely, she found herself picturing Paula again. It comforted her. Not that she had any illusions about a warm welcome from Paula. But even the thought of a fight with the little redhead was better than the thought of not seeing her at all.

Beebo touched Venus's long hair gently. "A few minutes ago you were telling Leo he'd have to kick you out, too, if he wanted me to go." It wasn't kind to remind Venus, and yet it was a relief in a way.

"Oh, darling, I'm such a coward," Venus said brokenly. "I can't bear it. Where in hell did they find out? Miss Pinch would never tell. The others don't like me, but they wouldn't do anything to ruin Leo. Besides, I was never around during the day and at night we were so careful. How in hell—?"

Beebo knew perfectly well how it got out. She touched the telegram in her pocket fearfully, and Venus saw her face change and guessed. "Your friends in New York?" she asked.

Beebo pulled out the wire. Jack had written: "Hope this catches you before the sky falls, pal. If not, chin up. We love you. I found out too late from Pat that Mona wired the Hollywood press. Come home and ride out the storm. This is a time for friends to help you, not lovers. Jack."

Beebo folded it with the meticulous care you give to the oddments of life that happen to be in your hands when pain strikes; each fold careful, straight, and neat—as tidy as her life was not. There is an obscure comfort in smoothing a small piece of paper to its ultimate neatness. It seems a symbol of order and reason that must somehow rescue you from the chaos of suffering. It eases the misery that wants to pour out of your eyes and wail from your throat.

"My friends in New York," Beebo said huskily, "are still my friends. My enemies in New York did this to me. Venus, Venus..." She shook her head. "I don't know what to say. I've been trying to tell you, but I didn't know how. I thought we could part lovers and come together again, still lovers, some day."

Venus reached up for her, both of them admitting tacitly that it could never have lasted; neither willing to say the words outright.

But Beebo rejected her arms. "I have to confess something terrible to you," she said. "I—I brought on Toby's attack. I was telling him I thought I would have to leave here, so you wouldn't be hurt by the papers. He got more and more upset and strange...he tried to answer me...and then suddenly he shot up and fell over."

Venus looked away. "It might have happened anyway," she said. "We know so little.... I'm going to lose him, Beebo. He'll never get over this."

"You're wrong. You've got to be! You can't lose all you worked for with him in one stroke like that," Beebo said.

"Maybe Leo can help me," Venus said, the dimmest spark of hope in her eye. "He always seems to put me back together. Maybe he can do it for Toby."

Beebo could see that she was floundering at the prospect of losing the props that had supported her for so long: Leo, Toby, her money, mass love.

"One thing you have I'll never have, darling," Venus told her quietly. "Courage. I'll bet you didn't know how much till now. Maybe you've got it because without it you'd have been destroyed long ago. Well...I hate to admit it, but Leo is my courage. I can't run away with you, even though my heart breaks to let you go." She stopped talking for a minute till her voice steadied a little. "I thought you'd given Toby to me at last, but I'm afraid you've lost him for me forever."

"I hope to God he has better sense than that," Beebo said, kneeling by the bed with her face near Venus's. "I hope he loves both of us more than that, and I think he does. He's brighter and steadier than you are, Venus. Besides, he's lived all his life with a condition that makes him different from ordinary people. Maybe that will help him understand me a little now."

Venus stopped crying and embraced Beebo. "Forgive me," she whispered. "All I want to say to you is, thank you. For the time I had with Toby, for the love you gave me."

For a moment Beebo wanted to stay so badly she was ready to sacrifice her life again—but only for a moment. It was easy to get carried away when you had your arms full of Venus.

"I love you, Beebo," Venus said seriously. "Some day you'll know how it feels when you're my age, and the girl you'll adore forever is yours. And you know it's going to end before long and you'll have to go on living somehow."

Beebo caressed her shoulders without looking at her face. "You'll never say you love me again, will you?" she murmured. "Will you say it to another girl?"

Venus's arms tightened around her. "Will you?" she countered.

"You'll say it to men as long as you live, won't you?" Suddenly it seemed unbearable to Beebo; bad enough to know that other girls would follow her, even if Venus never loved any of them. But intolerable that she would keep on climbing into bed with men, too. Her hands hardened on Venus's shoulders. "God, how I wish

I could make you choose!" she said. "Be gay or be straight. Don't be both. The only other girl I know who's both is contemptible."

Venus answered quietly. "Beebo, you knew what you were early in life. Some of us don't find out till after we've committed ourselves to a man and children. You're one hundred percent gay. You never doubt it. You breathe such easy contempt for me. But darling, believe me, you're the lucky one. You knew yourself in time to save yourself from housewifery and husbands—things the rest of us have to live with.

"But I didn't know till it was too late. It wasn't just all the men I've known that confused me. It was the way I was raised, too, and the girls I knew. It was having a man and a child and a career in my life to defend before I knew I wanted anything else. It was a paralyzing fear of the truth. I didn't have a body like yours that threw the truth at me whether I wanted to see it or not. I could pretend. I pretended with men and men and more men.

"And the more clearly I realized I was gay, the more terrified I was to admit it to myself, and the more I had to lose. Do you have to loathe me for it, Beebo? Am I a sort of second-class Lesbian, is my love a second-class love, because I live with a man and I've borne a child?"

Beebo shut her eyes. "I'm your lover, not your judge," she said, pulling Venus's head down on her shoulder. "All I know is, I hate it—sharing you. If it were another girl, I could fight back on my own ground. But Leo confronts me with marriage and motherhood and morality and…God, what can I say? Tell all of society to go to hell?" She kissed Venus disconsolately. "If you'd known what you were when you were young, would you really have given up all this for the life of a Lesbian? The kind of life I'll lead?"

"If I'd known I could be as happy with a girl as I've been with you, Beebo…and I didn't have my son or a name to worry about… I could have given up anything to be with you."

Beebo couldn't hate her, in spite of the distressing knowledge that she had been used. Venus was no Mona Petry. Venus proved her love and did her utmost to go beyond her limitations for the sake of that love. But she had lived too long in the world of safety and social acceptance that is the normal woman's—a world Beebo would never know—to leave it now. She was imprisoned in the only security she knew, just as Beebo was imprisoned in her body and her strong emotional needs.

"You despise me a little for hiding behind my husband and child," Venus said, seeing it in Beebo's face. "What do you want me to do with them, darling? I love Toby and I need Leo. I can't wish them out of existence. They existed for me long before you did."

"Venus, I don't know what's right or wrong," Beebo said. "I only know I love you—and it's made me miserable. God spare either of us another affair like this one." She caught Venus in an impassioned embrace, holding her hard enough to hurt her and crying soundlessly against her cheek.

Then she released her, walking swiftly to the door. Venus gave a small scream and rushed after her. "Oh, not like this! Wait, stay with me a while. There's no need to go just yet. I need you more than I ever did. Beebo!"

"Don't make it hurt any worse, Venus," she said. "Let's not cut it off an inch at a time." Beebo was the strongest and it was up to her to make the break physical and final.

"Say it one last time, then," Venus pleaded wildly. "I'll never see you again! Beebo, darling—say it!"

"I love you," Beebo said huskily. "Goodbye, lover." She reached out and put her hands on Venus's shoulders to draw her near; kissed her ardently on the lips and then chastely on the brow.

Venus gazed at her, afraid to believe it for a minute, and then dropped her face into her hands with a sob. Beebo left her, running down the curving stairs to the front door. If she were to move at all, it had to be at top speed.

It was raining in New York when Beebo landed at Idlewild, a standard, sharp November rain: liquid ice tumbling out of a dirty sky. She reached Jack's familiar door early in the evening and rang his bell. The answer was immediate, as reassuring as a personal word.

She dashed up the stairs and saw him leaning in the open doorway, waiting for her. Neither of them said a word. Beebo went up and hugged him against her damp jacket. He fit neatly under her chin, letting himself be squashed in the name of friendship.

"Come in, pal," he said.

"I should have wired you. I left in such a damn hurry," she said. "Jack—you aren't even surprised to see me!"

"I read the garbage in this morning's paper," he said. "I didn't think Venus would keep you around long after that. But I have to admit I wasn't prepared for her phone call."

Beebo's mouth fell open. "Venus called *you?*" she said.

"About four hours ago. Said you were flying back. She remembered my name and had her secretary try every Jack, John, and J. Mann in the Manhattan directory," he chuckled. "She sounded very sweet and sad. I was impressed with her—I really was. She said to tell you she loves you."

Beebo leaned forward on the sofa. "Poor Venus," she said, too tired even to feel surprise at her compassion. "She's so afraid I won't believe her. You know something, Jackson? She does love me. That's the craziest part of it. She just isn't strong enough to snap her fingers at the world. And God knows she had more at stake than I had—mostly a son she's just beginning to know and love. I have no business condemning her. But oh my God, it hurts so much. She was so lovely."

Jack sat down beside her. "I know the feeling," he said. "I guess it's the one pain on earth you can always remember perfectly, down to the last mean twinge."

Beebo smiled a bit, putting her head back on the sofa and accepting gratefully a lighted cigarette from Jack.

"How about a peppermint schnapps?" he said. "Or would you prefer Scotch and water?"

"That's more like it."

"It'll warm you up a bit. What a rotten day for a homecoming." The rain pelted the roof and windows with an endless muted rattle. He handed her the drink, making one for himself.

"Thanks, Jack," she said. "You know, it was sunny in California. Eighty-two degrees and not a cloud in the sky."

"I was stationed there a while during World War II. I remember that weather."

The small talk comforted Beebo and the drink relaxed her. They had another, and it wasn't till Beebo had been there several hours and told Jack all the highlights of her life with Venus, that she became aware at last of a void in the room. She sat up. "Where's Pat?" she said.

Jack glanced down into his drink. "Pat left," he said simply.

"Left?" Beebo looked at him incredulously. "Jack, he couldn't just leave, he was so fond of you!" she said. "I'm so sorry."

"So am I. But it's winter, after all. Spring will bring somebody new. It always does."

Beebo's heart turned over for him. "But you...really loved him. Oh, Jackson," she sighed. "And you let me deluge you with my problems."

"Yours are worse than mine, pal," Jack said kindly. "And newer. Pat left me about four weeks after you did. First of October."

Beebo shook her head, still half-disbelieving. "Why?" she said.

"He found somebody else," Jack said, and when Beebo exclaimed in protest, he added, "A woman." Beebo stared at him. "I guess you put that bug in his ear," Jack said wryly. "He began to brood about being gay. He thought if he could be so attracted to you, maybe it would work with another aggressive girl. And he was a bit lost when you left, anyway. Then he met Sandra and got quite a crush on her. She took him on. It all happened in a few weeks' time. They're living upstate, running an antique shop. She's teaching him the business. And I guess he's exterminating her termites. Now and then he comes down to see me. We get along fine."

"And I thought he was so happy here," Beebo mourned.

"I think you meant more to him than we realized. He moped around after you left and wanted to follow you to L.A. I talked him out of it, but it seemed to relieve him to talk about you. Frankly, he talked too much. I warned him, and he really tried to stop, but he'd have a drink or two and open up. And he always got around to you. It was complimentary—what he said—but there was too much of it. Mona or Pete managed to get most of the dope.

"And when Pat realized he was hurting you, he began to blame himself for all your troubles. He felt guilty about living with me— 'off me'—when he couldn't give me his whole love. He's a damn nice kid, Beebo. It's best for him that he look around a bit more."

"What's best for you, Jackson?" Beebo asked fondly.

"Somebody new, I guess."

"I hope you don't have to wait till the spring."

"I'd rather. It'll give me time to get over Pat. Besides, I'd rather fall in love in the sunshine than the rain."

He fixed another round while Beebo mused, "I hope Venus's son gets through this all right. It's tough enough on Leo and Venus...but Toby. I was his best friend. He thought if I ever left he'd lose his mother again."

"He didn't lose her," Jack said. "Venus said Leo explained things to him at the hospital. It shook him up pretty badly, but he came out of it on Venus's side. That Bogardus must be a wise man. Venus said he didn't say one bitter word about you. Anyway, Toby ended up wanting to comfort her. She said it saved her life. She couldn't have stood to lose you both in one day.

"Toby doesn't know what to think about you, and maybe he never will."

"That will draw him closer to Venus, at least," Beebo said. "I don't like to think he'd ever hate me. But there's some comfort in knowing I brought him and his mother together. It's a funny thing…all of a sudden she seems as remote and inaccessible as—as the California sunshine. The end of the rainbow. Jack, I hate to give up the pot of gold."

She bent her head and shut her eyes a moment. When she looked up she asked, "How's Pasquini doing?"

"Got a new driver—a boy," Jack shrugged. "Marie can still cook. I don't know about Pete. He's a scared little man. I guess that's what makes him so vindictive. He feels brave hurting somebody who can't hurt back."

"He and Mona sent the scoop to Hollywood, didn't they?"

"They did. They called me about it later. They were that sure of themselves." He studied her face. "Venus told me about the boxing match with Leo. He must have given you those bruises."

"It's all right," Beebo said, touching her face. "I gave him some, too."

Jack lighted a cigarette. "There's one more thing, honey," he said. "Your brother." He spoke carefully in an effort to keep from alarming her.

"Jim?" Beebo said, grimacing. "God, I suppose he read about all this, too. Did he tell Dad?"

"No," Jack said. "Somebody sent your father the news, but he never saw it. I suppose it was Mona."

"Damn it, why does that girl enjoy persecuting me? All I ever did was get my wires crossed on a date with her once. I can't understand—"

"You will," Jack promised her. "Beebo, listen to me. Your father…never knew."

She looked at him, suddenly white-faced, and whispered, "Oh, Jesus. Oh, God. Jack? He's dead, isn't he?"

"I guess I shouldn't have told you tonight," Jack said. "Coming on top of the rest, maybe it's too much."

"No," she said, breaking down and crying a little. "Do you know, Jack, I'm almost glad. I'm sick that I wasn't with him at the end—if I'd known it was so close I'd have come back. But that poor unhappy man went through too much over me as it was. I think—I hope—that he knew why I left him. Maybe he seized the chance to lay his burdens down.

"Oh, I don't mean he'd kill himself. But he kept himself alive through sheer will power, to help me out of my scrapes. After I left, he was free to surrender. For all he ever knew, I ended up the doctor he hoped I'd be." She shook her head. "Such a good man. So kind, so humanly frail. I loved him, Jack."

"I got quite a biography of him from Jim," Jack said. "His drinking, his poverty, his tantrums. Jim's bitter as hell."

"I was the cause of most of it," Beebo said. "What happened to Jim?"

"He sent me a letter from the University of Wisconsin. He said your father didn't have any money, but you could have any of his belongings you wanted. If he doesn't hear from you before the end of this month he's going to sell what he can and throw out the rest."

"Is that all?"

"He said he was sorry for you but he never wants to lay eyes on you again."

She laughed sourly. "I'll bet," she said. "That's the nicest he's ever put it, too. I never loved him, Jack, but he's all the family I have, and he's no family at all. It's too bad…but he's right. We're poison together. I guess I'll let him sell Dad's things. I have his picture and my memories. They're worth more to me than some worn-out furniture."

She fell into bed soon after, lying in the familiar warmth and watching Jack move around the room. She envied the fullness and strength of his arms and chest.

When the lights were out she asked him softly, "Jack? How's Paula Ash?"

"Pretty lonesome."

"Do you see her at all?"

"All the time. We shore each other up."

"What do you do together?"

"Talk about Pat and Beebo."

Beebo smiled faintly in the dark. "Is that all? Does she hate me?"

"No, little pal."

"Does she...love me?"

"You'll have to ask Paula that one."

"Jack, is she living with anybody?"

"She was. The girl with the Plaid Pajamas moved in for a while."

Beebo felt an odd melancholy that had nothing to do with her father or Venus. "Have you met her? Plaid Pajamas?"

"Yes."

"Who is she?"

"Nobody you'd go for. Didn't Paula tell you about her?"

"Not much."

"Well, you'll meet her one of these days," he said.

That was all she could get out of him.

Beebo spent the next week resting and living quietly out of sight. She had no plans for wild revenge against Pete and Mona; only the wish to forget, to learn to live with herself again.

Venus was often in her thoughts and would be for a long time. But more and more, as the hurt faded, she found herself preoccupied with Paula. Paula, so real and so faithful; so unlike the fairy-tale princess, Venus, who had vanished inevitably into Never-Never Land. Beebo had crashed back to earth, and she wanted a real girl in her arms.

The cackling in the papers about the Bogardus-Brinker affair made life awkward for her for a while, with reporters trying to scout her down and people whispering about her wherever she went. But the talk was slowly yielding at the other end of the country to Venus's surprising dignity. She appeared in public at Leo's side emphasizing the duration of their life together. Both of them swore that their marriage had never been stronger, and in a way, it was true. They needed each other extremely then.

The official story was that Beebo was a young woman who had taken a job on the household staff and subsequently became a close friend of Toby's. Nobody was aware that she was harboring a feverish crush on Venus. When the situation blew up in their faces, Venus and Leo were as startled and shocked as the rest of the movie colony. They expressed their sympathy for their unfortunate young friend and hoped she could find a happier life somewhere else.

"No one who knows me will believe that there was anything between this poor girl and myself except a friendly relationship based on her closeness to my son," Venus was quoted. And Beebo, reading the statement, could picture Leo writing and rewriting it at the desk in his library, with a cigar fuming in his mouth and a glass of orange juice nearby.

Somehow, Leo brought it off—partly by expending huge sums on public relations and partly by exploiting Toby's illness: he hinted broadly that unless the furor died down, the boy's health was in danger of permanent damage.

Beebo shed a few tears over it in private. But it was, after all, as merciful towards her as Leo and Venus dared to make it. Her picture was kept out of the papers. She still had some anonymity in this biggest of all big cities.

It had been two weeks since she returned to New York; weeks spent resting and job-hunting. Beebo was tense throughout the day, for that night the second segment of *Million Dollar Baby* was scheduled for showing. It was the one in which Venus sang "I'm Putting My All on You"—the song Leo and Beebo had coaxed out of her that night in the recreation room.

Beebo tried all day to forget about it. But when she came home again that night without a job, Jack had to cheer her up with a cold martini. "When are you going to call Paula?" he said casually.

"Paula who?" she said with a little smile.

Jack pinched her amiably in the arm. "She wants to see you. This would be a dandy night not to watch television."

"How do you know Paula wants to see me?"

"Well, if she hadn't called to say so, I'd still know. I'm telepathic."

"You're psychopathic. What am I supposed to do, go over there and beat the daylights out of Miss Plaid Pajamas? You said they were living together."

"*Were*—past tense. I don't know what the situation is now, with you home. Anyway, pal, what's the matter with you? Afraid of a little fight? Or isn't Paula worth it?"

"What are you promoting it for, Jackson? Taking bets?"

"If the Pajamas are still hanging around, you can take her with one hand behind your back. Leo must have taught you *something*."

"And after I kayo her, then what do I do?"

"You claim the fair damsel, stupe," Jack said. "Jesus, you're thick sometimes, Beebo." He chuckled at her.

Beebo sobered slightly. "Jack, I'm not so sure. I mean, I hurt Paula. I was damned unfair and unfeeling with her."

"Really? *Unfeeling?*"

"I ditched her for what must seem like the cheapest kind of affair, when Paula needed me and Venus only wanted me."

"You're ashamed of yourself. Is that why you're stalling? Beebo, don't you know a girl in love is always ready to forgive her lover?"

"Provided the lover's in love with her," Beebo said.

"Well, aren't you? Not one letter did I get from California that you didn't fret and worry over Paula Ash."

Beebo looked at him. "I've been thinking about just two people for the past two weeks: Venus and Paula. And every day, it's more Paula and less Venus. And yet I think if Venus were to call and say, 'Come back, I can't stand it without you—I'd go."

"No, you wouldn't, pal. You've learned too much." Jack nodded at the phone. "Besides, she'll never call. Venus Bogardus isn't real any more. She's the doll millions of us will watch and covet tonight on TV. And you're just one of the millions now."

Beebo felt momentarily swamped with frustration. Gradually she became aware of Jack's voice saying, "Paula doesn't belong to the public or a bank or a one-track husband. She doesn't have any of those things. Paula can get up when the show is over and turn the set off, and come back to your side, ready for love. Venus will be gone forever with a turn of the knob."

Beebo lighted a cigarette to cover her emotion. "Maybe I should call Paula. The least I can do is apologize. But I don't want to see her till I'm sure—"

"Sure of what?" Jack said. "Loving her? Beebo, you can wait a lifetime trying to be sure of love. You didn't wait to be sure of Venus. I didn't wait to be sure of Pat."

"And look how those affairs turned out," she said.

"If we had waited, we wouldn't have known any happiness at all with them. I still love Pat. We're friends and I think we always will be. Venus loves you, Beebo, and the things you gave her are the most precious in her life. Because of her, you're growing up a little, at last. Would you rather it had never happened, just because it hurt?"

She glanced at him, puzzled. "No. But I don't want to hurt Paula any more. She doesn't deserve anything but my love, and I don't know if I can give her that yet."

"Well, she can give you hers. And right now, that makes her the strong one. You need love and it's her joy to give it. Maybe the gift will transform the recipient. That's what happened to Venus."

"God, if I could make myself love her, I would," Beebo said, but Jack laughed at her.

"Hell, honey, that's *her* job," he said. "Be honest with her and she'll take it from there. If she's willing to risk a love affair with you now, knowing all she knows, you have nothing to be ashamed of."

Beebo doused her cigarette. "Can you eat all that hamburger by yourself?" she said, pointing at it.

"Without the slightest strain." He smiled at her.

"Okay," she said, answering the smile reluctantly. "I'm going calling. But if I come back here tonight with two black eyes and a broken heart, by God, Mann, you're going to pay for it."

"I can't wait," he said.

Beebo threw a plastic saucer at him, which he fielded deftly, and left with his laughter in her ears.

She walked through the night air, crisp and cold enough to crack if you just knew how to grasp it, all the way to McDonald Street. It was easy enough to find Paula's building. Not so easy to go in and ring her bell.

Beebo looked at the small black button for several minutes before she pressed it. When the answer sounded at once, she wondered if Jack had called to forewarn Paula. She opened the door and walked down the hall with the feeling of reliving in life what she had once dreamed an eon ago.

Paula's door was open as it had been the night they met. A slice of light lay across the hall. Beebo felt her heart beating higher in her chest. Soon Paula would appear in a pair of plaid pajamas that weren't hers, and say sleepily, "Yes?"

But she didn't. Beebo stopped at her door and waited. She could feel Paula's presence somewhere just inside the room. Finally she glanced in, blinking at the light. Paula was leaning against the far wall, facing the door. Her hair had grown quite long in the few months since they had seen each other, and it washed over her pink silk shoulders in an auburn tide.

Her eyes were enormous and there was a flush of love and fear in her cheeks. She wasn't just pretty. She was so lovely that Beebo's breath caught in her throat. Everything Paula felt and feared and hoped for shone on her face.

Beebo stood in the doorway, her hands characteristically shoved into her pockets, her bright blue eyes fixed on this gentle girl who, incredibly, learned to love her in three days and loved her still after three months.

"Paula," Beebo said. "Are you still my Paula?"

"Still yours," she answered.

"I don't see any plaid pajamas around," Beebo said, but it was no wonder: she didn't see anything around that room but Paula Ash.

"She left," Paula said. "The day you came home. I told her to leave. Oh, Beebo." Paula shut her eyes, and when she opened them, Beebo was standing beside her, hesitating, absorbing the mystery of their attraction.

"Paula, I feel as if I'm seeing you for the first time," Beebo said. "I swear I do."

"I'm no match for the goddess," Paula said, smiling without any malice. She was prompted by an innocent little-girl need to be admired and loved, so transparent that it charmed Beebo completely.

"The goddess was no match for you." Strangely, all at once, it was true. "Jack was right—you're the real woman." She closed the small space between them, taking Paula's shoulders in her big hands and kissing her suddenly on the mouth. Paula put her arms around her, so hard Beebo could feel her quivering.

"Paula—darling—I want to know just one thing," Beebo said. "Where are your damn sleeping pills?"

"I gave them to Jack the day you left," Paula said. "Kiss me again, Beebo." Beebo obeyed her gladly, over and over, rediscovering with her all the things they had learned to need and love in each other months before.

When Paula took Beebo's hands and turned them palms up to kiss, Beebo groaned with the delight she couldn't hold back. "Paula," she said, "oh, Paula. I came here like the self-centered idiot I am, thinking I could pay you off for what you've been through with a few silly kisses. Honey, I'm the one who wants them. I'm the one who needs them. I just didn't have the sense to see it."

She was full of crazy joy that was part nostalgia, part relief, and mostly desire. The touch, the fragrance, the feel of this marvelous girl were beyond anything Beebo had remembered.

Beebo picked her up and carried her into the bedroom, bending over her on the bed, her hands supporting her weight on either side of Paula's face. "Oh, that hair, that mouth—Paula, I came so close to loving you before. And then...Jesus, she dazzled me. Honey, I was helpless with her."

"Don't explain, Beebo. I got through it somehow, and it's over. Jack practically adopted me. We talked all night every night for a week after you left. He told me you'd be back, and he was so sure of it that I believed him. I knew you weren't in love with me, but I knew you wanted me. And because of Jack, I never despaired. I wasn't even afraid of Mona any more. She thought I was nuts, but—"

"Mona! Has she been after you, too?" Beebo flared. "Hasn't she hurt me enough? Does she have to take it out on you?"

"You stood her up for me, remember?"

"How could I forget?" Beebo leaned over to kiss her. "Unbutton me, Paula," she whispered.

Paula complied with a tremor. "Mona thought she owned me," she said softly. "She shucked me off months before, but I wasn't supposed to love anybody new for the rest of my life."

"Paula..." Beebo seized her hands and looked at her searchingly. "Are you trying to tell me—oh my God!—was *Mona* the girl in the plaid pajamas?"

Paula nodded, still opening buttons until Beebo's shirt slipped off. "She came back this fall when you left. She wanted information about you at first, but then she decided to live with me again. I let her do it. I supposed I was looking for a way to hurt you both. Make you jealous, and get even with Mona for the pain she gave me. She was astounded when I told her to get lost two weeks ago. She's still waiting for you to snub me, and then she'll come back to say, 'I told you so.'"

"That's one thing she'll never say," Beebo said emphatically. "She won't have the chance. How could you fall for a girl like that, darling? You so sweet all the way through, and Mona so sour?"

"It's you I love, Beebo. Let's not talk about Mona."

Beebo kicked her slacks off, lying down beside Paula. "Did you know Mona was going to send that smear to the gossipists?" she asked.

"Yes," Paula confessed and shocked Beebo. "I'll be truthful. This is the hardest thing I have to tell you, Beebo. I knew, and maybe I could have stopped her, I'm not sure. But I didn't even try. I knew it would separate you and Venus. It would have come sooner or later, but I wanted you so awfully and this was the fastest way to do it. I couldn't have done it to you myself. But when I found out what Mona and Pete were up to, I didn't have the guts to stop them."

There was a long silence. "Beebo, I forgive you everything. Can you forgive me this?" Paula's voice, slight and sweet as herself, hung close to tears. This was the test.

Beebo turned Paula's face up to hers finally and kissed it. "You have far more to forgive than I do," she said. "If you can, so can I."

Once again they held each other, immersed in the swell of love. Paula lay beneath Beebo, letting her work a while; letting the ardor slowly take fire inside her, until the urge to respond became irresistible.

Then, suddenly, her head went back in a beautiful arch, into a pool of auburn hair. Her body heaved against Beebo's, and one of her legs slipped between her lover's. Her hands began to wander through Beebo's close-cropped curls, over her broad back and trim hips, caressing her everywhere. Beebo answered her with gratitude, amazement, and the first warm thrill of real love. Not an infatuation that knocks the breath out of you and dislocates your life for a while. But the slow sure kind, strong and reassuring, that holds together. Honesty, trust, respect, all were growing between them.

When they had slept a little, Beebo raised herself up on one elbow to light a cigarette and talk. "You know something, Paula," she said. "I tried to tell you this our first night together, and you wouldn't believe it. But it's true, and it has a lot to do with the way I feel about you now."

"What, darling?" Her look of love, so womanly and so complete, moved Beebo warmly.

"You brought me out, Paula. You were the first. I spent my life back home saying no to everything but my daydreams. There wasn't a soul I could have touched without the whole town finding out. It would have killed my father. That's one of the reasons I had to leave. Paula, you precious girl. God, how lucky I was that it was you."

"It might have been Venus," Paula said.

"If it had, I'd have botched it. She would have laughed at me."

"Her show is on," Paula said, looking at the clock-radio by the bed. "Want to watch it?"

"No thanks."

"I think you should. Come on, I'll watch it with you." Paula got up smiling and pulled her halfway out of bed.

"Paula, honey, I don't give a damn—"

"No fibs!" Paula cautioned, throwing her pink silk wrapper around herself. "Come with me, Beebo." She stood at the bedroom door, waiting, and Beebo couldn't turn her down. She stood up, but not without misgivings.

The show had already started and the commercial was in progress. Beebo took Paula in her arms and together they settled back on the sofa.

"If you had refused to look, I would really have been scared," Paula admitted. "I would have thought you were still tied to Venus emotionally—too much to bear to see her, even on the screen." She twisted around in Beebo's arms to look at her face and kissed her swiftly a dozen times till Beebo was suddenly embracing her tightly and murmuring her name eagerly.

Paula was trembling with the immensity of her feeling, full of whirling thoughts hard to word. "I know you don't love me yet the way I love you, Beebo," she said at last. "But God, I hope you will. It's kept me going—that hope—all this time. You felt so right to me."

Beebo stroked her hair and gazed at her, unaware that Venus, in black satin, was singing, "I'm Putting My All on You."

"You've only seen the rough side of gay love," Paula told her. "People can be so cruelly selfish. Even the people who try to be good to you, and I guess Venus tried.

"Darling, Lesbian love doesn't have to be brief or heartbreaking, just because it's a love between two women. I want to teach you that. I want to live with you and do things for you and even let you do things for me.

"Oh, Beebo, don't you see it? Women have a special knack for loving. Even Venus, in her way, found that knack. There's a tenderness, an instinctive sympathy, between two women when their love is right...it's very rare in any kind of love. But it comes near perfection between women.

"You haven't known that tenderness yet. You've only known a hectic affair with a fantastically difficult actress. I want to give you a home. I want you to come back to me every night and know you'll be loved and cared for and spoiled. Beebo, darling, I want you to spoil me a little, too."

"Paula, it'll be a pleasure," Beebo smiled.

Paula relaxed in her lap and Beebo put her hand back on the cushions. They watched the end of the song as the camera closed in on the face of Venus Bogardus. She was talking the words the way Beebo had suggested, her head tilted to one side and her eyes full, glittering with a give-away brilliance of real tears.

At the end, she let her head drop so that her gleaming hair swung around her face and hid her eyes. The tune—just a gimmicky little love song to begin with—had become a torch. And for just one moment, Venus was living flesh for Beebo again.

Beebo moved Paula off her lap and got up, going to the TV and turning it off. "It's not that I'm still close to her, Paula," she said, coming back to the sofa. "It's just that that was goodbye. From her to me."

They looked at each other. "Did you really love her, Beebo?" Paula whispered.

Beebo sat down and took both of Paula's hands in hers and kissed them in a gesture that had become special to them both.

And then she pulled Paula down on the couch in her arms and kissed her neck until she squirmed and laughed. "I won't know for sure what love is till I've spoiled you for a while, sweetheart," Beebo grinned.